THE CRITICS KNOW WHAT'S RIGHT WITH JOHN SCOTT
SHEPHERD AND HIS ACCLAIMED DEBUT NOVEL

Henry's List of Wrongs

"*Wall Street* becomes *It's a Wonderful Life.*"

—*People*

"Smooth as silk. . . . [A] charming, sweet story."

—*Kirkus Reviews*

"Winning and sincere . . . bound to enchant readers."

—*Booklist*

"If you can put this book down after the opening scene, then you're a lost cause."

—Aint-It-Cool-News.com

"Shepherd taps successfully into the universal fantasy of revisiting the past. . . . Should twang the heartstrings of readers."

—*Publishers Weekly*

"A hip, brash, stylish page-turner with a surprising amount of heart."

—Kristin Hannah, bestselling author of *Summer Island*

ALSO BY JOHN SCOTT SHEPHERD
Henry's List of Wrongs

The
DEAD FATHER'S
GUIDE
to
SEX &
MARRIAGE

A Novel by

John Scott Shepherd

doWn
tOwn
press

New York   London   Toronto   Sydney

An *Original* Publication of POCKET BOOKS

 DOWNTOWN PRESS, published by Pocket Books
1230 Avenue of the Americas
New York, NY 10020

ISBN: 0-7434-6626-8

First Downtown Press trade paperback edition July 2004

10 9 8 7 6 5 4 3 2 1

DOWNTOWN PRESS and colophon are
trademarks of Simon & Schuster, Inc.

Manufactured in the United States of America

For information regarding special discounts for bulk purchases,
please contact Simon & Schuster Special Sales at 1-800-456-6798
or business@simonandschuster.com

For my father, who I met in the nick of time.
I love you, James Homer Shepherd.

PART ONE:

Home Study

ENTRY 1: SATURDAY, OCTOBER 9, 11:06 P.M.

(CLICK.)

Is this thing on? Yeah? Okay, let's give it a shot. . . .

Joseph Way, self-made millionaire, community icon, and mayor of Cleveland, is the older, deader one in the tastefully trimmed wooden box. I'm the eagerly anticipated sequel, the thirtyish, ruggedly handsome, more upright one at the microphone in front of the box.

I'm Joseph Way, Junior. They call me Joe and, frankly, if you're Joe Anybody Else in this town, you might consider a catchy nickname. And having said that out loud, *I'm* considering kicking my ass.

Anyway, the box filled with my dead father is perched regally before a poster-sized photo of the deceased looking like Clint Eastwood and Brian Dennehy blended.

Me and him. Father and son. Block and Chip. Best friends

and confidants. We're a smash hit here in the First Episcopal Church, centerpiece of historic St. James Square, centerpiece of postcard-perfect Benton Heights, the most affluent suburb of Cleveland, Ohio. The venue is standing room only, with some three hundred well-heeled admirers anxious for assistant district attorney and local hero Joe Way—that's me—to eulogize his superfantastic father.

It's fervently hoped that I'll also weave in that I'm running for mayor in my namesake's place. The plan was congress in 2006, at least last I heard, but all that changed when Dad hauled back his Big Bertha driver and dropped dead on the first tee last Saturday.

No, the faces before me aren't ashen with grief and loss; they're lit with conviction for their way of life and the God- and Reagan-given right to it, with the hope that the broad-shouldered, ruddy-cheeked young man in front of them will fortify that right as their next mayor.

"Ruggedly handsome?" "Broad-shouldered?" *"Ruddy-cheeked?"* Jesus, I never realized how absurdly pleased with myself I am. Have others noticed?

Know this: It's not the number of people in the church that matters, it's the tons of lead they swing. And they're ready and willing to wield it over the hundreds of thousands of employees they commandeer if only I ask.

Even my mom, the Sturdy Widow Rita Way, holds her chin up, a proud smile creasing her taut face.

I clear my throat and hold the room in the steady grip of my steely stare. To them, I radiate a calm, confident resolve. I know this because I practiced in the mirror.

"My . . . father," I begin. It's a statement in full, and many of the assembled nod, basking in the eloquence of those two small words as wielded by yours truly. I go on in due time: "Where the hell do I begin with a guy like Joseph Way?" This is good, the nods and chuckles say. This is *perfect.*

Emboldened, I say, "Holy *shit,*" and then chortle. From somebody else it might be off-putting.

In the front row next to my mom, Jacob Moore, the seventy-year-old retired chairman of OhioBanc, tilts his head, one jowl swinging lower than the other. Men like me are always watched by men like Jacob. It's the way of the tribe.

On my mom's other side, my fiancée, highbred whiplash blond Beth Pruitt, twenty-eight. She fingers her pearls, recrosses a toned, black-stockinged calf, and mouths, "What are you *doing?*"

"You said it, Joe," a voice yells from the back, breaking the silence. Why, it's unimaginably successful realtor Mark Stranad! At just thirty-two, he's chairman of the ultraprestigious Western Reserve Academy's school board and, more impressively, *my best friend!* Of course, it's an honorary position, since everybody knows my father was my real best friend, a notion so cute it got me laid more times than I can count.

Mark smiles and his cheek twitches, breaking through the drugs to betray his lifelong anxiety disorder. He successfully compensates for ordinary looks with pinpoint grooming and that "good listener" thing I could never nail down.

So now a chuckle oozes smugly across the room. "Holy shit" is inappropriate, yes, but now it's *wonderfully* inappropriate, right? It's *boardroom icebreaker* inappropriate.

So I nod appreciatively at the support and scan the room once more. Then I say, "So here's the thing: My father was a lying, manipulative, adulterous *fuck* who betrayed everyone who loved him."

For a couple of heartbeats, nothing. Silence. Beyond silence— negative noise. Antinoise.

On perfect cue, with the earth's rotation paused, enter stunning cocoa-and-cream hippie Mara Pinkett, the liberal mestiza Juliet to my right-wing Romeo back at Wittenberg University.

Mara's not just a liberal, she's a liberal *journalist,* so her I-knew-it-all-along expression is permanent as opposed to a reaction to something I've said. But for that sliver of time, the only thing that matters is that she and her self-involved dreadlocks are here. In the room. In my life again.

Only then does it occur to me that in a mind-boggling display of faith, the assembled *have not freaked out!* Believe it or not, they're actually waiting for a punch line they can really get behind.

You've heard of The Jordan Rules, right? A few years back, if Michael Jordan traveled four steps and bricked a lay-up, they called a foul on some poor guy sitting on the opposing bench. Lebron James gets the same treatment, now. That's sort of what my life is like.

So I wallow in the anticipation. I smile and nod, taking in each and every one of them. "Yeah," I say like a stoned teenager. "You heard me."

Even coming from me, this is *not* a punch line they can get behind. So a gasping, choking sound echoes off the chapel walls. An older tree trunk of a man staggers from a pew, takes a few wobbly steps down the aisle toward the heavy wooden doors, and falls to all fours. A panicked huddle forms around him, frantically doing precisely nothing.

His daughter-in-law, 1989 Western Reserve Academy prom queen Cammie McCalister, looks back at me with the high-grade hatred often accessorized with a burning torch or pitchfork. You'd assume she's pissed because I just caused her wealthy father-in-law's heart attack at a funeral for a man who had a heart attack, but honestly I think it has more to do with my never calling after our postprom boffing, for which she insisted we both keep the crowns on.

Considering that maybe it's a little of both, I continue: "It took me a while to get the words just right, so I just wanna make sure I didn't leave anything out." I review notes I scrawled on a cocktail napkin, the first clue that my steely stare is more shitfaced than confident.

"He's drunk," hisses a stern soccer mom from one of the newer developments just outside town as she covers her computer-designed son's eyes.

At this point, I turn to address my father's casket and say, "Hope you packed linen, shithead, because the forecast for hell is hot, with occasional flesh-searing flames." Then I point at the casket with both hands and yell, "Yeah! Burn, Daddy, burn! *Whooo-hooo!*"

When I turn back, literally every mouth is agape with silent horror. Undaunted, I hold my hands high, forefingers and pinkies extended. "Hello, Benton Heights," I barely manage through my wheezy, drunken laugh. "Are you ready to *party?*"

My mom does her thing where she sucks in her cheeks and exhales through her nose, fluttering her eyes in disapproval. She turns to cry into Jacob Moore's shoulder, but never actually does, of course. Jacob exhales in resignation and calmly retrieves a pistol from his breast pocket as he stands.

"You're decidedly unelectable, Joe," he says, shrugging apologetically. I nod back because, you know, it's tough to argue with.

Jacob takes aim at my forehead to remove me from consideration with one clean kill shot. But he's really not much of a marksman, so he shoots me in the shoulder.

"Ow!" I yell indignantly, staggering out from behind the lectern. Jacob cringes in faux embarrassment and the mourners laugh a little. He takes aim again and the shot takes me in the thigh. Jacob rolls his eyes and an artificial sitcom laugh track bursts from the gathered. He steps forward and fires over and over again until finally, at last . . .

I drop to my knees amid the howling laughter. For some reason, I try to find Mara at the back of the chapel, but she's gone. Beth screws up her face and looks that way and somehow she knows. "Shoot him again," she stage-whispers to Jacob. He shrugs amiably—if you say so—and finally puts one directly into my heart.

And at last, I fall. And you know what? It feels good. I should've tried it a long, long time ago.

Well, *that* was queer. What is this, therapy?

Oh, right. Of course. You wanna know what "this" is? It's two scotches, two Valiums, and about three fingers of good cabernet. God, that explains so much.

I'm gonna sleep a little and try this again later.

(CLICK.)

(CLICK.)

Okay, I'm back. I just had a hiccup of a dream that I was at a Browns game with Beth. People were pointing and whispering, and it turned out that I was not only naked, but I'd shaved all the hair off my body, even my eyebrows. Beth acted put out and mortified, but frankly I was pissed at *her* because it really seemed to me she could have said something in the car or maybe even before we left.

The point of lying here in a single bed in my childhood bedroom beneath a poster of Heather Locklear still tacked to the angled ceiling above me, of talking into this tiny little tape recorder, is to find some way to deliver a eulogy for my father Thursday night. My older, gayer brother Nathan had suggested that I do some visualization and try to imagine the funeral. Clearly, *that* turned into something else entirely, so let's take another tack: Let's review the past couple of days and maybe figure out where it all veered into Crazyville.

The last time things were the way they were supposed to be forever was Thursday, so let's start there.

The day started early, trouncing Mark Stranad 6–1, 6–0 at the Carriage House Tennis Club. We play every other day at dawn, like a recreational execution. I'm not sure which is stranger—that Mark keeps showing up to play Washington Generals to my Harlem Globetrotters or that I keep letting him. But there I am, hitting the laser-beam serves . . . and there he is, shaking his head in wonder. Every other day. From where I lie now, there's something a little perverted about it.

I wonder what it would be like if Mark beat me one morning. And then beat me again. And what if he just started kicking my ass on a routine basis? The world would be off its axis somehow. My tee shots have always bounced off a tree, out of the rough, and onto the fairway. Yes, I know we were talking about tennis and then I abruptly veered into a golf metaphor, but I couldn't make it work with tennis. If you hit a tree with a tennis ball it's just out, right?

So life is more like golf, I guess. My life, anyway.

The point is, I can't think of a time when I was in a state of *wanting* for very long. I don't even recall any substantial periods of *establishing goals*. I had trouble sleeping a couple of weeks ago and I was flipping through channels and saw Fran Tarkenton pimping self-help tapes and figuring out that *what you want* is apparently a big horking deal for ordinary people. When Fran said the first step to figuring out what you want is to really know *who you are,* I flipped over to ESPN Classic. Fucking yourself in the ear can cause headaches, man.

And now, a message from our sponsor, the corner of me that, in spite of all efforts, has become eminently more self-aware in the past eighteen hours: I am not an asshole, but now I'm beginning to understand why somebody might wish humbling, stumbling catastrophe upon me.

I guess we're into semantics here. I may in fact *be* an asshole, but I am *not* a dick. I don't wish bad things on others. I never do anything for the purpose of causing grief or discomfort to another human being. I'm not mean or malicious.

But if a man who glides smoothly through his life with a carefree sense of entitlement and terrific hair is your idea of an asshole, well then, I'm your man.

I'm also the assistant district attorney in these parts. It's like my preseason before I'm a congressman and, if all plays out just so, President of the United States. The Plan, otherwise known as My Life, is admittedly an ambitious endeavor.

On Thursday morning, I strode confidently across the marble, three-story lobby of the downtown courthouse with plans to head a few blocks south to speak at a rally. In my life, as part of The Plan, *striding confidently to speak at a rally* isn't a big deal. It's called Thursday. Just another day.

I heard clicking heels and knew Jessica and Carl were running to catch up to me. Even though I don't walk all that fast, it always seems people can't catch up.

Jessica's young and pretty enough but she's spreading out left to right even though she's always on some macabre diet. On

The Warrior Diet, for instance, she would starve herself all day and bounce off the walls from caffeine and cashews before eating her way into a coma each evening. I think her metabolism is pretty well shell-shocked by now.

Carl? Carl's fodder, a one-man test group, the guy you wave at on your way to better things. He'll end up somebody's Mark Stranad, I think. Everybody should have one.

I'm not putting Jessica and Carl down, mind you. Each and every Jessica and Carl is important, not just these two. You know why? Because everybody's a constituent. That's what Jacob used to tell my dad so my dad started telling me. It's like running for prom king your entire life.

Which, again, defines an asshole. But *not* necessarily a dick.

So they finally catch up to me, breathing like they started about a mile back, and Carl says, "So?" And Jessica says, "How'd it go?"

I smile cool and say, "That breeze you feel is everyone on Macaluso's payroll turning away from him." Which basically means I'm locking up this crime dude left over from the Gotti era.

So Carl gets in front of me and grabs me by the shoulders and he's smiling all crazy and he says, "Have you *ever* tripped up the stairs with people watching? Huh? Maybe you shook the last drop onto your linen trousers and didn't notice until it was too late?"

Very calmly, I say, "Of course I have, Carl." But you know what? I was lying. Because if I *had* dripped piss on my linen trousers, somebody would've erased the event, appearing from nowhere with identical replacements.

I looked at my watch and realized that a thousand people are probably waiting for me right now. It occurs to me as I lie here in this very small bed that most human beings are lucky to have five people waiting for them at any specific point in time. Maybe thirty if it's a surprise party.

So while I was hurrying for the exit, from behind me I heard Carl say, "And thus ends the portion of our program where we pretend to be Joe's relative equals."

The aforementioned rally was for a proposed new retail and entertainment district in the heart of thriving Downtown Cleveland, situated in the middle of the triangle created by Jacobs Field, the Rock and Roll Hall of Fame, and Cleveland Browns Stadium. The name, the Light District, really means nothing to nobody, even after a massively expensive publicity campaign about some mayor from a hundred years ago named Garfield Light. The point is there will be a big mall, even though they don't call it that, with a Starbucks, a Sunglass Hut, like two hundred movie theaters, and some overpriced office space.

Once the boring architects and public officials had been ignored by the thousandish in attendance, this old, gin-blossomed sportscaster named Gil Shanling took the mike and just started clapping, which seems sort of silly but it worked and everybody started clapping with him. People are odd that way.

So Shanling yells, "Aw-right!" He's been about half drunk since retirement, right there between sober and curbside. He whips out an index card and literally starts yelling my introduction: "Four-year starting quarterback at Wittenberg University, graduate of Case Western School of Law, assistant district attorney, and son of our fine mayor. But more than all that, he helped bring the Cleveland Browns back to Cleveland! Please welcome Joe Way!"

By the time I grabbed the mike from Gib (Gib? Gil? Like it matters?) and pretended to say something to him, the crowd was chanting, "Joe! Joe! Joe!"

I don't know, maybe it wasn't exactly the *whole* crowd, just a few dozen rowdy construction workers on break. But, anyway, I acted like I was overwhelmed even though this wasn't the first time I'd heard it.

Come to think of it, I'm not so sure there were a thousand people there after all. Odd that would come to me now.

I've never said this to anyone before, but sometimes I feel a little preposterous as The Man Who Helped Return the Browns to Cleveland, because it's not precisely accurate. The mayor before my dad, the black guy, he was the one who did all the heavy lifting with the NFL commissioner, Paul Tagliabue. But his term ended when they were still in the gritty phase, and by the time coaches were getting hired my dad was mayor and I was the faceman for the Sports Commission, playing hardball with the NFL, making sure they delivered everything they promised.

That's what everybody said, actually, but I don't remember there being anything hard about it, balls or otherwise. We shot memos back and forth, we had Tags in for an Indians game, that sort of thing. Maybe it just comes easy to me.

Well, whatever. In recorded history, I played a prominent role in giving the Browns back to Cleveland and I'm not gonna argue with it, right? It's not like I don't bring something to the table—I am, by all accounts, quite *charismatic.* Jacob says I'm the embodiment of the New Cleveland. I think that's a good thing. I really do. It matters in some indirect way.

Anyway, I threw my support behind the Light District, but everybody knew I was stumping for my dad. Plans are like train tracks—you remove a piece and everybody falls to a gruesome death in the valley, which in turn is televised on Fox as *The World's Most Gruesome Deaths in the Valley.*

Point is, a major component of The Plan had always been that my dad is mayor when I run for congress in 2006, not the guy who got his ass kicked.

I know how to milk it, so I basked in the applause and stepped over to give Beth a kiss. She raised a leg like she does, flexing her calf. She was dressed up in her Republican Wet Dream look—bobbing ponytail and white blouse over a black skirt, stockings, and pumps.

Beth's something of the shit in her own right, though I like to tell her it's mostly because she's with me. She's the youngest instructor at Western Reserve Academy's prep school, which is ranked as one of the best private high schools in America. She fought for and won the prestigious position of Faculty Representative on the Board of Directors, which is basically the Masters of the Universe. That's how she met and for a minute or two dated Mark Stranad before he did the right thing and stepped aside. Some things are just meant to be.

Okay, so if I'm the poster boy of the New Cleveland, Beth's the face of a more progressive, open-minded WRA, as it's known. Besides teaching social studies, she's way into marital arts and she fought really hard to be allowed to teach self-defense in girls' gym classes. They made a big deal out of that in *North Coast Magazine* when they put us on the cover of their special "Cleveland Tomorrow" issue.

So I pulled away from Beth and said, "Gotta go to work, honey," and she does that thing where she puts her hands on her hips and rolls her eyes like I'm just the *biggest dork.*

So I'm charming and funny, funny and charming, then I pull out a letter and say, "This is a letter from the League of Cities informing my father that for a record-setting eleventh straight year, Cleveland has been named an All-American City."

I realize nobody's gonna remember what I did or didn't say about that stupid-ass mall, okay? What they'll remember is that I shouted into the mike: "The letter should just say, *Cleveland Rocks!*" That's what people remember. Like Gore went on and on with his economic brainiac shit, but then Bush said, "I don't get your fuzzy math." Nobody else did, either, so Bush is president. Politics are just way simpler than people make them.

So I said some serious stuff with my brow furrowed and my voice low, and ended big again: "We've got the best football team, the best downtown . . . *and the best mayor this city has ever seen!*" They ate it up. I'm like a rock star. Not just anybody can do that. Like I said, I think that matters in some indirect way.

I was still smiling when I walked back into our offices at about 4 P.M. I carry a light caseload because my boss, District Attorney Ally Wong, is a good Republican who recognizes that my value to her department and professional future lies more at public rallies and on magazine covers than in some musty courtroom.

So I blew past my assistant Callie, fifty and strangely cute with some kind of Bolivian or something mixed in and these dark sun freckles across her nose. I vaguely noticed a teenage girl sitting in the waiting chair against the wall. I closed my door and then felt compelled to open it and look at her.

Callie said, "This girl needs to see you. I think you'll find what she has to say very interesting."

She was a little squat, maybe twenty pounds overweight, but there was something delectably naughty about her. I gave her my Ultrabrite trust-me smile and she let her eyes flutter hornylike and gave me the up and down with a rest stop at my trousers. I'm not making it up.

She said "Hello," like that, her voice all Marlboros and bad intentions. I tried to keep it together by more formally asking what I could do for her. And in that dangerous voice, she said, "My name's Jenni Sanchez. I need to speak to you in private."

I couldn't possibly have imagined how many times I'd hear that name in the next twenty-four hours.

Now, you're gonna think for sure I'm bullshitting but I swear I'm not: When she walked past me, into my office, she brushed the back of her hand against my package. I felt severely manipulated and that in turn gave me a raging hard-on.

In my office, Jenni kicked off her tacky Candy's platforms and curled into the antique swivel across the desk from me on a hip and a thigh, bare feet peeking out from under one arm rest. The nails were cherry red and she had rings on three chubby toes.

She caught me looking at her feet and my face flushed hot. So I said, "What can I do for you, Jenni?" All business.

She looked me right in the eye and asked, "Do you know who Lester Ratcovic is?"

Do I know who Lester Ratcovic is? The frizzy-haired liberal intellectual who's suddenly and inexplicably leading my dad in the polls?

That Lester Ratcovic?

Well, yeah, it was *that* Lester Ratcovic. She'd been temping at his election office for three weeks. And here's what she said next: "He's big-time horny for me. He wants to hook up real bad. He won't stop calling me at home. He came to my aunt's house the other night. I didn't let him in."

I couldn't control my breathing, let alone come off professional. I heard myself ask if he kept his feelings to himself in the workplace, and I got the answer I wanted: "Uh, I don't *think* so. He told me he'd sell his wife into slavery for one big bite of my ass."

I could taste it in my mouth. No, not her ass. Like when I know I'm gonna ace Mark Stranad to win the match. It's metallic, like blood, and it's intoxicating, man. I had to put my palms flat on the desk in front of me and breathe deeply.

So Jenni said, "Are you okay, dude?" I asked if he'd touched her inappropriately at the office. She said, "No, but if that'll get me paid, I'm willing to say he rubbed up against me or something."

Yes, for the record, I rolled it around. Tested it and tried it on. She raised her eyebrows, making sure I knew she was making a win-win proposal here.

And that's when I said no way. Can't do it. And I meant it. I really did. Whatever else I may be, I'm not *that*. And I guess that's something to build on.

Now she was bummed and looking at the door, leaking interest at an alarming rate. So I made an intense speech about how that man had done her wrong and she has an obligation to provide testimony about it for the sake of the girls he's yet to molest. It came out better than that. Edgier, I think.

She chewed at her lip and smiled a little, a poor barrio girl from the wrong side of Cleveland with a profound sense of her own power and what to do with it. I remember being more impressed than turned on. But a little of both, to be honest.

So I gave her exactly what I sensed she wanted: I said, "Please, Jenni." She relished it. Control is her currency. She accepted it hungrily, nostrils flaring.

Then she actually asked what I want from her. Forget that she'd come to me, right? Now it's, *What do you want from me?*

And so I told her this is complicated and asked if she knows who I am. She rolled her eyes and said, "I know it took me about a minute to give you a hard-on. In a half hour I'd have you washing my Camaro with your tongue."

That's when I told her she needed to leave now and come back in the morning. She's like, *Huh?* So I told her my father is Joseph Way, the mayor, and it hurts our case if I'm the one who takes your testimony. What I want you to do is go home and come back tomorrow morning with less makeup and more ponytail, understand? Ask to see Ally Wong, the district attorney, and tell your story to her.

But *just tell the story,* okay? That's what I said. Don't punch it up or embellish it in any way. Just tell the truth.

But I was losing her again. She stared at the wall over my right shoulder, thinking about beer or shoes or something. So I affected my father's voice and said, "You must never tell anyone you came to me first, okay? Neither of us has done anything wrong here."

Her eyes shifted just slightly to focus on me. She sounded about ten times smarter when she said, "If you're all about the truth, then why are you asking me to have a secret with you?"

So I just spilled it. I said, "God knows why, but my father is trailing Ratcovic in the polls right now. If you give your testimony to me, you arm Ratcovic to suggest it was some kind of setup. That's why I want you to come back tomorrow and tell your story to Ally."

Dead-on, she asked what's in it for her. And dead-on, I told her maybe nothing. Well, probably a little something when it's settled out of court, but don't get a fresh paint job for the Camaro just yet.

She stood, put her hands on her hips in what looked way too much like disappointment. She toed at her shoe, turned it over and slipped it on. Did the same to the other.

So I said, "Jenni, please."

She walked closer, mirrored me with her hands flat on my desk. "'Pleease,'" she said, mocking me. "Say it again, Mister *Do-You-Know-Who-I-Am.*"

God help me, I did it. I said, "Please, Jenni."

She smiled wide open like an actual teenager for the first time. She said, "Okay," and with that one word, Barrio Girl appointed Joseph Way mayor and sentenced his opponent to a live broadcast of his bloody, bone-snapping tumble down the rocky hill of infamy. On Fox, of course.

She turned her ass on me, like a bag of pissed-off cats, and swung it around on her way out. I nodded out a five count and practically ran out of my office to tell Callie, "That girl was never here."

"What girl?" Callie said without bothering to look up.

I literally levitated back into my office, behind my desk, and snatched up the phone. My father just had to hear this, right?

Wait . . . *wait*. I think someone's walking down the hall, toward my room.

(CLICK.)

(CLICK.)

Okay, whoever it was just sort of evaporated or something. That was weird.

Where was I? Let's jump to Friday morning, when I woke up with Jenni Sanchez's chubby fingers wrapped around my cock.

Well, sort of. I was lying there with Beth's breath warm in my neck and her fingers snuggled in the waistband of my boxers, so I just nudged her hand down to give her the morning news. She chuffed a little laugh and fondled me sleepily. Damn me straight to hell, but I couldn't resist fantasizing that it was saucy Jenni Sanchez who'd snuck into my bed.

If you've even *seen* Beth Pruitt, let alone had her suck your earlobe and groan softly like it's dipped in chocolate while she strokes you to full attention in the morning, you'd know how whack-ass crazy it is to be in bed with her fantasizing about a chubby Mexican teenager.

I can't explain it. I just can't.

When I turned over onto Beth, she opened her legs but not her eyes. She smiled a little and raised her knees, guided me in with both hands. She said, "Good morning. And so it seems you're fucking me." It was an absolutely perfect beginning to the end of life as I knew it.

When I get into work an hour later or so—for the sake of my reputation, let's say it was *two* hours—Callie said to me, "Just keep walking." Then Ally turned the corner and I smelled the Marlboro Lights off her. She'd power smoked, trying to huff it out the window. She waved wildly for me to follow her.

A quick primer on Ally Wong: She's fortysomething and surprisingly beautiful in photos, frozen in place. Agelessly Asian, smooth-skinned and sleek-haired. But in motion, her face is always post-tequila, twisted and angry. Jacob Moore summed her up when he called her "indelicate and decidedly unelectable." Apparently, she'd at some point expressed interest in succeeding my father and her hopes had been quickly dashed.

But, c'mon: Ally is a triple-shot espresso, slinging you right past perky to jittery and confused. I get the feeling it's by design. It's how she gets an edge on you.

We were barely inside her office when she started waving her hands and hissing, "Close the fucking door!" When I turned back, she was on me, twisting my lapels in her fists. From my vantage a foot above her, I could see the two pencils holding her bun together. One time, in a caffeinated fury, she'd reached up, grabbed the pencils in her fists, and speared them deep into a Big Mac, her eyes wide like a silent-movie samurai.

They didn't hold the special sauce. And so you must die.

She started out: "You're never going to guess what I just did. Go on and guess." When I tried to guess, she clamped her hand over my mouth so I said, "Wowowowowowoof." The thing is, Ally clamps her hand over your mouth so much that it's not always the right time. You'd have to know her to understand.

When she removed her hand, I said, "I'm thinking a speedball."

She goes, "Ha-ha-ha-ha-*ha*," deadpan, with a stone-cold expression. "*Or* I just videotaped testimony from a Mexican teenager accusing Lester Ratcovic of sexually molesting her."

Ally Wong will never know how close I came in that moment to throwing up on the top of her two-penciled head. I meant to say, "Did you say he *molested* her?" But my lips just parted a little and that was it. Ally knocked on my forehead with her knuckles and said, "Hello? Anybody in there? Lester Ratcovic is fucking dead in this town."

She went on to explain that he'd called the girl thirty times in three days and we'd have the phone records by the end of the day. Moreover, the girl had been humping an intern when Ratcovic showed up at her aunt's door, a white kid from Whiteville, "just like you," Ally said. The kid had already agreed to testify.

Still nothing new. Right up until Ally said, "The girl says he dragged her into the supply closet and started humping her."

I blurted out, "She said *that*?" It wasn't damning, but it was far enough out of place to make Ally do her little caffeine twitch. She tossed it off, found a remote on her desk, and punched the TV on. After some static, Jenni Sanchez appeared sans eye makeup and attitude, looking every bit the eighteen-year-old she was.

"He grabbed me by the arm," she said, her lower lip quivering all scared and weak. "He wanted me to help him find a stapler in the closet."

Wait, wait. Time out. Someone's walking around the house again. Who the hell's awake and why are they meandering about at this hour?

I'll bet it's Nathan. He would be profoundly stoned by now. Meandering and eating.

Well, okay. *Poof.* It stopped again.

So anyway, when I was driving home that evening, whipping down the highway in my very sweet Audi, I was beating myself up, wondering whether I said something to make Jenni Sanchez think it was a good idea to lie to the district attorney *on tape.*

Because that's exactly what she did. On Thursday night she admitted to me that Lester Ratcovic had never touched her inappropriately. On Friday morning, she told Ally he dry fucked her in the supply closet.

I broke it down in my mind: Nobody knows about her prior visit but me, right? Well, there's Callie, but Callie doesn't really count, I figured.

Regardless, while I was weaving smoothly between cars on the way to my dad's house, I realized that if I did the right thing, if I stepped forward and told *how* I knew Jenni Sanchez was lying, it'd be me sweating buckets under the naked, swinging bulb, not Lester Ratcovic. And that would doom my father's already flagging campaign.

Quite the dilemma, right? If I follow Dad's lead and hold to the "ethical imperative" he preached, I have to spill the whole gloppy mess onto the table for the whole world to pick through. But by doing so, by admitting I'd advised Jenni Sanchez, I'd blow it into some low-level scandal. People absolutely crave that shit these days.

In a way, *not* telling keeps things in perspective, right? The end justifies the means in some Lincolnian–Clintonian way. After all, Jenni Sanchez did what she did of her own volition. Nobody but her did anything wrong.

Right?

That settled, I did something I've been trying to stop for about five years: I thought about Mara Pinkett. Back at Wittenberg, we were straight out of a romantic comedy—we hated each other but we just couldn't keep me out of her. She's the house blend, this beautiful, caramel-skinned Rasta girl who thinks she's saving the world or something. She left to cover wars overseas but now she's back running a hippie rag over on the Left Side.

What I was thinking was, what if Mara got a hold of *this,* huh? She'd make a meal of it, boil the bones and serve soup. But what I was *really* thinking right underneath that was, what if that put us back in contact?

What would happen then?

And so this is the problem. Everything that happens to me,

in the end, gets funneled down to how it might draw Mara back into my life for a curtain call, a last dash of libidinous melodrama before I settle into the politically advantageous comforts of monogamy.

For the record, I have never cheated on Beth, and we're not even married yet, okay? Not once. I'm just a big talker with a vivid imagination. We have this whole life together mapped out and I don't want to screw it up.

Beth is perfect. I couldn't have drawn her up any better.

Okay, so now we're up to Friday evening, maybe thirty hours ago. My dad and I hung out on the backyard tee box between his house, this very hundred-year-old, six-bedroom Victorian, and a tree line that falls off quickly into a gulch, a creek, and then a stretch of woods. I can see the glow off the antique lamplight from here in my room, just barely illuminating Heather Locklear, eternally hovering over me.

Okay, you know what? I'm supposed to be recording notes that ultimately lead to a eulogy. I'm doing *something* here with this tape recorder, but I'm not sure what if anything it has to do with a eulogy anymore. I keep saying "you," like teenage girls do in their diaries: "You are *not* gonna believe where Bobby touched me last night!" But I have no idea who the hell *you* are.

I'm not sure of much right now. Not much at all.

Okay, Friday evening and the tee box in my father's backyard: It was warm for early October that night, still is. At dusk it was maybe sixty degrees. There was this crisp autumn perfection to everything, but I always felt that way when I was with my dad.

Two men, father and son, in untucked polos and carelessly mussed hair, sharing a bottle of Glenlivet single-malt scotch as they practiced their drives.

My dad, all barrel-chested and still wavy-haired handsome, bit a Cuban between his teeth as he smacked his ball into the trees. He said the same thing he always said: "Fucker went three hundred yards, easy."

If more men could say "fucker" like Joseph Way, it would be on third-grade spelling tests. He knew how to say it, and when *not* to say it.

So now I took my cut, and it fired off the tee like a bullet. I'm strong, man, like two hundred pounds and not an ounce of fat. And I said, "Using your math, that one should arrive in downtown Columbus any moment now."

Real scotch. Real men. Real rich. Women can have their *Cosmo* nights. This was an *Esquire* moment. I'm telling you, when my dad and I were together, testosterone dripped from the trees.

He prodded me with his driver and that set off a fencing match. The truth is, we were more than "best friends." More than father and son, too. There was just something *more* about us. I could feel a connection so direct it was like I began precisely where he left off.

I was never happier or more complete than when I was with him. Let me just say that.

But there was this matter of Ratcovic surprisingly jumping ahead in the polls. There was some visible scurrying and hand-wringing going on lately, perfectly executed by the people mayors pay to scurry around wringing their hands.

So he said, "You been reading *The Independent?*" It was a matter of time until he brought up Mara Pinkett. He went to the wooden bench beneath an antique street lamp and I'll be damned if a copy of the rag wasn't lying right there. In Joseph's world, there are no accidents. He picked up his prop, handed it to me, and said, "Have you read it since the communist you used to fuck started running it?"

I had, of course. But I still snorted at the pretentious tagline under the banner: KEEPING IT REAL. It bears mention that Mara had been *way* more terrified of our college canoodling being found out than I was. She couldn't have the other revolutionaries knowing she was taking a ride on a Republican, but that didn't keep her ragged jeans on her perfect ass, now, did it?

I knew what he wanted, so I read the headline out loud: *"Is Lester Ratcovic Too Good to Be Mayor?"* Beneath it, frizzy-haired Lester Ratcovic smiled warmly and looked endearingly rumpled, educated, and apolitical in his smart-guy glasses. That's his shtick, in a nutshell. Everybody's got one.

"I guess we know the answer to *that* now, don't we?" my dad said while he checked his grip on the driver.

It occurred to me, so I said it: I couldn't figure why he wasn't more stoked about the whole Jenni Sanchez thing. He hadn't even brought it up. So he growled, "We would've kicked his ass on our own. Now everyone'll say we got it handed to us when that liberal perv finally got his wanky in the ringer."

It was the "finally" that struck me even more than the casual use of "wanky." My dad read it off me and said everyone knows

Lester is one sick Democrat who doesn't even golf, like that was just as damning as his taste for teens.

When I handed the rag back to him, though, he shook his head sadly as he stared at the photo under the headline. He said, "Guy's got a pair of fourteen-year-old daughters. Imagine what this'll be like for them."

That's when it hit me: Joseph Way didn't have to know Ratcovic's girls to care about how this affected them. And that's why he wasn't celebrating. He was actually *saddened* by the whole affair.

So what the hell is wrong with *me?* Did I ever stop to think that when shit like that happens—whatever actually *happened*—flesh-and-blood human beings suffer? What about his wife, man? What'd *she* ever do wrong?

So I clinked the glass in his hand and said, "Here's to you, old man." And I'll tell you right now: While I was knocking back my scotch, I had the first sense of loose footing. Like sod slipping under your golf cleats. Something was in motion, something out of my control. I could just feel it.

And just maybe I'm the one who set it all in motion.

So my dad slapped his thighs as he stood, which means the meeting's adjourned, basically. He said, "So we'll keep your profile high and The Plan rolls on."

The Plan, remember? My life. The sequel to his.

He started toward the house and I asked if he and Mom were kissing babies tonight. Most of the mayor's so-called social life is perpetual campaigning at some event or another. He turned and said, "My *God,* man. Campaign or not, it's the second Friday of the month. I'll have a scotch in one hand and a full house in the other."

Poker night is the second Friday of every month. It's his break from public life. Then he asked what *I* was doing, but he didn't ask it in that polite way, like he was returning the favor. He'd abruptly developed deep and sincere interest in my plans for the evening. I told him I was having dinner with Beth.

He asked that I be a little more specific and I explained that Beth made the reservations so I didn't know. He gave me shit, asked if she was picking out my clothes, too.

Then he kept standing there. And one more time, he said, "You really have no idea?"

Finally—*finally*—he walked away and I turned into one more drive. For some reason, my right foot slipped on the grass and I sprawled backward, did a jerky, arm-waving 360, my club waving up in the air until I used it to poke at the ground and steady myself.

I didn't go down. I didn't fall. But it was weird. That never, ever happened before.

Three hours later, Beth and I were on the chimanea-heated patio at the Savoy Riverfront Inn, this really gorgeous historic hotel and restaurant on the Rocky River, which is admittedly more of a stream. With rocks. But the reopening of the restaurant was something of an event and, while I'd passed on the party the night before, Beth accepted their offer of a reservation and gratis meals the next night.

The steaks were great and the red wine was going to my head. Jenni Sanchez is on her own, I decided, and there's nothing in it for her to reveal our meeting. In all probability, as Ally hinted, they didn't have a molestation case against Ratcovic anyway. He'd be charged with harassment and a deal would be struck for a minor cash settlement that would keep Lolita in condoms and beer for no more than a year or so. Best of all, Ratcovic would pull out of the race, my dad would forge on as mayor, and I'd become a U.S. congressman in a couple of years. As the man himself said, the Joe Way Plan rolls on.

So I stared across at Beth, looking mouth-watering good in the lantern light, and said we should smoke a couple of almost-Cubans. Beth asked if I was actually celebrating the very public moral disintegration of another human being, but she knew the answer.

I mean, *of course I was.* So was she.

Everything has always been easy like that between Beth and me. One assumes there's more to practically everybody than meets the eye, and with Beth you're sure of it. I guess that's always been good enough for me.

We looked at each other for a while, making silent bedroom promises, and then she said, "So, you're gonna be a congressman, huh?" It's funny how we all just assumed I would win. Like there wasn't a shred of doubt.

So I made a joke about her being my dutiful and photogenic wife, and she went off on an overacted girlfriend rant: *"Excuse* me? Must I remind you that I'm the youngest instructor at the finest prep academy in the entire state of Ohio? I have a master's degree from Brown University and blah-blah-blah . . ."

I leaned in close enough to smell the vanilla-and-spice perfume she has mixed just for her and said, "Most importantly, you have the most inspirational little ass I've ever seen."

Beth likes being hot, like someone who wasn't at one time. I figured someday I'd get around to asking her if I'm as insightful as I think. Anyway, she slipped into a low, slow simmer that nearly made me forget the whole cigar idea. But not quite.

I said, "I'll get two cigars and we'll celebrate your ass." She said she'd smoke to finally getting approval to teach self-defense in the girls' gym classes, if I didn't mind.

When I stood up, I leaned in close again and whispered in her ear, "Smoke to whatever you want. I'll be thinking about your ass the whole time."

I heard her throaty chuckle—more promises—as I headed in through the restaurant. I went past the reception desk, toward the small gift shop off the lobby, and smack into the Twilight Zone.

Just before I curled into the open door, I heard a wide, familiar laugh from inside.

My father's.

And in that moment, I knew without the slightest doubt that there had never, *ever* been a standing poker game the second Friday of every month. At times like these, you simply know what you know.

I peered around the door frame and there he was, standing at the cash register, shirttail hanging out. He'd made a quarter-assed attempt to disguise himself in sunglasses and an Indians ball cap, bill pulled low over his forehead.

He bellowed at the middle-aged clerk behind the counter, "Come on, let's go!" He snapped his fingers, but he smiled like they'd played this out before. She did her part, pretending to be irritated when she said, "Hold your water, old man," and took her sweet time pulling a pack of cigarettes off the shelf and sliding it across the counter to him.

He turned quicker than I'd expected so I ducked around the corner and watched him step into the elevator, tossing the cigarettes up and catching them, over and over. He seemed like somebody else.

I moved quickly, located the stairway but watched the numbers on the elevator until they stopped at three. Only then did I bolt up the stairs three at a time. When I hit the metal door marked 3, I took a deep breath and nudged it open a little and peered through: I saw him walking jauntily down the hall, still tossing the cigarettes up and down and whistling to himself. Halfway to the end, he slipped a key into the lock of room 324.

The door clicked shut behind him and I tiptoed up to it, listened to the muted conversation and laughter inside. My dad and a woman who wasn't my mother. And right there, I stopped loving my father and started hating him.

It was *not* a gradual transition.

I banged on the door three times. When he yelled, "Yeah," I said, "Room service."

It just came out. I didn't plan it.

The door opened and life locked into freeze-frame. Joseph Way looked right into my eyes, his mouth hanging open. In the silence, I could hear the faint ding of a distant elevator.

And then my father actually said, "Don't tell me you're out of Rolling Rock again."

I didn't want to crawl out of my skin. I wanted to explode and cover my disgusting, adulterous father in human chum. "That's a joke?" I said in a shaky, low, homicidal voice. "You're making a joke?"

A woman's voice came from inside: "Joey?"

I was turning in tight, angry little circles before I knew it and my dad pulled the door nearly closed behind him.

I said, "You're having an *affair*? Are you kidding me? Mayor Joseph Way, the moral stoic, is having an affair right here in the Savoy Riverfront Inn? Could you *not* get directions to the seedy part of town?"

He calmly explained that this wasn't exactly an affair, at least not in the traditional sense. Furthermore, it had very little to do with being the mayor, or a stoic, or even my father. My reaction to his thoughtful explanation was a blinding need to smack him right in the face, really hard.

Instead, I spoke in a shaky teenager voice, saying, "Is that right?" while I edged backward, toward the elevator, retreating from this unspeakable horror. I asked him what exactly this *is* about, then. And the fucker holds out his hands like some fucking fucker of a shaman and says . . .

"It's about love, Joey."

This I know I said: "You won't mind if I just vomit right here in the hallway, will you?" I meant those to be my last words, because, well, it was pretty damn cool under the circumstances.

But he said, all warm and calm, "Listen, Joe. I'll come to your apartment tomorrow and we'll talk. Your mother and I have an eight A.M. tee time, but then—"

So I'm striding back at him stiff-legged, thrusting my finger at the air, and saying in this bitchy voice, "Shut up! You shouldn't even speak of her, let alone golf with her. I forbid it!"

Those were my last words to my father. The elevator arrived with a ding and I went into it with one more damning thrust of my finger. I could see him standing there, his hands still held out as the doors closed.

Damn.

(CLICK.)

(CLICK.)

Sorry. Let's get back to it, okay? Whatever happened between then and the sun coming up Saturday morning was basically lost in the martinis. Next thing I knew, I was trying to open my eyes but they were *encrusted.* It crossed my mind that if you're too drunk to wake up and actually regurgitate the vodka, it has no other recourse but to seep out your eyes and ultimately crystallize there.

While wiping my sandpaper tongue around my Styrofoam mouth, I swore to never, ever drink again. And it hit me that I am not the guy who wakes up entirely uncertain of what happened last night. I drink, but I drink well. It's my honest opinion that if you're bad at drinking, you should focus your efforts elsewhere.

But here's what happened: I smelled my dad's aftershave. The thick, cloying one only available at "vintage" barbershops frequented by older men who don't really care how their hair looks or at least don't know any better. It has a little green lid and a jaunty homosexual on the label, which seems to contradict its manly reputation and core ingredient of cheap bourbon.

But the point is, I definitely, positively smelled it. More than that, I could just *feel* my father there, his warmth nearby on the edge of the bed. Although I will admit that beyond "bed," I didn't exactly know where I was.

All thoughts that I might have been dreaming disappeared when he spoke to me. He said, "Get your ass out of bed. We've got work to do." He was very close, almost whispering it in my ear.

But the next voice I heard was Beth's. She said my name, once and then again.

I woke all at once, and for reasons I don't understand, I dug my heels into the king-sized bed at the Savoy Riverfront Inn and pushed back against the headboard, trying to get away from something.

There, in panties and a Cleveland Browns jersey, Beth sat Indian-style on the bed beside me, her elbows resting on her smooth, even-toned knees. She was intensely watching the TV in the armoire across from us as if something significant had happened. I couldn't register the objects on the TV yet—they were just colorful blobs.

I asked if my father had been there and sucked in a deep, hungry breath because my head was spinning. Once I asked, though, I realized how profoundly unlikely it was that my father had been sitting there with us in our hotel room.

Beth had turned away again to the TV and didn't hear me. I reached out for her, tried to touch the wavy trendle of golden hair escaping her scrunchy, desperate to know this self-induced horror would end and there would be beauty in the world again.

Abruptly, ice water coursed through my veins and into my chest cavity. Last night was there, available on demand. I pressed it back down. Not yet.

When Beth turned I could see her red eyes and tear-stained face. She sobbed and threw herself on me, knocking me back onto the pillow. She rocked me a little.

It's important that you know I had no idea what was going on just yet. Plus, I already had a hangover hard-on and now it had made its way into the crack of Beth's panty-covered ass and she was rocking on it. Involuntarily, my hips elevated and I heard a quivery sex breath escape me.

Beth was horrified. She said, "What the hell are you doing?" and practically rappelled off of me, wiping her eyes with both hands.

Here's the thing about Beth: She wasn't originally from Benton Heights. But no girl had ever been more *of* Benton Heights, and there was a time and a place for everything. And for whatever reason, this was clearly not the time for me to dry hump the crack of her ass.

And that's when she blurted, "Your father is dead!"

I had to agree that was an excellent reason not to have sex at that exact moment.

Her eyes grew cartoonishly huge, then, realizing she'd just jammed the information into my face like wedding cake. I froze into a statue of a horny, hungover man reaching desperately for his panty-clad fiancée.

Your father is dead. That's what she'd said. You only say that kind of thing if it's true. It's never appropriate as a practical joke. She wasn't going to say, "Just kidding. Now that you're awake, let's order bagels and mimosas."

So, I realized, my father really *is* dead.

Beth climbed back on the bed, on her knees, straddling me but not touching me. "I'm sorry," she whispered. She looked at the TV, leading me to look, too. A grim-faced male reporter held a microphone, the stunning, PGA-quality golf course in the background.

He said, "By all accounts, Mayor Way hit a terrific tee shot down the middle of the first fairway and then suddenly grabbed his chest and collapsed on the ground. Joseph Andrew Way, the mayor of Cleveland, is dead at sixty-nine."

Nobody knows why the mind does what it does under extreme circumstances. But when Beth turned back to me, what I saw wasn't her deep sense of sorrow or commitment to helping me through, but that her Browns jersey had been cut into a V at the neck, exposing the freckles at the top of her breasts.

She noticed and raised my chin with her hand, looked me in the eye and said, "Honey? Do you understand what's happened?"

I didn't, exactly. I knew on a technical level that a heart attack had erased my father's name from the People Who Are Alive List. But "understand"? No. I wasn't quite there yet.

I'm still not, I guess.

But then this laugh burst from me and Beth flinched like I'd sneezed at her. And I say, "Jesus, is his timing unreal or *what?*"

After a round of blinking and twitching her head to understand, Beth just said, "Um . . . w*hat?*"

I couldn't help it—I laughed again and shook my head at it all. Beth struggled and finally confessed that while there were many ways she imagined I might cope with my father's death, this wasn't among the finalists.

She asked if I was still drunk. It seemed hopeful. I shrugged. And then she started crying again and said, "Oh, God . . . oh, *baby.*" She was on me again, rocking me, and my erection was still very much in the room with us.

Finally, she said, "You're in shock. It's too much to absorb, so you're covering it in this very strange, horrifically inappropriate way."

I told her she was absolutely right and maybe she was. At that exact moment, though, I was not at all sad that my father had died. He deserved it. Sometimes God works in mysterious ways, and sometimes he puts an M-80 in your heart if you cheat on your wife.

So Beth was rocking me again, unintentionally elevating my "inappropriate response" to a significantly higher and more turgid plane. Because we'd agreed that I was in shock, she didn't stop me when I hooked my thumbs in her panties and started working them off.

You know what? I'm just gonna cut ahead a half hour or so, when I'm in the shower. I turned off all the lights and made the water skin-flailing hot, just trying to cook off the film encasing me, I guess.

The thing is, not only had I laughed at the notion of my

father dying the morning after I caught him in an affair, but I'd coaxed a perfectly good fiancée to have sex with me, leaving her there in the bed, wallowing in the obscenity of it all.

As I was heading into the shower, she'd said, "Whatever this is, Joe, I suggest you get over it before you see your mother."

No shit. I knew Rita Way, the Woman Behind the Man, simply wouldn't swallow "shock" as a response to my father's death. A life is defined by moments like these, goddamm it, and one does not sleepwalk through them. One seizes the moment and performs. One falls hard and rises swiftly, with dignity and grace.

And this wasn't exactly shock. Not really. I just didn't feel *anything*. I didn't want to fuck Beth because my dad had died. I wanted to fuck Beth *in spite of* my dad's death. I didn't care enough about it to *not* fuck Beth.

The monumental breadth of such a thing occurred to me there in the shower and I had to slide down the wall and sit there in the void. I mean, until the night before, I'd known what I'd always known: Everything good about me came from Joseph Way, Senior. The most noble and worthwhile human being I'd ever met just happened to be my father.

If my dad had died one day earlier, they would've had to sedate me, pure and simple. The pain would've been unbearable. I'm not sure how long it would've taken to get it together and wash myself, but off the top of my head I'll go with a month.

And somehow, as excruciating as it would've been, I felt cheated. He'd taken something from me.

He'd taken my grief.

Okay, you know what? I want to tell you about my father now, whoever you are. I want you to at least know the basics because I think it matters to your understanding of what I may or may not do between now and the funeral on Thursday.

So here's what I used to know: Joseph Andrew Way graduated college in his twenties without ever graduating high school. How? His small-town's minister had helped him get into the military early to escape an impoverished childhood. And back then, war heroes went to college where they wanted to, diploma or no diploma.

Soon after college, he founded J. Way Home Security by pilfering catalogs for a top security-system company, banking that they wouldn't turn away the unsolicited contracts he was sending along in droves over the measly 10 percent he was asking.

He grew his plucky scam into Northeast Ohio's largest home-security provider, complete with 280 patrolling security guards and exclusive marketing rights to the three most prestigious in-home systems available.

By 1987, gross revenues had topped $25 million. A minor celebrity at the peak of his powers, fifty-five-year-old Joseph Way retired with more money than most people can even comprehend.

At the time, my older brother Nathan was a Romance languages grad student at Berkeley, which, of course, proved beyond a reasonable doubt that he was queer. My dad was basically absent for Nathan's teens, and while he never actually said it, he was convinced that being bestest friends with his own mother may have at the very least been the nail in Nathan's heterosexual coffin.

It bears mention that Joseph Way had literally outlived his daughter, my sister, but I don't want to talk about that right now, thank you. And by his way of thinking, he'd lost his oldest son, too. He wasn't about to take any chances with me.

So Dad was there to enjoy my senior year, help me choose a college, and get to know me before it was too late. Oh, and in his spare time he co-chaired the local Republican Party in Benton Heights, the densest concentration of rich white people this side of Dearborn, Michigan.

The King of Kings, he was. The epitome of the Cleveland Conservative. How lucky you are, they all told me, to be the most important person in such an important person's life.

And I bought into it, didn't I? Just like I'd believed every word Joseph Way said. I'd waited a long time for my busy, powerful father to take an interest. No way I would blow it now.

How lucky I was, indeed.

Four years later, there I was with my right hand flush against a fat boy's ass, everything on the line; Wittenberg was trailing Dennison 17–16 in the league championship game.

After a touchdown, Coach Erickson sent the squatty South American kicker waddling out to tie the game with an extra point. I shoved Eduardo or Gerardo or whatever he was back to the sidelines and headed into the huddle with my ten gape-mouthed teammates. *We're going for two.*

It was my moment to seize, and it came down to this: Either I would be carried all the way back to Benton Heights as a folk hero like my father, or be reviled as the most narcissistic dick-head in the history of forever.

I took the snap, having already decided to fake the handoff I'd called. After all, if the back didn't get in, I'd still be the one taking shit for epic levels of boorishness.

I got hit by a defender just as I pulled the ball away from the runner, who then dove empty-handed and confused through a wide-open hole into the end zone, further enhancing my potential infamy. I'm really not that fast, so I staggered, dragged my foot awkwardly, and missed taking a knee by about an inch. There were no TV cameras for a Division III league championship, so those minor details aren't part of the official truth anymore.

So I broke away and, well, let's say I *sprinted* toward the front corner of the end zone. But then, to my horror, it became clear that while I could outrun a fatter, older man, I couldn't outrun the lean, young safety angling at me. So I put my head down and ran right into the kid.

Barreled, staggered, *fell.* Like I said, there were no TV cameras. Everybody says I barreled.

For a second, we were standing bolt upright together, frozen in place. So I played out my final card and left my feet, tried to launch us both across the line.

I scored. The safety tipped back and ultimately fell over with me on top of him. By agreement, the way the tale is told properly, I changed the play and flattened a safety to score the winning two-point conversion.

The first person to reach me, even before my own dumb-struck and from-then-on inconsequential teammates, was my dad. His eyes were moist with tears and he could only say, "I love you, Joe. I love you!"

And in that moment, in my father's arms, I knew who I was without the slightest assistance from Fran Fucking Tarkenton. It was all so clear and simple because there was just this: the two of us, the victors, holding each other in the end zone.

Forever captured in glossy black-and-white, that would be the only necessary record of the event.

As my father smoothly ascended to the mayor's office, my path unfurled in front of me, gold and straight, clear and true. I would follow where he led. That's the way it would be, forever and always. That's what he took from me by not dying two days earlier.

That's it for now, I think. I'll tell you more tomorrow. Whoever you are.

(CLICK.)

(CLICK.)

You'd really think a couple of scotches, two Valiums, and three fingers of red wine would just lay me out, wouldn't you? But I could swear someone was in my teen time capsule of a bedroom, watching me, and it freaked me out to the nth. Clearly, since I'm back talking to you, nobody was really here.

Well, I'm awake now, so let's get back to whatever the hell this is, shall we?

Later this morning, Beth drove my Audi to Benton Heights and my parents' house once I'd pulled myself together a little. Under a low, slate-gray Ohio sky, she eased into our circular drive and pointed out that Jacob, Mark, and even Crane Parker were already there. She looked me over and seemed convinced my unshaven, bleary-eyed, and broken-down look just might play, under the circumstances.

I knew my father's unofficial advisory panel wasn't collected just to exchange anecdotes. These are men aligned by purpose. Every action, even death, initiates a reaction.

Beth took my hand and traced her fingertips over it. And she was the first to say, "You do realize you'll be expected to deliver the eulogy."

Well, yes and no. As in, yes, I clearly knew they'd expect that of me. And no, that would not be a good idea. See, the guy everyone assumed knew Joseph Way better than anyone now knows *too* much. So who's my backup?

Sitting there with Beth petting my hand, waiting patiently for me to say we could go in, that was the first time I realized I wasn't just pissed at my dad for cheating on my mom and stealing my grief. Suddenly everything I knew about the world and my place in it was under suspicion.

Let me put it this way: Two days ago, I would've bet every penny in my trust fund that my dad would never in a million years be unfaithful to his wife. If I was wrong about that, what else was I wrong about? Not just about him, but about everything and everybody that just forty-eight hours ago seemed so thick and permanent and *definite*?

And here's the thing took me upside the head, then: The fundamental Me is built on assumptions. Assumptions about right and wrong and good guys and bad guys and which flag I salute and which colors I wear. What I believe in and what I *want*. If it turns out too many of those bricks are cardboard, I'm destined to come crashing down, right?

And from all of this profound thought, I put together these

words in response to Beth: "Really? You think they'll want me to give the eulogy?"

Even under this sky and these circumstances, she couldn't resist the dead-eye "duh" stare. Because, c'mon! I'm Joseph Way, Junior, for chrissakes. That's who I am.

Just the same, I asked about Nathan. I mean, he is the oldest son, right? Isn't there an official guide somewhere that says that's a viable option?

So Beth nodded very sincerely and said, "Yeah. He could sing his favorite Bette Midler song. That one from *Beaches*, maybe."

I made the mistake of saying Nathan's not that kind of gay—he's not—and she laughed and wondered when, exactly, that had mattered in Benton Heights or anyplace like it.

Life is so much simpler here, or at least it was. Straight or queer. Conservative or page-fucking, tax-raising, baby-killing, draft-dodging, queer-loving liberal. And if you don't play golf like every other right-thinking man, you might be latently predisposed to any or all of the above.

Since I can remember, if ever a person said to me, "It's not that simple," from that point on I had them pegged as a navel-gazing pissbrain. Because it was *precisely* that simple, man, if not a little more.

Not anymore, though. Now it's all slippery and hot, liquid pouring through my fingers.

I turned to Beth, hoping in some way she'd just get it, because she always seemed to just get it, and I said, "I'm not entirely sure what I'd say right now if I gave a eulogy."

She looked at me for a very long time, somewhere between sympathy and irritation, and finally said, "Let's go in."

Our house, the house I grew up in, had been dutifully restored to its original 1912 state. Actually, it was made to *look* like it had back then, like a movie set or something. And once the phrase *movie set* locked in my head, it made me see everything through a lens.

When I walked into the great room, I could've said Jacob's line with him: "We lost one of the good guys." I nodded tightly to him, which was dead-on the right thing for me to do. The room is dark, woody, and authentic. Just perfect for that day's crucial scene.

The three men closest to my mother and the center of the room were far more important to my father than the ambitious suits that made up his actual staff. The suits were necessary, because a mayor is expected to have a staff of qualified and reasonably photogenic up-and-comers standing behind him when he talks.

But the truth for almost every leader, whether he's a governor or mayor or even president, is that he takes his real cues from people you'll never know. In my father's case, those people were Jacob, Crane, Mark . . . and me. At least I've always included myself on that list.

Mark had been a fixture in this house since we were both kids, so we also communicated in manly man nods. Mark patted my back and held my shoulder for a dignified moment. His cheek twitched like it always does, even with the meds, and it reminded me of the time we were teenagers drinking warm beer stolen from my father's garage and he emptied one of his capsules into my can. I woke up on the front lawn, soaked by the sprinklers and my own piss. I couldn't remember what happened for about three days. Then I knelt on his arms and slapped his cheeks crimson and made him say stupid things.

But we were still best friends.

Also in the light, I realized I'd always known that Mark wore makeup, concealer that shows up too powdery in certain lighting. I'd always pretended not to know, because wearing makeup is kind of gay wherever you live and Mark isn't gay because he's part of our inner circle where gayness just isn't part of the program, okay? See, that's how you keep everything in its place and running as smoothly as Mark's made-up cheeks. It takes commitment, dexterity, and delusion, in precise dosages.

Crane Parker, by the way, was my dad's Honorary Alternate Best Friend and Golf Partner. His lot in life had always been to learn the playbook and stay sharp in case Jacob was unable to fulfill his duties. Crane is cut for an old guy and a little intimidating, even to me. He was military and I'm pretty sure he's killed people. I just hope it was *while* he was in the military but I wouldn't be shocked to find out otherwise.

I'm not sure *what* would shock me now.

So anyway, there were other people there but they just filled in empty spaces and nodded and stuff. Day players at best. I picked up a never-filled brandy snifter and felt Beth's eyes on me. I didn't mean to say it out loud, but I did. I said, "It's a prop."

Before I could ponder too deeply if I was alone, the only one who could see that none of it was real, Beth cleared her throat and nodded at Rita, my mother. She was sitting there in the corner of the overstuffed couch, reduced in size and gripping a framed photo. All I could feel then was love for her and everything else mercifully receded for the moment.

I said something and she looked up at me. She covered her mouth and darted her eyes between me and the framed photo in her hand. She laughed and said, "He made you in his own image."

At that, Jacob and Crane exchanged glances and did this little move where they seemed to fade back into the satiny walls to wait their turn. It's really impressive.

I sat down next to my mom and looked at the photo, a weathered black-and-white of my parents at some sort of yard party at a lesser home, grinning broadly and toasting beer bottles at the camera. They looked to be early thirties—Rita effortlessly pretty, Joseph handsome if a bit goofy, black hair falling across his eyes.

My mom touched the image of my dad and said, "I remember you." It bothered me somehow, something I sensed I would figure out later, although I didn't know that blathering into a microcassette all night could be part of that process. For the time, I took her framed photo away from her and set it on a table and held her.

She said, "He was a good friend." Before I could roll that over a few times, Jacob patted my back, a signal that a quota had been met but not exceeded. There *was* business there. I was right.

As I stood, my mom wondered if Nathan would come and I promised that he would, even if I had to fly to Berkeley and drag his skinny ass back. Beth stayed behind and I looked back to see her watching me.

For a moment, we locked eyes and we were saying something, having some conversation. She sensed danger, felt the rumble of impending *something*. When she exhaled, it was shaky and scared.

Still the choreography was truly magnificent and Beth played her part as scripted. Just as Jacob and his meaty hand guided me toward the study with the others, Beth gave Rita her picture back, helped her to her feet, and rubbed at her Dinah Shore shoulders as she guided her up the stairs toward her bedroom. I heard my mother say what sounded a lot like "more Valium." At the time, I assumed I'd misheard.

In the pine-walled den, we skipped the heavy leather furniture in favor of standing while Jacob and the other two took turns suggesting what I already saw coming: They wanted me to use the eulogy to declare my candidacy for mayor in my father's place. After eight years, I would run for governor and then eight years later for president. After all, governors were doing better than Beltway insiders these days, so it's all for the best.

Not my father's death, Jacob was quick to point out. Not that, of course.

When Beth pushed through the double doors, I had yet to say my first words. I took her by the elbow and said, "Do you know what they want me to do at my father's funeral?"

And it turned out she did know and didn't seem horrified in the slightest. In fact, she shrugged because, well, it seemed to make pretty good sense. In truth, I would probably win, right? And I had a clearer path from very young mayor of Cleveland to governor than from congressman to president, right? She has a quick mind, Beth, and she has a way of just saying things others won't.

It seemed ghoulish to me and I said so. Even for adulterous phonies, your funeral should probably be mostly about *you*, right? I left out the adulterous phony part for their benefit. Honestly, it would be like telling them Jesus was a black chick.

Beth shrugged and bit her lip, which means what I said sounded real nice but was ultimately just bullshit. My speechlessness gave Jacob an edge and he grabbed it, waded in a little, and revved back up with the rhetoric. It all ran together in my vodka-clouded brain, but let's say it was something like, "We simply can't let this be an ending, Joe."

In the flurry, one or the other said, strange as it sounds, this is an opportunity . . . we can't let four years of hard work go to waste . . . we have to make damn sure *that pervert Ratcovic* never holds office in this town.

And that's the moment I began to connect Jenni Sanchez's decision to lie on camera to my family and the people who surround us. Because the only other person who knew outside of Callie, who doesn't count, was my father. And if my father knew, Jacob probably knew. And if Jacob knew, it was quite possible that everybody in this room but Beth knew that I had sent Jenni Sanchez home on Thursday afternoon.

And, hell. Who said Beth didn't know?

It was like caffeine injected into my temple, and I realized that until just then I'd been gradually emerging from drunk. I woke up all at once, standing there in the middle of my dead father's study.

So I steeled my eyes—which I can do at will, after years of practice—and asked Jacob, "Did you say Ratcovic is a pervert?" Like I'd caught him in something, liked he'd accidentally revealed his knowledge of the Jenni Sanchez Affair.

He spat out a laugh and said everybody knows that man likes his meat rare. I must've missed that meeting because I was apparently the only one who *didn't* know.

Beth pointed out to me, quite correctly, that my father would've stepped into the void and run for mayor if our roles were reversed. I almost laughed, because Things Joseph Way Might've Done had recently become a *much* longer list.

With that, I found myself fleetingly imagining my father at my age, like he'd been in that framed photo in my mother's hands. Would I have loved him back then?

Or hated him?

Mark stepped forward with his eyes twinkling and the corner of his mouth twitching and delivered a really great speech, never realizing that in this light his makeup was too light, too dry, and altogether too evident. He said, "We live in a world that can't afford to lose Joseph Way. A world so morally vague that Lester Ratcovic isn't laughed out of town for having the fucking audacity to run for mayor. So it's not enough to honor your father with words. You need to do more with this space in time."

Mark had an edge on me this morning. He clearly hadn't thrown back 323 martinis last night. And though I could still obliterate him in tennis—hell, I could ace Mark from a hospital bed—my verbal sword was more of a butter knife.

So when I was back on my heels, Jacob the Elder closed in for the kill. He said, "Ratcovic gets his grimy little hands on this thing, he'll never let go. Cleveland's a big wave right now, and he'll just ride it for a good eight years. Do you really want it all to go to waste? Do you really wanna let the legacy end?"

I looked out at the pool, at the water, and that made me think of my sister and the fact that 40 percent of my family is gone. It came over me like a tidal wave and I very nearly cried. I heard myself say, "Everything's changed."

Jacob appeared in front of me much more quickly than seemed possible, based on time and girth and other mathematical factors. He was playing hardball now, like, "Straight up, what we want you to do come Thursday is go up there in front of all these rich powerful people and tell them why your daddy was just this close to being Jesus Fillmore Christ. And then we want you to pound your fist on that goddamn lectern and proclaim that you will *not* let his death be in vain. And that's why you're officially declaring your candidacy for mayor in your father's place, if for no other reason than to keep it from a man who, with every breath, insults the memory of all that Joseph Way accomplished."

Beth edged into the narrow space between us, looked me in the eye, and said, "You're meant for this. I believe that."

And you know what? She does. She really, truly does. Damn.

And between that and the memory of my sister, I couldn't hold back the tears much longer without suffering an aneurism. So I just turned and walked out.

I barely remember stripping down to my underwear or jumping in. The next clear thought I had, I was exhaling to sink to the bottom of my parents' well-heated pool. It felt every bit as good as I'd hoped. I sat on the bottom in my boxer shorts and looked straight up, into the gray of the water-rippled clouds.

I tried to imagine what my sister's accident might have looked like from beneath. It's the only angle that would've told the whole truth of it.

When I broke the surface, Beth was standing at poolside with an oversized towel in her hands. She knelt closer as I waded to the side. She said, "Is this another peculiar twist in your already distinctive emotional meltdown?"

I *like* Beth. I sincerely do and so would you. And now that I say it, it sounds like an apology. But there at the edge of the pool, earlier today, I just told her I wanted to go to the Big Park.

The Big Park, by the way, is what I called Travers Park when I was little. And that's where my older sister Kate died when I was six years old.

I'm gonna take just a second here, okay?

(CLICK.)

(CLICK.)

I don't like sneezing *or* crying. I hear people talk about how much better they feel. I don't believe it and I didn't cry just now. I nearly pulled a muscle, but I didn't cry.

Anyway, twenty minutes later, Beth stood beside me on the near bank of the pond in the center of Travers Park, just outside of Benton Heights. Glimpses of the sun came through the clouds, making the surface sparkle. Past the tree line, a barren Ferris wheel stood as the last remnant of a small summer carnival I never had time for.

Beth waited patiently until I talked about my sister for the first time in the eighteen months we'd been together. Kate was fifteen, pretty as an angel with a laugh that made me want to follow her around just to hear it again. Nathan was fourteen and I was six. Somehow, she flipped her paddleboat and hit her head on something. Nobody even noticed.

Such a small, quiet way for someone so necessary to die.

But what I remember best is my mom bringing me here every day the rest of the summer, like she was looking for Kate. I'd play, and she'd sit near the water on a blanket, drinking cup after cup of lemonade that smelled like cough syrup. And she'd wait for the daughter who was never coming back.

Beth asked about Nathan, and I told her that at fourteen, he was way too busy clinging to the absurd notion that he wasn't gay to hang out at the park with his little brother and drunk mommy.

Beth asked when he was coming; I told her I was picking him up at four. And that's when I saw my father on the far side of the pond with his trademark knock-kneed stance, chipping one after another from a row of golf balls directly into the water.

My instinct was to assume it wasn't my father's ghost, which left the nagging question of *who in the hell does that?* So I chuckled to Beth and said, "What's with *that* guy, huh?"

My blood chilled when she asked what I was talking about. I wasn't ready to let go of reality just yet, so I described the guy she couldn't see, told her he was chipping into the pond right there in plain view.

When I pointed at him, he waved, tossed his nine iron into the pond, and dove in after it. He hacked at the water like Jerry Lewis drowning before going toes-up and disappearing. The wake dissipated and the surface went to glass far too quickly.

When Beth pressed, I had to tell her he was gone, now. When she asked where he'd gone, well, I told her that, too.

In the middle of my attempt to laugh it off on last night's martinis, she got me by the jacket with both fists and her voice dropped into a severe no-bullshit register. She said, "I hate to do this, Joe. I really do. And maybe it's not fair that you don't get a chance to wander around glassy-eyed but you just don't, okay? That's not who you are. You have a eulogy to deliver and a candidacy to declare and come Thursday night a whole lot of people are going to be looking to you to tell them how they feel and what to think, okay? *Okay?* So you're gonna need to pull your shit together, hon. That's just the way it is."

I waited for some salve to soothe the flogging, some sympathy or maybe a hug, but she just shrugged. The thing is, she was all over it, man, even without knowing the details. So you caught your father in an affair and suspect that just maybe he got to Jenni Sanchez that night and used her to run his opponent off the mayoral road, through the guardrail, and into the murky death of his dreams. And, okay, maybe you get the sense that the man you apparently never knew is still lurking around the edges, trying to get your attention.

Put a Band Aid over it and let's move on already.

My cell phone chirped and scared the piss out of me. I am *so* close to being literal. Ally Wong wasted no words, cutting right to this:

"Jenni Sanchez is dead."

(CLICK.)

ENTRY 4: SUNDAY, OCTOBER 10, 1:41 A.M.

It was my bladder this time, not the ghosts. While the Valium and wine aren't putting me to sleep, they did a smashing job of making me list to the right and piss all over the odd little afterthought of a bathroom off my former bedroom.

Back to yesterday: The home Jenni Sanchez had shared with her thirty-year-old aunt Jackie on the yellowed fringes of downtown didn't have a bombed-out El Camino in the front yard or a Harvest Gold couch on the porch. But it *could* have.

A handful of barrio boys—all torsos and heads in their oversized T-shirts and baggy pants—loitered in the front yard across the street, passing their gray Saturday with fists wrapped around quarts of beer. They were all show, gangsters of boredom, sons of secretaries in a neighborhood that isn't good enough or bad enough to matter or make the news.

When I pulled into the driveway, six cop cars were lined up

the gravel berm in front of the one-story pillbox of a house. Too many cops pooled into small groups in the patchy front yard while just one kept watch over the woman crying and guzzling from a tall-boy on the porch swing. When I got closer, I heard her ask the squat female cop, "Can you get me another? They're in the fridge."

I'm totally fucking serious.

The female cop shrugged and headed through the creaky storm door. They don't cover stuff like that at the academy.

I asked this very young black cop I recognized who the woman was. He told me it was Aunt Jackie, and turned his back to her before saying, "I'm pretty sure the party's back on after we put her niece in a drawer."

I asked the kid his name, thinking that he looked more like a high school running back than a cop. He said he was Jason or Justin or something and that it was an honor to meet me, *sir*.

He called me *sir*. Someone called sir should have their shit in a much tighter knot than I do. Seriously.

I asked and got my answer about Ally's whereabouts—back at the creek. When Jason or Justin told me they'd just taken the body out five minutes ago, his voice quivered. He still cared, that one.

The backyard dropped a sudden thirty degrees for roughly twenty yards off the cracked slab of cement that serves as a back porch. A tangle of trees blocked the creek, but you could hear its gurgle blending with murmuring cops. The yellow crime scene tape stretched between an old tetherball pole and a stump, but it was mostly a formality. Only four teenagers—two girls and two boys—were in the backyard. They sat on rusty metal chairs near the charred remains of last night's fire, haphazardly bricked in. Crushed beer cans littered the party perimeter, along with a few overstuffed Busch boxes.

I'm good at seeing things. I don't just look; I *see*. I lock the images in my mind. Now I'm wondering about blind spots on the personal stuff.

One of the two girls, a slender Chicano in a hooded Indians sweatshirt, stared off with eyes tumbled over the arc of her Mayan nose. Her skin was creamy and the sadness was real.

In contrast, the boy next to her, in a flannel shirt and a soul patch, whispered something to a friend and they snickered together. The sad Mayan chick backhanded him square in the mouth, up under his nose. He called her a fucking bee-atch, but she dismissed him with a fluttering hand.

Ally yelled at me to get my ass down there. She was waving wildly, Marlboro Light between her fingers. The Mayan girl heard my name and when I looked back at her she was looking at me, too. Both of us knew we'd be talking soon.

I got to Ally just as Dan McCale reached her from the other side. He lit her cigarette, then his own. As always, there was something of a dark celebration to a crime scene.

McCale isn't ready for prime time and never will be, like most real detectives I know. He's twitchy and pale with orange hair pressed tightly to the side. He always seems to be turning back for the last thought, the last conversation, never ready to let go. A stuck needle skipping, skipping, and finally catching.

He's a smart guy, though, and a good detective. A ghoul disturbingly out of his element everywhere but here, under the dense, dank Ohio sky, with the heavy smell of stale beer and death. This is home for guys like McCale.

He mumbled something about being sorry about my dad. Ally fired off a me-too and added, "Jesus Fucking Christ, you know?" That's solace, Ally Wong style.

I asked if she got that from a Hallmark card. McCale made a whole bunch of half gestures and I decided he had something, maybe that Michael J. Fox thing. I figured McCale would die alone and not terribly mind. When you get to know people the way McCale does, alone is better.

I asked Ally what was up and she said the girl clearly had the fucking shit beaten out of her. She seemed legitimately disgusted, so I figured it was bad. But then McCale said we weren't so sure about that, and cut his shaky hand across the slope of the backyard. I knew he was suggesting that maybe she fell or something.

Ally pointed out that her head had been caved in and that Bulger figured she was hit like nine times. On cue, our aptly named, potbellied senior CSI made it up the rise, peeled off and tossed aside his gloves. At fifty, Karl Bulger is well into his last act. I'm sure of it.

He stood there wheezing and Ally turned her hand over in the air in front of him, urging him to get the fuck on with it already. He flipped her off with a sausage-sized finger and eventually managed to say, "Massive trauma to the head. Skull looks like an eggshell. Seven teeth broken at the gums, four broken ribs, and three busted fingers."

When I asked what she was hit with, McCale again said she could've fallen. Bulger said that was dumb-ass bullshit. You fall, you twist an ankle, bruise a cheek. He'd bet his career this girl was viciously beaten to death, and I was prone to believe him.

So I asked what he thought she was beaten with. Bulger guessed a baseball bat or even a hatchet handle. Something hard but not too hard. Not a pipe, for sure. Not a gun.

I asked about motive, figuring something romantic because it clearly wasn't a robbery. Me and Ally's eyes passed and snagged for just second or two. This smelled way worse than stale beer and damp, charred wood and she knew it just as much as I did.

Bulger said someone was either real pissed or having a hell of a good time bashing in that girl's brains. He pointed and I turned just as the body bag was sliding past. A few EMTs arrived with a gurney and met the coroner's goons, who hoisted her up and dropped her on it roughly. Bulger unzipped the bag and stepped back so I could look.

I pulled back the flap to see a fright mask of pain and fear. Her mouth was yanked down to the left, broken teeth and dried blood between her torn lips. One eyelid was ripped off to show the crushed eye beneath. The left side of her head was dented in like a melon.

McCale said, "It hurt, man. It hurt a lot." He was feeling it, too. I like McCale. I trust him. I heard someone say, "That shouldn't happen to anybody," then realized it was me.

Here's what I knew about Jenni Sanchez from our brief meeting the day before: She was a desperate, manipulative, dangerous girl. A girl who wanted things and found ways to get them. A girl who lied and made threats. A girl you found in a creek with a dent in her head. But still, a bullet would've sufficed. Why *this*?

I'm still wondering.

When I looked up, Ally was staring at me. She knew something and wanted me to know she knew it. Was she letting me in on it or fucking with my head? I couldn't tell. I still don't know.

I asked McCale if he'd talked to the Mayan chick and her friends. He said Elisa was "like" Jenni's best friend. I knew what he meant. Jenni Sanchez didn't have a best friend. It's not who she was.

McCale said none of them had the kind of marks you get for messing somebody up like Jenni was messed up. None of them was hiding anything, as far as he could tell. And all the while, Ally kept watching me, reading me. It was hard to pretend not to know.

McCale told me what he knew: Jenni was out, then came home and drank with them a little. She met a guy, had a fight, didn't wanna talk much about it. Everyone left her alone around 1:00 A.M. She was drunker than usual and in a mood, according to Elisa. It was how she got when she didn't get what she wanted.

My opinion of Jenni was validated. Like I said, I don't just look. I *see*.

Bulger said he guessed she died about 3:00 A.M. We all just stood there for a while, so Ally, never taking her eyes off me, said it would all still be here on Monday and I should go home to my family.

I never looked back at her. I just started up the hill. I felt someone following me and I was relieved that it was McCale. He said Jenni had something on her I might find interesting, and held up a Ziploc bag.

In it was a shred of paper. I had to tilt my head to read it. Right there, clear as could be, was the name Mara Pinkett. And then a phone number.

When I looked back at McCale, I knew that he knew all about me and Mara from the way-back days. I said, "Why does everybody always know about shit like this?"

McCale said, "It's my job to know shit like that, Joe." I got it. I understood. Navigating the system requires an understanding of the connections that pervert it. It's not right or wrong; it just *is*.

McCale and I locked eyes and nodded a little. This is how allegiances are made. Someday I would do something for Dan McCale. We would never have to speak of it.

I said, "Monday," and he said, "Monday." And then the thick green bag of broken Lolita bounced by.

I looked at my watch. It was time to get Nathan.

(CLICK.)

(CLICK.)

The damn tape ran out. I found this one in the little case. I hope I'm not taping over Nathan's single most profound thought of his lifetime, a definitive Answer to it All found in an obscure Italian novel. Anyway, I need to buy more. I'm on my second tape and it's not even morning yet.

While I was digging around, I realized that somewhere in my mind I'd logged the right time for my dad to die: after his retirement as mayor but prior to me becoming president or something like that. There might be a seven- or eight-year window when we were both normal, relatively speaking.

Why would that be the right time? I don't know. I guess because we'd belong to each other for a little while. The house would still be filled with cronies, but there would be a deeper sense that we were a family.

This scenario assumed that my father had managed not to slip himself into another woman or in some way cause the death of Jenni Sanchez.

That's the thing, isn't it? I mean, clearly Les Ratcovic had the motive for having Jenni's head cracked open like it was. But he didn't know; my father *did*.

Some doctor involved in one of my cases told me that most patients know what's wrong with them when they walk in the door, so the shortest route to a diagnosis is to set aside your ego and just ask them.

It's the same with cops and prosecutors, I think. About a day into an investigation, whether you say it or not, you know who did it and why. About three-quarters of the time, that's what you find at the end of the trail.

So here's what I know: My dad knew about Jenni. The next day she smeared Les Ratcovic on tape and that night she was promptly bashed and beaten, spinning and staggering all the way into the creek behind her aunt's house. So something wrong turned into something *very* wrong. Where I lie right now, it's a matter of how, not who.

But still I can't stop asking myself: Why did it go down the way it did? If a killer for hire took her out before she could tell the truth, where did the sadistic rage fit in? The job done on Jenni's skull was anything but detached and professional.

One way or the other, come Thursday I'll bury a stranger. I'll never feel the exquisite, searing pain of burying my *father*. And that pain was owed to me. It would've been part of who I became. It would've given me gravitas, I think. I'd be more the leader I'm expected to be, because I'm no closer now than I was five years ago. I've picked up a move here, maybe a crossover dribble, but that's about it.

So anyway, I went for Nathan at four, like ten hours ago. Nathan's thirty-nine, I think, and he looked exquisitely tweedy if jet-lagged when he flowed with the river of other passengers into Terminal C of Cleveland Hopkins Airport and right past me without a glance.

I turned to watch him freeze in midstep as he realized that the unshaven, bed-headed frat boy he'd instinctively averted his eyes from was me.

When he walked back to me, he smirked like he has since he was twelve, because I'm the porterhouse steak to his delicate, more sophisticated baked cod. He finds me dull and amusing, I think, even if my ACT score was too close for comfort to his own. He asked if I'd seen his brother and I admitted not lately.

I'm not sure what he read off me, but he dropped the smirk and just hugged me. If Nathan had ever hugged me before, I don't remember it. He held on tight and his body spasmed just once against me and I knew he was swallowing a sob.

I have to admit, I was surprised. But then, as he pulled away, he made the mistake of asking how I was. I sucked in a breath and said, "Just before Dad died I found out he was having an affair and I think he may have directly or indirectly persuaded a teenage girl to falsely accuse his opponent of molesting her so he could hold office long enough for me to run for congress as the mayor's son and now I'm suddenly wondering if Beth might be the perfect little accessory he picked off the rack for me and on

Thursday I'm supposed to eulogize him and announce that I'll run for mayor in his place and . . . you know . . . I really should get my shit together by then. At least that's what Beth said."

Nathan waited a beat, then said, "And the weather?"

But I wasn't done, so I went on, "Oh, and the girl? The one who accused Ratcovic of molesting her? She was murdered late last night."

Nathan looked a lot like I imagined myself looking when Beth blurted out that my dad was dead. His bike chain had slipped off and he was peddling air. So I said, "Who's up for pretzels and bourbon?"

The conversation we had a few minutes later in a little airport bar was the first tug at the loose thread. The emperor's new sweater is coming undone, leaving me naked and confused like in my dream a few hours ago.

Skies was a great setting for this sort of thing. It's a place for lost travelers who've forgotten who they were thousands of miles ago. But at least *their* existential angst came with business-class upgrades.

The first thing Nathan said, while I was throwing back a drink, was that he always knew "that fucker" was stepping out on Mom. I informed him that I found it quite a bit more shocking than he. I think I was less eloquent at the time and I may or may not have called Nathan a cunt.

Nathan laughed, amused that I bought off on the whole cut-rate Patton performance. Then he apologized, remembering that I'm basically a Xerox of a photo of a highly inaccurate self-portrait. His words, not mine, and I didn't take it as a compliment.

Somewhere on his next riff, he mentioned Medina, where everyone but me had lived over Uncle Roy's garage. Well, actually I was there for a bit but I was too little to remember.

When he saw me hook on to it, he said things were better there, before Kate died and he got queer and Dad became the great man. I know what he was going for: He was telling me that I never really knew our father, something I realize now he'd hinted at before.

But is it necessarily true that you're more authentic when you're poor than rich? Anonymous instead of famous? Aren't some people born to be important and everything prior to achieving that is, well . . . just everything prior?

That's what I'd chosen to believe, squeezing everything into a plain brown box labeled EVERYTHING PRIOR. Prior to me, prior to Benton Heights, prior to Dad getting elected. It was all quaint enough but ultimately pretty insignificant.

So then Nathan looked at me and softened like he was going to say something kind and big brotherly. But it came out, "I had to figure out who I was all by myself, precious. You never had a chance. And there are consequences to not knowing who you are."

His expression was like he was saying, I love you and we'll get through this together. He was sincere. He believed what he said and it saddened him.

And while I was reeling, he said that watching his father slowly turn away from him had been hard, but of all the specific injuries, the worst thing Joseph Way had done was ignore him.

For the first time, I could see that wound had never healed. I'd never bothered to use my aforementioned *seeing* skills on Nathan before, I guess. I always figured that there were far more dramatic falling-outs between Republican fathers and their gay sons. A little chill wasn't so bad, right?

Maybe it is bad, after all. Maybe it's *forever* bad. And while that settled over me, making it hard to breathe, Nathan said, "He also hit me, but that didn't hurt much."

Between a spit take and choking on my scotch, I went for the choke. It amused Nathan to have made such direct contact, and he went on to tell the story. He said our father was "looming" over Mom, holding her with one hand, the other pulled back to hit her again. Nathan, the skinny little hero, got in the middle of the scrum somehow and Dad hit him. He realized out loud that it was the last time his father had looked him fully in the eye for more than a few seconds.

He'd turned fifteen three days earlier.

Nathan laughed and said that he got over it. In fact, on the flight in, he had a healthy, cleansing cry for his father.

I told him that must've been nice, drank my scotch, and stood up too quickly. I bumped a nearby table and the two businesswomen there steadied their drinks and averted their eyes with tight little smiles.

I was piteous and absurd. And I'm surprisingly okay with that.

The drive from the airport is about a half hour. Nathan insisted on driving and without realizing it, I drifted in and out of sleep. I was in between when Nathan turned on the radio and found the Elton John song "Daniel."

My father had liked that song and so had Nathan. It was one of the very last things they ever had in common. I turned my head to mention it and instead of Nathan at the wheel, my father smiled back at me.

You heard me.

He said, "Hey." It was tentative and unsure, just as it would've been if he truly had appeared as a ghost to me. And then he said, "Seriously, we're gonna need to talk, you and me. We've got so much to do."

I knew it was a dream, so I stared right at him, seeking imperfections in the rendering. His eyebrows flared up just so and his top teeth were slightly less yellowed than the bottom, thanks to the peroxide strips he'd been using for a couple of weeks.

I heard myself saying, "You look so real." And the car hitched a little or went over something and I truly did wake up, hearing my own voice. We were in our driveway and Nathan was looking at me like I'd shit myself. He kindly recommended that I consider an Altoid. Or five.

I caught up to him as he reached the garage. He spun back on me, clearly upset, and asked if I really believed that Dad had something to do with this girl's death. Ever the politician, I said things might've gotten complicated because she was *that kind of girl.*

It wasn't political enough, because Nathan said, "Jesus Christ, Joe," like he was pissed at me. When I tried to defend my stance, he raised a hand to me just as he had when we were kids and turned his attention back to the garage and what we both knew was inside.

He asked if it was in there and *I* asked if he meant the Mercedes. "No, Dad's corpse, you moron," I think he said.

I told him, duh, yes the car's in there. Where else would it be? Like a switch was flipped, he was suddenly all intense when he said, "It's mine." So I just held my hands up in surrender.

He gestured to the keypad, so I knew he'd forgotten the code. I punched in the numbers and he even bent over a little to get sight of it just as soon as he could: a silver 1975 Mercedes convertible.

I told him it might look pretty but it needed work. He said he could handle it and I laughed because, well, he's gay. Nathan walked up to me, amused by my naïveté again. But whatever he was thinking, he asked about Mom instead. I told him to go on in and I'd bring his bags. I warned that she was a little Valiumized and, without a filter between her brain and her mouth, seemed quite a bit like Dorothy Parker.

Nathan went on and I heard something and somehow I just *knew* when I looked back at the car it wouldn't be empty. I was drunk all over again and my peculiar breakdown, as Beth called it, had enabled me to accurately dimensionalize very startling illusions: My parents, more than a couple of decades younger, were in the front seat. Me and Nathan, seven and fifteen, were in the back. Our hair blew in the nonexistent wind as we headed off on an obligatory summer vacation none of us really wanted. It was all part of getting back to normal life, as I remember my mother explaining in a slurred voice.

Kate had died a year earlier, and everything was a struggle

for my family: Driving trips. Cooking. Getting up in the morning. Breathing.

But Nathan had to pee. Dad angrily dug up a huge plastic water bottle with a screw-on lid and threw it back at him without a word.

Even back then, at seven, I understood that Nathan was not a pee-in-the-bottle-at-65-mph kind of guy. He whined and complained and finally my father yelled back at him, *"Could you just once act like a man?"*

The first time around, I have to admit I thought it was mean *and* funny. But this time I was looking right at Nathan's face and the unimaginable pain there. I wanted to reach in and grab the little-boy me before he laughed but I couldn't.

Just as he had back then, Nathan glared at me and tried his best to pee in the bottle. But he locked up and we had to stop after all.

The ghosts dissolved then and the car was empty again. The lights were on in my mother's room for the first time. Nathan always has that effect on her.

I could hear the laughter all the way from the opposite end of the hall. I considered skipping the party, but the notion of a nice, fresh Valium was starting to interest me. I had plans to sleep for fourteen hours or so and wake up as myself again. I was starting to fear that I would keep waking up like this, over and over and over.

I opened the door to see my mom propped up in bed, glassy-eyed and grinning. Beth was curled up beside her, wearing her future mother-in-law's wash-softened flowered nightdress. They held glasses of wine and the mostly empty bottle rested on the bedside table alongside the open prescription bottle.

Beth and I exchanged a long, strange stare. After what seemed like a minute or so, she said, "You always know just what to say, don't you?" She seemed mad at me for something I hadn't done yet but almost definitely would.

My mom said they were trying to decide what to bury Dad in, but it was like she was describing a party game. Then Nathan exploded out of the closet, so to speak, wearing a wide-lapel canary-colored suit, white-white shoes, and a loud, splattery tie that made me think of Jenni Sanchez just before they zipped her up.

Beth and my mom laughed and slapped the bed, but their train had left too long ago and I'd just made it to the station. Maybe I'm always late for the party, just like Nathan enjoys insinuating about the happy days in Medina.

I took a shot at dry humor and suggested he try on our dad's army uniform and do a Village People thing, medals and all. After the notable lack of laughter, my mom squinted at me and said, "You don't really think your father got medals, do you?"

Well, I knew he did, specifically for dragging four wounded guys out of a foxhole in Korea, thank you very much. But my mom explained that the story had been just a little embellished over the years.

I reluctantly asked what really happened. She said he dragged one drunken friend out of a bar before the MPs showed up, which she figured was heroic in its own way.

I should explain here that my initial plan was to be really

pissed at my dad and then, over a period of years, decide that he was an otherwise great man with a historically forgivable flaw: Daddy dug the fine booty. With so much precedent in politics alone, was that really so horrible? I was even opening up the idea that my own distinctive taste for the minorities among us could be fed without really diminishing *my* overall greatness.

Now, hearing my doped-up mother good-naturedly reveal that Joseph Way was less the brave soldier and more the Partying Private, I was getting that whole disintegrating-sweater feeling again.

So I just kept tugging on the thread, pointing out that he *was* an Eagle Scout, right? And my mom started laughing like it was the single most outrageously stupid thing she'd ever heard. In her slurred words: "Joey was the Bad Bell of Wellsburg right up until he was the Big Man in Cleveland, know what I'm saying?"

One thing at a time. First I had to express my shock that my mother had just said, "Know what I'm sayin'?" Then I decided *not* to ask what the "Bad Bell of Wellsburg" meant, assuming "bad bell" was some kind of goofy-ass, postwar slang. They were known for that kind of thing. Some movies of that era should have subtitles—one wacky teen exclaims, "Scooby-doo Larue!" or some shit and everyone laughs like it means something.

While I was still absorbing the notion of my father as a bad boy or bad bell or bad whatever, my mom thought it prudent to stare off whimsically and remember his ass. I think the line was, "But baby could he fill out those khakis."

At that point, I threw up my hands and asked if anybody

here was monitoring my mother's Valium intake, because it damn sure didn't look that way to me.

From their sheepish expressions, it was pretty clear that they had *joined* her, not monitored her. Beth admitted to taking one and Nathan copped to two.

So I washed down a couple of Vs with the last quarter of the wine bottle. Beth said something like, "You've *got* to be kidding," which made it clear that she does not regard me as someone who could ever be a bad bell. Well, Scooby-doo Larue, baby cakes, the party lamp is lit!

The notion was to just do it and walk out, which would've been fairly dramatic, right? But my exits have really sucked the last couple of days and I found myself locked in another stare with Beth. She was sleepy and sad, reading me and not liking the story at all.

So I said, "I'm sorry." I don't know why. It just came out like that: "I'm sorry."

She asked for what, of course. I quickly laughed it off and said we'd all be normal again tomorrow.

Beth said, "You think so?" And no matter how hard I tried, I couldn't hold my smile. Nathan saved me by leaping out of the closet again in a hideous red jumpsuit my mother had worn to a Christmas cocktail party when I was about ten. He struck that Charlie's Angels pose with the hip jutted and his hand's gripping an invisible gun and said, "Freeze, turkey!"

I tried to make my escape while they were all still laughing, but Nathan said my name. He knelt down and dug in his backpack, which was next to his suitcase, and I asked why his stuff was in Mom's room. He looked at me like I was ignorant and explained that he was sleeping in her bed, under the circumstances. It made me feel very alone, a leftover from another era in the Way family. Things had gone back to the Medina days and I had no point of reference.

Anyway, Nathan handed me a leather case with the microcassette recorder and a couple of extra tapes. He said, "Just start talking. Maybe in a few days it'll add up to a eulogy."

That was three hours ago and damned if I'm not *still* lying here, awake. And talking.

Shit. Okay, that was a casserole dish hitting a beer bottle. Somebody is absolutely, positively digging through the refrigerator, and I'm guessing it's a stoned college professor with the munchies. Nathan's like a sorority girl; he does the serious eating when nobody's looking.

Well, you know what? Nathan's been wandering around for about two hours so he could probably use someone to talk to. That will *not* prevent me from scaring the living shit out of him though.

I'll tell you all about it when I get back.

(CLICK.)

(CLICK.)

Um, okay. Excuse the shaky voice, but it turns out it wasn't Nathan foraging for leftovers in the fridge.

It was my father. That's what I said: my father.

I tiptoed my way down the stairs and in the arched doorway to the kitchen and I could see that the tall door of the Viking was open. The person on the other side was too impatient to actually carry the plate of chicken legs to the counter, which only reinforced the plausible theory that Nathan was stoned, which makes him totally indistinguishable from a half-starved dingo.

I figured I had him right where I wanted him, hyperfocused in the middle of a feeding frenzy. So I got to within a few feet of the stainless steel door without making a sound and yelled *"Ahhh!"* with zero regard for the others in the house. Collateral damage is acceptable in these matters.

I saw the plate of chicken legs crash to the floor and that's when Nathan's wide-eyed head shot up over the door.

Except, like I said, it wasn't Nathan.

It was Joseph Way, Senior. And as if that weren't sufficiently mind-blowing, he was down to about sixty years old, where he was when I was Mr. Quarterback at Wittenberg. He was thicker, fuller-faced, and his hair was still more black than gray. He was wearing his favorite yuppie suit from back then, tie loosened to midchest.

I circled around to face him, my arms frozen out at my sides like they'd been when I'd tried to nuke Nathan, who was apparently all cuddled up in Mommy's bed still. And my dad grinned a little and said, "What're you trying to do, Joe, give me a fucking heart attack?"

And then he started chuckling, all pleased with himself. Like, "Heh-heh-heh." I don't recall my dad *ever* acting like that, at least not in front of me.

I tried to say something but it came out more like the last sound you make before you start bawling like a baby. My dad— my *dead* dad—laughed at me and shook his head. I never realized how much he looked like Older Paul McCartney at sixty.

When words finally came out, they were "Jesus shit fuck!" My dad pointed out that you don't hear *that* every day. He bent down and picked up a drumstick from the smashed plate at his feet and said, with his mouth full, that dying is *really* hungry business.

The line popped into my head so I said it: "Good to know. Now go back to hell."

At that, the son of a bitch actually held out his arms for a hug. He said, "You don't mean that, Joey. Come on. Give me some."

I told him no fucking way, but he just kept calling me in, tinkling his fingers. "Come on, Joey," he said. "Don't leave me hanging here. Where's the love?"

The lines were really clicking now: I told him it was in room 324, last I looked.

That one got him. He was finally off his feet. By way of apology, I guess, he said, "Did I ever tell you how deeply in *like* I was with your mother?"

Yeah, whatever. I tried to wake up and said to myself, "Three scotches, two Valiums, and a little wine. That's all this is." Somehow he heard me and said, no, I'm totally real. And I'm like, *right*. My dead, adulterous, never-was-a-hero father is scrounging in the fridge for leftovers.

So that's when he admitted he's in something of a predicament. I hopefully asked if he was talking pitchforks in the ass, that sort of thing, and he said not exactly. But he was stuck. And then he said it was *my* fault. *I'm* the one keeping him around, chipping into the pond at the park and scamming all the leftovers.

I told him I would far prefer that he moved on to his eternal damnation, since he'd not only cheated on my mother but somehow influenced Jenni Sanchez to lie to the district attorney. And that fucking bastard had the unmitigated gall to get pissed at me. His eyes got all intense and he said, "Christ, you pampered little fetus! What the hell do you know about *anything?*"

Yeah, I tried to point out that philandering dead men can't jump attitude, but he kept going. He said, "Nothing's ever happened to you. *Nothing.* You never had to work for anything because, like an idiot, I just handed it to you. You're educated, you're white, and you're rich. What could you possibly know about life? You haven't even skinned your knees yet. Put your head through a few windshields and maybe then we'll talk."

He even turned away from me in disgust and went for the hardboiled eggs. I told him I don't even know how to think of him anymore. I don't know who he is.

Was.

And you know what he said? He said, "You don't even know the half of it yet."

So I fired back that I hate him. That's *one* thing I know. And at least he had the decency to be hurt by that. He said that's what's keeping him here: He can't move on until I forgive him or some bullshit like that.

I said fine, whatever. If I forgive you, you can get out of the leftovers and I can wake up, take some more Valium, fall into a dreamless coma, and then set about proving you're an accessory to murder?

He said what the hell. Let's give it a go. I said, "I forgive you for fucking around on Mom and being a complete phony of a father. Now shoo. Go 'way."

He leaned his head back, spread his arms, and looked toward the heavens. We both waited.

It didn't take. He said, "Aw, shit. I think you have to mean it."

That's when I woke up, back in my bed, with this itty-bitty recorder on my chest. But I remember it so clearly. Every step down the stairs, every single . . .

Hold it. Gotta go.

(CLICK.)

(CLICK.)

Well, that couldn't have gone any worse.

Beth heard me talking and came in. She sat on the edge of the bed and asked if I was okay. It took me a second, but I realized she thought I was talking in my sleep.

She was still in my mom's nightgown so, like a genius, I pointed out that she'd clearly spent the night. She said my mom insisted right before she sang "Just the Way You Are" and passed out. All three of them had been sleeping in my parents' king-sized bed until Beth heard me "going on and on."

Then she sniffed at the air and blinked back tears and called me sweetie. When I asked her what all that was about, she said it was adorable that I'd put on my father's aftershave.

Which, of course, I hadn't.

I didn't say anything, though, so she kissed me and said, "I love you." And guess what came out of my mouth?

I said, "Really?"

She jerked back like I'd stuck a pin in her hand, eyes all wide and everything. Her voice went homicidally low and she said, "I beg your pardon?" I tried to laugh it off, which turned out to be a sorry-ass job of damage control. I reached out to brush a lock of hair from her eyes and she smacked my hand away so hard it left a mark. It's still there.

She just said it again, only slower: "I . . . beg . . . your . . . pardon?" I didn't have a choice. I had to press forward. So I asked if she thought we were really in love or maybe just *deeply in like*. And I just kept yammering on and on about how maybe that's better in the long run and after a while I don't know *what* I was saying. I know I heard the word *companionship* come from me, and women under fifty don't take that as a compliment unless they're in a wheelchair. Permanently.

Her eyes were slits and between her lips I could see her teeth clenching together. It would not have surprised me if she'd fired off some kung fu punch right on the bridge of my nose and left me there crying like a schoolgirl. She was that pissed.

So with my life or at least my dignity in peril, I came up with, "You know what? Forget I said that."

She smiled and nodded as she stood and said, "Oh, okay. It's totally forgotten." It seemed just a bit sarcastic to me. I begged her not to take anything I said seriously after the booze and the prescription muscle relaxers, but she wasn't having it. I swear to God I could see her breath. She said, "I didn't know how or when or where, but I knew someday it would bite me in the goddamn ass."

I asked what and she said, "Your dad introducing us."

I couldn't think of a response because in a very specific way, she had cut right to the nut, hadn't she? The chill between us is all about her prominent place in the now very suspicious world my father constructed around all of us.

She raised her eyebrows, like, you got *nothing*? And I finally managed to say, in a very obnoxious soap opera whisper, that I was *so* sorry.

Needless to say, she was not impressed. She said, "Wow, Joe. I was a little worried you'd stroked there for a minute, but how can a girl stay mad when you hit her with *that* material?"

She even mocked the soap opera whisper as she turned away: "I am *so* sorry." It really was pretty queer.

When she flung my door closed, the Heather Locklear poster on the angled ceiling above my childhood bed curled and fell for the first time ever. While I was fighting it, she looked back in and said, "Do me a favor, okay? When you're done sifting through everything in your life that isn't quite what you thought it was? Let me know if I make the cut."

Then she slammed the door again and left for real. And I'm way too scared now to sneak into my mother's room and lift a Valium so I'm just gonna lie here and think about how the week of my father's funeral was *supposed* to be.

Oh, fuck it. I'm getting that Valium.

(CLICK.)

ENTRY 7: SUNDAY, OCTOBER 10, 11:25 A.M.

(CLICK.)

Hey, guess what? I just smoked pot in the woods with Nathan. First time since I was in high school. I think I did it maybe four times before I became, you know, *Joe Way.*

I just made those little quote marks with my fingers and there's nobody here to see them. So that's Level Two stoned, at the very least.

And I still have no idea what me and this little tape recorder are trying to accomplish together. Something important, I think. Part of it's that I can't remember who I was before I was the guy who gets to have his name chanted, if only by a couple dozen beer-buzzed construction workers. I was a swirling, muddled mass of inconsistency and uncertainty, sort of like now. Maybe that's really me and everything in between was just bullshit. Seems entirely plausible all of a sudden.

I'm hiding out in my room while Nathan showers and makes something of his thinning hair and then the two of us are driving to Wellsburg, where my dad grew up and eventually met my mom. We came to that grand plan in the woods and it would've been significantly cooler if we'd just jumped in the car and drove. Unfortunately, Nathan's a raging priss, but it gives me time to catch you up.

When I walked into our dining room a couple of hours ago, everybody tried to pretend I wasn't unshaven and generally unkempt in a paint-splattered Wittenberg sweatshirt I found in my dad's closet. The dress code for Sunday brunch here is usually informal but clean and sporty. I'm significantly closer to hungover and mostly cloudy.

It took some of the glare off me that my mom, usually torqued up in a culinary frenzy and wearing her crispest oxford and corduroys, had wrapped herself in an old, fuzzy robe and a haze of muscle relaxers. She held Nathan's hand and leaned against him dreamily.

Beth, having achieved functional cuteness in spite of her hangover with a light V-neck and jazz pants, finished lighting a row of candles down the middle of the table just as I made it to my chair. We sat at the exact same moment and I instinctively leaned in for a kiss. She recoiled and whispered, "You're kidding, right?"

My mom squinted, vaguely aware of the mood, and Nathan quickly jumped in and told me Jacob was cooking this morning.

I looked around the room—it hasn't changed one bit in my whole life, from the endearingly tacky primitive of St. James

Square to the weary oriental rug with its family timeline of faded spills and the strange mix of Hummel birds and fake flowers. Every Sunday, my dad walked in and demanded that the whole mess be torched and rebuilt from scratch. My mom would level him with her slate-eyed stare that can numb your extremities and he would wave his surrender. The dining room is hers to ignore, to let settle into an embrace of unfashionable predictability and permanence.

Jacob barked hello to me as he entered with an industrial-sized vat of Italian sausage, potatoes, and onions. He'd become something of a comfort-food gourmet since his wife Lydia fell to cancer, figuring he owed nobody a diet after all he'd lost.

So as he set the delicious-smelling mess down, something occurred to him and he looked at Nathan and said, "You still eat meat, don't you, Nathan?"

Nathan about spit his coffee out. I chewed the inside of my mouth hard enough to draw blood. And then my mom said, almost defiantly, "My Nathan eats meat." Those were her first words of the morning. Then she said, "He eats meat *all the time.*" I'm just really glad I wasn't stoned yet.

I didn't even realize Beth was speaking to me at first because she never came close to looking at me. She said something about having faxed the obituary to the paper and that I needed to take my mother to look at caskets on Monday, if I could squeeze it in between not shaving or combing my hair. Again, I swear I could see her breath, man.

Jacob lumbered back in with what amounted to a barrel of eggs with cheese and chives and asked if I'd thought about the eulogy. He started to press it but my mom cut him off hard and said we weren't going to talk about that now. She fell into a half-senile smile and said we should each share something we loved about Joseph Way. Wouldn't that be nice?

So Beth jumped right in with, "He was the strongest man I ever knew. He had such *clarity*." She was pretty smug about it, like she'd been the only kid in class to raise her hand. But then my mom goes, "I said loved, dear. Not respected. It's different, you know."

Beth arranged her napkin and said, "Well. I guess I get an F then, don't I?" She and my mom exchanged bitchy looks for a second and then out of nowhere, Nathan said, "I liked the way he smelled." Beth whispered, "Momma's boy," and threw a tiny piece of sausage that tagged him right on his massive fivehead.

Nathan dipped his fingers in his juice to spritz her, but Jacob cleared his throat and put an end to it all.

In the silence, Nathan's glibness flaked away in layers, right before our eyes. He said, "On Saturdays, his golf day, Mom would go down to put on the coffee and I'd sneak into the bed and curl up against him. He was all warm and sleepy and smelling of Clubman and I'd press my face into his back and just hold on.

"He'd reach back and pat me and say, 'Good morning, Natie.' He'd try to get up, but I'd just hold on.

"I'd hold on . . . until he pushed me away."

It was so quiet you could hear the sausage still hissing. Nathan said he bought some in a drugstore in Berkeley a few years ago, but it didn't smell right.

The pain flickered in Nathan's eyes again before he caught it and put it away. The same look I'd seen in the backseat of the Mercedes almost twenty-five years ago. I think that's what a broken heart really looks like. It's not showy or overacted and if you don't look closely you won't notice it at all.

Nathan said my name, like it was my turn. I nodded and pretended to be thinking about it, buying time. Mostly I nodded a lot, though, so Beth kicked me in the leg and told me to just pick something I loved about my father and say it. She called me "sweetie," but it sounded so much like "fuckhead" that I thought for a moment she'd actually said it.

I opened my mouth and nothing came out. Jacob cleared his throat and looked straight into my eyes and said, "I remember answering the door that day thirteen years ago."

He told the story directly to *me:* "When my Robert died up in New York, in some dank, dark shithole with a needle hanging from a scab in his arm . . . just a week after I told him not to bother coming home again . . . nobody could even look me in the eye. Nobody but your father."

At that moment, *I* couldn't hold his stare, either. My father had just come home from a business trip and Jacob saw him out the window. My mom said something and Dad dropped his bags right there on the sidewalk, started walking across the street. Jacob opened the door and my dad just grabbed him. He held him so long that Jacob thought maybe, just maybe, he might be able to stand the sight of himself one day.

Jacob finally looked away from me and wiped his eyes. He said, "I think he would've stayed there with me forever if I wanted him to."

Nathan looked at me, like he was getting it, you know? Like he'd figured out where I was coming from. So he grabbed the massive serving spoon and shoveled a load of the sausage and potatoes onto his plate. And he said, "I don't know about the rest of you, but I'm gonna start eating Jacob's meat now."

Jacob went home right after breakfast to be alone with his grief. On the anniversary of that day—that humid July day in 1989—he stays in the house and pulls the blinds. In all that time, only my father and a bottle of single-malt scotch were welcome.

Beth and I rinsed and loaded dishes together without exchanging a word. I could see Nathan through the back window; he sat alone on the glider, smoking boutique cigarettes, staring at the tee box, probably imagining the last evening of his father's life and digesting the fact that I'd been there and he hadn't.

Beth passed me a plate but when I grabbed it, she held on. She refused to let go until I looked at her, which I could take only in small doses. She whispered, "Jesus. Who *are* you?"

I very earnestly admitted that I wasn't entirely certain anymore. To which she shot off a quick, cold laugh and said, "Oh, that's just *precious*. Who writes your lines? And what shitty soap opera was she fired from?"

I wasn't ready for her to let go of the plate, so when she did, I flung it hard over my right shoulder to explode into a thousand pieces against the far wall, just about three feet above my mother's head. She was standing in the doorway with two water glasses, which she promptly dropped to smash on the floor.

She pondered for a moment, nodded very tightly, and said, "Yes. Well. I'm going to go back upstairs now." She did a tidy little turn and left, taking the express train straight back to Valiumville.

I was going to use it as source material for some tension-breaking humor, but I turned and found my jaw clenched in the wet rubber glove on Beth's right hand. She went up on her toes and covered my mouth in hers and it's the first time I've been kissed with so much passion and disappointment all at the same time. It made me dizzy.

Then, just as suddenly, she harshly pushed away my soppy face. She said, "I've gotten pretty much accustomed to being disappointed by people I love. I never thought I'd be adding you to that list."

And then she was gone.

Like I said, I know Beth has a story. Some part of me probably knows *I* do, too, but I'd managed to carve out a stern opinion on that sort of thing. I'd decided each of us is only what you see, not the messy sum of everything we've been through.

All I know is Beth left home very young for an elite boarding school in New England or somewhere leafy like that. She didn't return for almost a decade, after college, after her stepfather died and her mother had her stroke. That's when the two of them moved to Benton Heights, into the Victorian fixer-upper just off the square.

I realize that fourteen-year-old girls don't just leave home for a decade. It doesn't happen, not without some cataclysmic event that shapes you and keeps reshaping you forever.

But wasn't my father's relative disappearance from my life, from our family's life, roughly the same length? Hadn't he quietly slipped out the door after Kate's death and returned just in time for my senior year? Hadn't his space at the table been filled by a hologram and sometimes just a cardboard cutout with a fork permanently poised above his plate, eyes flat and disinterested and *absent?*

It's always seemed simpler that I am Joe Way and she is Beth Pruitt and our story begins right now, right here, and we make it precisely what we want it to be. Clean and simple with a predictably cheerful ending.

That's another thing my father took from me: my blissful ignorance. I'm turning pages now and I'm not sure I can stop. I'm talking into microcassette recorders and having *internal dialogue,* for God's sake. Only, you know, out loud.

So I went out to Nathan at the glider, still staring out at the tee box. And I asked if he still loves Dad. Nathan answered not yes or no, but, "He was what he was."

I told him that was precisely my problem. He *wasn't.*

Nathan asked, "What about you?" Meaning, what does all this mean to *me,* right? If the original was a fake, what does that make the Xerox?

Nathan left that broader issue rest, and directly asked if I felt at all culpable for Jenni Sanchez's death.

I'll tell you what I told him: I did, right up until somebody killed her. Because that meant somebody else got to her between me and Ally. Somebody coached her. Somebody had a plan that went very wrong. And because that somebody wasn't me, I'm not responsible for what she did or where she ended up.

Nathan stared at me for a long while and I knew he was

palming a card to play later. For now, he looked into the woods with a laugh and asked if I ever knew what he really did out there. I told him I didn't need to know about his transgressions with God's woodland creatures, thank you very much.

That's when he pulled the tightly rolled joint out of his pocket. At least one of life's great questions was answered: How could anybody get *that* happy collecting leaves?

Nathan held the joint between his fingers, raised an eyebrow, and said, "Wanna?"

I'm not sure why I went along, except that maybe things couldn't get any weirder. And a few minutes later, we were down in the gulch and I was floating instead of walking.

I remembered the last time I was high, before Wittenberg and The Touchdown and becoming the Great Son of the Great Man. I was just Joe Way, the house alarm guy's kid. A promising if unspectacular football player, a solid student, and an enthusiastic cocksman. At the WRA, none of that made me glow, exactly.

Jesus, how in the world did I ever get into Wittenberg? It's like the most elite college in all of Ohio. Oh, yeah—the test score. I blew up the ACT, like a 32 or something. I was accepted while some of the finer eggheads weren't and then I went on to validate that choice by getting a 3.75 and acceptance to one of the state's finest law schools. It wasn't even hard, you know? I barely had to study.

In fact, you know what? Sometimes I didn't study *at all*. It didn't seem to matter. It was all coming together—the clarity of me. The clean lines and absolute connections.

I said something—I really don't know what—and Nathan started laughing. I laughed with him and we did that stoner nod like we both knew some exquisite secret.

When we finally settled, I became fascinated with seeing my breath but being unable to capture it. I said, "Cool," and Nathan corrected, "No, *cold.*" And yes, in the moment, that qualified as clever, maybe even profound. We both nodded some more to confirm it.

Then Nathan got serious and asked why I didn't tell a story about Dad, and I admitted I couldn't think of anything at the moment. So he found a golf ball, threw it into the woods, and told me I was a fucking asshole.

I took exception, of course. He shook his head and said just because Joseph Way wasn't the bullshit icon I'd believed him to be doesn't mean he would have a girl killed. There's a lot of available real estate in between.

He was pissed at me, for real. He said, "Yesterday he was a god, today he's a demon. Maybe if you judged him as a flesh-and-blood person, you could forgive him like a grown-up instead of stomping your feet like a child."

That's when I chose to tell Nathan about our father chipping into the pond and raiding the fridge. He pressed me for details—the age regression, the aftershave Beth could smell, and the fact that he needs my forgiveness by Thursday or he has to take the Down escalator.

Nathan nodded and pondered in his gay-professor way and finally played the card he'd held before. He had an alternate take on the whole thing, which was this: If I'd taken Jenni

Sanchez's testimony as I was supposed to, perhaps none of this would've happened and that girl would still be alive. Perhaps then I wouldn't be covering it all up with this grotesque disdain for my father and dumb-ass dreams that his afterlife is completely dependent upon my forgiveness.

I was doing it before I *knew* I was doing it: I spun and lurched forward, lowered my shoulder into Nathan's midsection, and just folded him over. When the top half snapped back, he went flying backwards with me on top of him until I planted him in the soft earth and felt all the air leave him. He turned and twisted desperately, gasping for breath.

And then I was kneeling over him, sitting him up, rocking him and crying. I was crying, "Dammit," like I'd broken or spilled something. "God*dammit!*" I said.

Nathan fought me at first but somewhere along the line it stopped being me holding him and started being *him* holding *me*. And he was rocking me, now, and it occurred to me that it *wasn't* for the second time after all.

This was my big brother. This was my Natie, who'd held me and soothed me long after my father had stopped. Maybe *because* my father had stopped.

When I settled a little, he asked me to repeat the part about the chicken legs. I told him Dad had dropped the plate but reached down and shook the shards off one anyway.

Nathan stood up so I did the same, asking why he wanted to know. And he told me: *Because there was a broken plate of left-over chicken on the floor when he came down in the morning, complete with a half-eaten chicken leg.*

I mean, Jesus Christ, right? So it's real? Nathan said again he had a slightly different take on it: He figured I went down and busted the chicken plate and maybe I needed some serious therapy. Like the kind you pack a bag for.

In the end, there was nothing more to say about that so we walked up the hill. At the tree line at the peak, we stopped and looked at the only home I remember before my loft downtown. That's when Nathan laughed like a stoner, turned to me with his red-rimmed eyes, and said, "Hey, Joe. Wanna go for a ride?"

See what I mean? We should've been in the car a minute later, right? Instead, I'm lying here waiting for him to fluff his lame-ass thinning hair into something presentable.

I hear him coming. I'll let you know how it goes.

(CLICK.)

ENTRY 8: SUNDAY, OCTOBER 10, 4:32 P.M.

(CLICK.)

I'm whispering because I'm driving home from Wellsburg and Nathan is asleep in the passenger's seat. He's exhausted himself keeping up the whole bullshit "at peace with Dad" act, I think.

Me? After what just happened in Wellsburg, I'm not sure I'll ever sleep again.

It took us about eighty minutes to cross into Pennsylvania and right then you can see my dad's birthplace of Wellsburg on the hillside just a mile up the highway. Nathan's herbally enhanced mind had spun it so that there was a realistic chance the storied "old minister" who got Joseph Way out of town and into the military might still be there, might be able to reveal something about Dad's growing-up years that could inspire an acceptable eulogy for me to deliver.

Nathan summed up the town by saying he would've joined the military, too. Or found a way to go to prison. Or accidentally fallen in front of a Camaro.

The low, gray sky enhanced the East of Bumfuck gloom, but Wellsburg is plenty depressing in its own right. Just a half mile from expressway fumes, several rows of slender Archie Bunker houses are scalloped up a hill, all painted in drab greens and yellows over crumbling cat-shit brick.

The "neighborhood," such as it is, seems loosely patterned around a main street, such as *it* is. A tiny cinderblock church with a half-cocked steeple serves as the centerpiece to the entire dismal presentation.

When we passed the wonder of Wellsburg and approached the actual exit, a monstrous manufacturing plant revealed itself, tucked farther back into the next rise. The towering smokestacks weren't belching out smoke these days. It seemed like it might have been a while, now.

Nathan eased my Audi around the circular exit and headed up the rise, back to Wellsburg. We passed a sign that once said, ALL'S WELL IN WELLSBURG! But a little modification had changed it to, ALL'S HELL IN HELLSBURG.

I suggested we head for the church so Nathan hung a late left and we cruised the strip: a Handy Dan hardware, a convenience store, and a Hardee's hosting caterpillar-lipped teenage boys and sneering, thick-hipped girls clustered around a hand-painted monster truck. A stencil in the back window boasted, I SEE YOU LOOKING!

A decaying strip of alleged Main Street came next, with a

barber shop, a greasy breakfast joint, a Laundromat, and a painted-over storefront where a faded neon sign proclaimed BUNNY's as *the* place to ogle naughty parts.

Naturally, that's where all the pickups were parked.

Nathan pulled to a stop in front of the church. WELLSBURG COMMUNITY CHURCH was painted black-on-white on a board affixed to the cinder block.

We walked down the driveway toward what looked like a residential entrance next to a carport, weaving rain-filled potholes to reach three cement steps to a doorway. A 1960s sedan was parked there, painted sky blue with tufts of clouds.

My rap on the metal storm door echoed across the entire town. Half alive but mostly dead, as one folk singer put it. The door swung open and a Mickey Rooney clone stood there, eighty if he was a day. His strained smile matched the glaring yellow of his Izod golf sweater.

He was grappling with something we couldn't see, and finally he produced a yipping wiener dog. He laughed and said, "Oh, my," again and again as the dog lapped at his cheek.

I asked if he was the minister and he said, "At your service." When Nathan asked if he'd been here awhile, the little man pointed out that *everybody's* been here awhile, son.

True enough, it seemed. So I asked if he was here in the fifties, and he said he was. That and longer.

Finally, I told him we were looking for someone who knew Joseph Way. He started laughing again, wedged in one or two "oh mys," and explained that it's kind of funny that anybody would go to a church to find someone who knew Joseph Way.

Just then, rain began to pelt the awning over our heads. The old man waved us in and said he just *had* to hear this.

We entered the residential half of the cinder box through a hiccup of a TV room with a tattered La-Z-Boy, a clean but open TV tray posted against the wall. A twin bed covered in pillows and a quilt wedged in beside an old console TV topped with framed, misty-lensed photos chronicling a young woman's gradual descent into obesity from mothering what appeared to be about forty-six children.

The cramped kitchenette came next, and the old man directed us to a blocky wooden table with mismatched chairs. On the wall, next to a ceramic Jesus, hung an out-of-focus snapshot of him and his bride some fifty years earlier.

Rigid and proud, their lives ahead still a thrilling mystery ride. Anything's possible. Even escape.

The old man identified himself as Reverend Hal while he mixed instant Folger's coffee at the Harvest-Gold stove. I finally revealed that we were Joe and Nathan, Joseph's sons.

Reverend Hal laughed some more and said, "So they let him procreate, did they?"

Reverend Hal noticed Nathan's twitch and explained that he actually kind of liked "the nasty little pecker." While we were still reeling from his choice of words, the good reverend settled in between us and said, "Okay, now. Two young men journey to their father's childhood home. He must've croaked, right?"

Nathan crisply admitted that while we try to avoid the words *pecker* and *croaked* in front of our grieving mother, yes, indeed, our father had died.

Unphased, Reverend Hal kept nodding and said, "He croaked and you're here to figure out how many of his fish stories were real." And while he was saying this, he reached to the back of the table, shifted an enormous bottle of ketchup, and retrieved what could only be a Ziploc bag of pot.

He explained that he suffered from glaucoma, but then smiled sideways to admit that at least one M.D. had been bamboozled real good. He pulled a rolled joint from the bag, lipped it, and lit it up with a pink disposable lighter.

When he offered it to me, I said it was a little early. Nathan rightfully mumbled the word *hypocrite,* so I punched him in the arm.

But when Reverend Hal said it's never too early in a place like this, I had to agree. He sighed in ecstasy as the first glow enveloped him and asked us to tell him what we *think* we know about our father. I said what I'd been told: Joseph Way grew up here in Wellsburg, the son of a coal miner. He got involved in the church after his father died. A minister—Reverend Hal, I assumed—helped him get into the military under age so he could go to college on Uncle Sam. He came back a war hero and met my mom, then a high-school senior from a wealthier family. They dated while he commuted to college, then got married and moved to Cleveland, where he started his business.

Minister Hal was looking down into his coffee when he started a long, wheezy laugh. Nathan said something like, "I take it that's somewhat less than accurate," and glanced at me while Hal's laugh got bigger and wheezier by the second.

And he just kept on, his face going crimson. His "oh mys" were reedy little whispers, now.

I crossed my arms and said, "I think we get the point, Hal." He clamped his eyes shut, overcome by the laughter. When he opened them, they were wide with terror. He clawed at his chest. Nathan and I looked at each other, but before we could do anything, Reverend Hal stood up and became trapped between the table and the wall.

He never made it out. As in, *never.* Instead, he dropped straight down, bouncing his chin off the table, and fell sitting on the floor. Nathan and I had to stand to look down on him: He was stone-cold still, both hands clamped to his heart, the burning joint still pinched between his fingers.

The yippy little wiener dog clicked his way over, put both front paws on his master's thigh, and cried.

Reverend Hal's mystery ride was over at last.

The Wellsburg police arrived within minutes; the ambulance took longer. Clearly, it's a lot easier to get arrested here in Wellsburg than saved.

A small crowd gathered on Main Street in front of the church, lured by the gratuitous sirens and the prospect of seeing a dead body. Only the seventy-something, all-day java swillers from Kate's Coffee actually seemed saddened by the loss, but I detected undertones of envy. The Hardee's boys and their girls were buzzing with excitement and the half-dozen perverts who tumbled over from Bunny's squinted their eyes against a cloudy sky and pretended they'd been somewhere else.

Nathan and I sat on the curb where the unshaven young cop

told us to wait. In the end, we agreed we did the old man a favor.

Scruffy Young Cop, not a day over twenty-three and looking a little overwhelmed by what he'd found inside, finally stopped working the crowd and talked to us. He quickly ascertained that we weren't from around those parts, as the cliché goes, and then identified himself only as Tim. Make that Officer Tim. At last, he settled on Officer Pollard.

So Officer Tim pulled out his notebook and pencil and started by asking if we were the last to see the deceased alive and blah blah blah so Nathan got impatient and just spelled it all out for him: We came to find someone who knew our father when he was younger. We found Reverend Hal here, and soon after he smoked his lunch he grabbed his chest and fell over dead. The whole thing took about ten minutes.

Officer Tim scribbled, flipping pages every fourth word or so. We waited while he scribbled and flipped, scribbled and flipped. . . .

Finally he asked, "Did anything happen to get him laughing? Because sometimes Reverend Hal would get to laughing during a sermon and couldn't stop."

I explained that the reverend asked what we thought we knew about our father and we told him, and Officer Tim said he wasn't surprised because "the old dude" thought damn near everything was funny. Once, in mass, something about lepers and whores got him so worked up he just kinda left and never came back. After a while, the congregation gave up and left, too.

Nathan wondered if Hal might've been on some kind of medication. Instead of answering, Tim asked what we'd told him about our father. I knew it was a mistake, but I admitted we thought our dad was the son of a coal miner who got involved with the church after his dad died, and a minister helped him join the military so he could go to college.

"A coal miner," Officer Tim said flatly. "Here?"

When I looked around, I noticed I'd become a source of great amusement to the bystanders. Great amusement probably doesn't visit Wellsburg that often. Nathan whispered, "I'm getting the notion that there's no coal here."

Officer Tim guffawed and said, "Hell no, there ain't no coal here," and I knew he'd be telling this story to his grandkids, over and over. And over.

And then I heard a gravely woman's voice from the crowd: "The only time Joseph Way 'got involved' with the church is when the cops made him paint it."

Nathan and I turned slowly. The woman standing there, hands on hips, simply had to be Bunny. Midsixties with a smoke-puckered mouth, a leathery tanning-bed glow, and a mop of Popsicle-orange curls framing her face, she couldn't have been any more "Bunny" if she'd had a big cotton ball on her ass.

Nathan asked the young cop if we were done here. He said we were, assuming we never saw that big bag of pot.

Done deal, Officer Tim.

Predictably, Bunny's smelled like a Schlitz and Clorox cocktail. Here, darkness was a necessity: The fleshy women undulating lazily on the stage at this hour should never be exposed to full daylight.

Bunny read my thoughts and said this is what happens to widows and divorcees in Wellsburg. She nodded at the pair of thirty-five-ish would-be soccer moms with slathered makeup and barren smiles and said that's why a good husband here is any guy decent enough to use an open hand.

The six unemployed customers had given up waiting for Reverend Hal's corpse to make a showing and returned to watch Nora and Laurie crawl for their kids' lunch money.

Bunny made her gradual way behind the bar and Nathan and I grabbed a couple of stools. Without asking, she loaded up a couple of tall, foamy ones for us. I realized that after a twelve-hour run of cocktails and my morning back-off, I probably looked exactly like a guy who would fancy a beer this time of day.

The bar between us was a carved timeline, including the announcement that Lisa does indeed give head, as it turns out, and here's how you can contact her if you're interested. Bunny couldn't stop looking between Nathan and me and shaking her head. Finally she said, "I guess she did save his ass that day."

Nathan asked the inevitable—she who?—and I asked exactly what day she was referring to. Bunny leaned in, lit a Pall Mall, and blew it from her bottom lip, sending the smoke straight for a fan in the dropped ceiling.

Then she growled, "Let me try that again: I guess your mama did save Joseph Way's ass the day she dragged him outta bed with me and put a mitt upside my head so hard my ears were ringing for a week."

From the corner of my eye, I could see Nathan's mouth make a perfect O, probably just like mine. Bunny fell into a phlegmy laugh, pleased to have shocked us.

While we were sorting out our eyeballs, she forged on, explaining that our grandfather hadn't died in an imaginary coal mine. He got up one morning, packed his lunch box to head over to the plant, and figured he'd just drive on by. And that's the last anyone ever saw of him.

Nathan asked what they made at the plant and she said it was bells, which is why the town was known as Bellsburg for a long while. You know, before it was Hellsburg.

She said when Jack Way worked there, it was industrial hangers. Wasn't until "those boys came over from Pittsburgh" that they started making bells. First for the old house alarms, the ones that went in the attic and rang like a motherfucker. Then it was doorbells.

Then it was nothing.

I pointed out the coincidence, that our father worked in a factory town where the factory made bells, then went on to become a home-security tycoon.

Bunny hardly saw how that was a coincidence, since Rita Carter's daddy was one of the fellas who bought the plant and started making bells. Turns out Rita's daddy then set Joseph Way up as a sales rep in Cleveland.

So much for Joseph Way's "plucky scheme," huh?

Considering that Nathan and I were pretty much turning

into furniture from the shock, Bunny kindly offered to just tell us a story. In turn, I'm gonna tell it for you because it feels very much like another piece in the puzzle.

Joey, as she called him, was all of ten when Jack Way slipped away that winter morning. My dad told everyone his daddy died, and everybody just went along with it. After a while, that's just the way everybody spoke of it, like it was gospel.

It seems Joey grew into a fine-looking piece of property with the sweetest blue eyes Bunny had ever seen. And with what his mother made answering phones over at the plant, that's about all he had to work with. He and Dan Somebody got to be pretty fair little thieves, slipping into houses and making off with enough cash to keep themselves in cigarettes and Pabst Blue Ribbon.

Yes, there's some damn solid irony in there: My father, the home-security tycoon who became mayor, was a small-time thief back home in Wellsburg.

Anyway, Bunny said Joey was a bad boy and she was the official class slut. Now she runs a low-rent strip club. Not a lot of irony there, I guess.

Thing was, Joey was the only guy in town who treated her like a human being. Before she became Bunny (a much longer story), she went by Linda Slessinger, since that was her name. By junior year, a few of the clever types charged with such responsibilities in any high school in any decade took to calling her Linda Sleaze-inger.

The difference is, in 1952, in a town like Wellsburg, that kind of thing mattered. As she put it, that kind of thing put a stain on you that don't come off. She went to school one morning and someone had painted it across her locker in red paint: SLEAZE.

Bunny wanted to die. She quickly planned to wash down a bottle of aspirin with her father's cheap bourbon that very night. But then Joseph Way walked up, saw the poodle-skirt girls and the football boys all standing around laughing at Bunny, and did this amazing thing: He grabbed a chair from a classroom and pulled it out into the hall. He stood up on it and started yelling, "Anybody interested in hearing which of these girls I've felt up? Any of you guys positively sure your girlfriend isn't one of 'em?"

As you can imagine, the poodle-skirt girls weren't laughing anymore. In fact, at least half of them were going shit-ass crazy, mouthing to Joseph, telling him what they'd do to him if he told. Or what they'd do *with* him if he didn't.

At this point, our hostess demonstrated a certain nonverbal with her tongue pressed into her cheek that might haunt me for a decade or so.

But then Bunny said this: "To this day, whenever I wake up at night and see real clearly what a total flaming shitpile I've made of my life, I just have to picture Linda Orbison's pretty little face all screwed up in horror that the truth would have out. But Joey wasn't done."

My dad, at sixteen, said if somebody didn't fetch some turpentine real quick and get that locker cleaned up, he was gonna make an announcement at lunch in front of the whole school. By the time Bunny got back from first period, the locker was shiny clean.

But stories don't end happy for white-trash kids like Joey in towns like Wellsburg. This was real life, not a movie, so somebody or somebody's daddy got to this Principal Walton guy and he came down hard on Joey. It only took a couple of weeks before Walton found some reason or another to expel him: something Joey said, something he did. It was over before it was over, really.

I could only imagine what it felt like to be Joey or Bunny. Born on the outside lane, running the race in shackles, dragging a Buick.

Anyway, she said, there ain't much for a fatherless dropout to do around Wellsburg but get in deeper. And that's just what Joey did. He got liquored up and threw a big metal trash can through the front window of Walton's house, just like they hoped he would when they put the boot on his neck.

At this point in her telling, Bunny said, "That's what people do when nothin' matters. That's why I never call nobody a nigger or a beaner or nothin' like that, you hear? 'Cuz if anybody's a nigger, it's me. I know what that shit's about."

She shrugged because it was what it was. Still is. They were gonna run Joseph up to the juvey in Lancaster for a few months, but Reverend Hal talked them out of it. He put Joe to work painting the church instead, cleaning it up and stuff. It's a matter of who you ask, but maybe he even talked to him a time or two.

(When we snickered, she pointed out that this was well before Hal boarded the Yellow Submarine.)

So, yeah, it was Reverend Hal who got our father into the army, even though he was just seventeen. Hal figured that for every day Joey spent in Wellsburg, he was another day closer to doing something he couldn't fix by painting a church.

Bunny said my dad changed some in Korea, figured a few things out. She cleaned up a little, too. Got a job right where we were sitting, back when it was a little burger shop. She spit in the shakes of every single person who had ever called her Sleaze. What goes around comes around, and sometimes it swims in your food, right?

So whatever else Joey was now, he was also a vet, so he didn't have any trouble getting a job making bells. The town had taken a turn of sorts, now that it was Bellsburg. The new company did well, what with all the 'burbs springing up around the big cities like Pittsburgh and Cleveland and Youngstown, all filled with people wanting to protect their shit from the people who didn't have any.

Rita Carter was a senior at Wellsburg High at the time, one of the flock of upper-crust kids who came in with the owners and their toadies from Pittsburgh. She wasn't exactly a pretty girl, by Bunny's way of seeing things, but she was smart and strong, like a boy. She didn't giggle like all the others. She had plans, that one.

Long and short of it, she and Joey started getting on some at a company picnic. He said she made him feel smart and decent, and he liked that. They started hanging around and she convinced him to go after his GED and start driving up to Lancaster a few nights a week for business classes. All this time, mind you, Bunny and Joey are still getting nasty together just about every night. It seems he just didn't feel that way about Rita.

"Deeply in like." That's how he would describe it a half century later.

A girl going to college was something Wellsburg hadn't seen much of. A girl and a guy being best friends? Forget about it.

Then one day Joseph came into the restaurant and said he needed to talk to Bunny. That usually meant they were gonna sneak up to her place over the Laundromat for the high hard one, so she pulled off the apron and took his hand.

But this time, they really just talked. Bunny knew she had a grip on Joey's stick shift, as she worded it, but his engine was out of her reach. Still, she couldn't help dreaming that one day he would take her away and make her an honest woman. So when he said Rita's daddy was setting him up near Cleveland, that he and Rita were gettin' married in just a week or so, Bunny took it hard. She fought back with the only weapon she had, luring him up to her place for a pity fuck.

That's when our mother came in and "rang her bell," she said. When we squinted, she clarified that Rita Carter, our mother, smacked her from one end of that apartment to the other. When Bunny tried to huddle on the floor, Rita kicked her a few times to make sure she got the message. Bunny ached in places she didn't know she had and it burned when she breathed for almost a week.

Nathan finally found the ability to speak again, and used it to say: "Our mother kicked your ass."

Bunny knocked down one shot, deemed it insufficient, and backed it up with another. She lit up a Pall Mall, looked between me and Nathan, and said, "Any questions?"

Nathan's twitching, having some kind of nightmare. I'm gonna wake him up.

(CLICK.)

ENTRY 9: SUNDAY, OCTOBER 10, 11:30 P.M.

(CLICK.)

I'm in bed. Everybody is. My mom's not real clear on when Beth left, but she did.

After I dropped Nathan at the house, I went out and bought a six-pack of microcassettes at the drugstore. I'm still not sure who you are or why I'm telling you everything, but I am. I'm taking you all the way through with me because something *is* happening here. Something is changing and it's never going back to what it was.

At some point, I'll be where I land and the only way I'll know how I got there is this tape recorder.

I can't tell you what kind of story this is. Is it a sordid crime novel, pulp fiction? Is it heartfelt family drama? Is it about a father and a son? Is it my story or my father's story?

I don't know. But at least part of it is a ghost story. I'm convinced of it now.

Nathan woke up in the car and jerked like he was falling. He was pale and disoriented. I tried to be cool and ask if he was sick or something and he said he just got over the flu. I said it looked like a little more than that and he gave me that bitchy-queer sideways look. Honestly, I'm not being homophobic because I sort of wish I could pull it off. Anyway, he said, "Oh I get it. You think I have AIDS because I'm gay, right? Because all gay guys in the movies get some kind of STD and that's pretty much your complete education on homosexual behavior?"

He was precisely 100 percent correct, so I said he was totally fucked in the head and should get over himself. To put my mind at ease, he told me in no uncertain terms that he does not have AIDS or any flesh-eating, God's-damnation-of-the-homos disease of any kind. I should save the drama for my mama, he added, which made me point out that he might want to make a black friend or two in the very near future, just to keep up on the lingo.

And, no, brainiac Indian professors don't count.

It was starting to rain and the rain was starting to freeze. Nathan began humming and I asked why he wasn't as freaked by the day's events as I was. After all, we'd seen a pot-headed octogenarian minister drop dead and found out our father was a Katzenjammer Kid whose greatest achievement in the first half of his life was meeting my mom.

Nathan laughed and said, "Oh, alert the media if you must: Dad was never quite what he made himself out to be. All we got today was confirmation of that. He and Mom collaborated on some impressive revisionist history. Maybe as much for themselves as for everybody else."

Still, I said, *holy shit.* Our mom practically dragged his ass out of the gutter, combed his hair, and shoved him out the door to work. And all Nathan said to that was that people are complicated, even when they're parents.

I thought about that as the swirl of freezing rain made me feel more like I was falling than moving forward. I never would've used the word *complicated* to describe myself before. Now, I think it's entirely possible that I am no more the man people think I am than my father was.

And then, behind me, I heard my father singing: *"Torn between two lovers, feeling like a fool."* I still felt ice water flowing into my fingertips and to the top of my head.

The dead dropping by never becomes entirely commonplace.

When I looked in the rearview mirror, I could make out the suit and loosened tie, but his face was hidden in shadow. Then he leaned forward—toothy and narrower-faced with slightly longer hair. Not much over fifty, I'd guess.

Even dead, he sang off-key: *"Loving both of them is breaking all the rules."* He scooted up between the bucket seats.

I said, "Terrible, awful news, Dad. You still can't sing and Grandpa was never a coal miner."

He acted shocked and said, "That bastard!" It sounded too much like that kid on *South Park.*

After a lot of consideration, I gave him his props on the high school hallway thing with Bunny and it occurred to me that

Nathan hadn't screamed like a princess under siege yet. When I looked over at him, he was staring out the window, only half there.

My dad shook his head and smiled, lost in the memory. He said, "God damn, if I'd listed all the Daddy's Girls I defrocked, I'd still have writer's cramp today. The ladies sure dig a bad boy, don't they?"

That's right. My younger, deader father now talks like Kid Rock in a Budweiser commercial.

He went on to posit that the most ingenious trick of the twentieth century is how women convinced men that they're more in touch with their feelings than we are. He didn't miss a beat when I rolled my eyes, explaining that we've got books and lectures and TV shows about what women want, entire careers built around telling men what women want. But there's a fatal flaw in the entire program.

I said the same thing you probably just did: Oh? And what's that? To which *he* said, "Women have no fucking clue what they want. They're as confused as we are. Their minds tell them they want men to be more like they are, to be less confounding and frustrating and more sensitive and verbal or whatever. But everything below the neck just keeps wanting the bad boy with nothin' on his mind but all-night pussy."

And now my father had said the phrase *all-night pussy*. I asked if he would be offended if I slammed my head into the steering wheel until I lost consciousness. He told me to grow up; he was trying to teach me something here.

I wasn't ready to play Bad Bell with my adulterous father. So I reminded him that starting in the morning, I was gonna do a little research on my own to find out if the deceased mayor is also an accessory to murder.

And you know what? He didn't flinch. Not a bit. He just said, "Well, that's great, Joey. Good luck with that. So, anyway, women, in all their advanced emotional wisdom, devised this brilliant solution: Snag the bad boy, bang him until that kind of thing slides down the priority chart, and then reprogram him. Turn Errol Flynn into Jimmy Stewart."

This lesson was starting to sound more and more like an excuse, and I told him so. And he just smiled and said, "Take it for what it's worth."

I asked if he ever loved my mother, which finally cracked his act. After chewing at his cheek a little, he said, "Everything I got in life, I owe to her. Everything about us made sense. She made me better. I made her laugh."

I said that was a very long "no," right? He said he thought we'd made some nice progress here and patted my shoulder.

But when he looked at Nathan, my dad's smile looked like it was propped up with toothpicks. He wanted to reach out and pet Nathan's hair, but he turned it into a gesture.

I didn't say anything. My dead dad shook it off and said we needed to pick up the pace a bit: "We're tight on time and I don't have the right wardrobe for hell."

I told him the tie looked about right; he shot me a quick "good one" smile, and then disappeared. No slow dissolve or twinkle-twinkle; he just wasn't there anymore.

I thought Nathan was crying next to me, but it turned out he was sniffing at the air. He said, "Is that *Clubman?*"

I looked back at him. He got it slowly, laughed a little, and said no way he was getting sucked into my delusional breakdown. They don't give twofers at the Jellyhead Ranch.

But he smelled it, just like Beth had. Which means my father really was there, in the backseat of my Audi, using the phrase *all-night pussy*.

Like I said, this is really happening. Shit.

(CLICK.)

(CLICK.)

I'm on my way into work and traffic's a bitch. It's amazing how life rolls on outside the window of your own finite universe, utterly disinterested in your existential crisis or the ghosts who haunt you and eat all the chicken.

We'll all meet today, the keepers of justice, the lawyers and the cops. We'll talk in ways nobody should hear, establishing priorities as much as mapping a strategy. My relative involvement in the case will probably rank high on the agenda, as will how blatantly we connect Jenni Sanchez and Lester Ratcovic at the get-go. Investigations aren't so simple as finding the truth. There are opportunities and consequences to every move and you ignore them at your own risk.

I always thought I enjoyed the game, which is exactly what it is. The stakes seem high, but with a longer view, a decade or a lifetime, they recede and wither and the details dissolve. Who is or isn't mayor or chief of police or district attorney in Cleveland or Omaha or Providence doesn't add up to much when you take a millennial view, does it? And if none of that matters, where does that put Jenni Sanchez?

Or maybe, as my high school football coach Jerry Shackleford said, when you don't know what's going to end up being important, *everything* matters. Championship games are lost over indigestion, man. A defensive back winces just a second when his mother's spaghetti repeats and in that instant the receiver hitches and then sprints down the sideline, wide open, and hauls in the touchdown pass.

There's a college scout in the stands who came to see that defensive back and now he's shaking his head and wondering about strip clubs. Instead of getting a scholarship, the kid ends up peddling pot for his cousin. He sells a bag to a twenty-three-year-old high school student who isn't really a high-school student at all, and because he lives in a mandatory-sentencing state our defensive back goes to the House with the rapists and the other monsters. One night, one of those monsters decides to get a grip on our boy's natural and ride him a little. But he pulls just a little too hard and snaps the defensive back's neck.

All because he had indigestion.

You know what matters to me? *The truth.* Yeah. The truth matters to me. I think that's about all I have right now. It's all I know. The truth *always* matters.

So here's some truth: I am damn well not going to see Mara Pinkett, which would require me to get off the highway one exit earlier to get to the Left Side, as it's called, the liberal kingdom where she often holds court in Y.J.'s Coffee Shop, where the windows are blanketed with photocopied fliers promoting poetry readings, spiritual speakers, and lost dogs.

I went in there once. I sat for three hours. She didn't show. Not that I was just sitting there waiting for her, right? I read the sports. I made a couple of calls. I did some business.

There was a picture of her, though. A Polaroid on a massive bulletin board, along with dozens of others. There she was, her smile impossibly white in the flash. She wore the tossed-on, oversized flannel shirt, reined in the dreadlocks with a hastily tied bandanna. The nose ring. The threadbare jeans, her thumbs in the pockets. She was what she always was: kick-the-back-of-your-knees, caramel-coated beautiful. Green eyes against latté skin. Sixty-four inches of insomnia.

I wondered then how the other customers in Y.J.'s handled her entrances. Construction worker double-takes are the opposite of coffeehouse cool, right? Did they nod and smile like she was just another hippie chick wandering in?

For what it's worth, Y.J.'s namesake, Yamin "Y.J." Jiminez, can probably pull it off because he's gay. He's something of a folk hero on the Left Side, an African-Cuban activist and former stripper who now goes about 6'6" and 380, most of that covered in tattoos. He's an artist and a lot of his stuff hangs in the coffee shop—newspaper clippings and doodles and blood and three-dimensional objects. It's confusing and disturbing and beautiful and you can't stop looking at it.

Like Mara.

The Left Side. Four square blocks of health-food stores, coffee shops, cluttered art galleries, cultural bookstores, and an African grocer derogatorily tagged "the Left Side" by a witty *Plain Dealer* columnist. Much to his dismay, the community embraced the name and embedded a ceramic marker in the sidewalk at the corner of Ohio and Fourth.

The Left Side is Mara's earthy, organic, all-natural empire. She's the queen, now, and her castle is a former Baptist church that serves as offices for *The Independent*.

Which, coincidentally, is exactly where I am now.

Fuck.

(CLICK.)

(CLICK.)

Okay, so *that* was a bad idea.

When I told the fortyish, overweight, muumuu-clad hippie in *The Independent* offices who I am, she took me directly to Mara's office. The woman rapped at the door frame and Mara held up a finger instead of turning and started reading from her computer screen in her raspy, Peppermint Patty voice: "Just when our downtown should be reaching back to its own history for a sense of permanence and cultural identity, the Light District raises only one salient and sensible question: Who had the *balls* to suggest that this monolithic temple of consumer excess has anything whatsoever to do with us as taxpayers?"

She held her hands out, but still didn't turn, and said, "I am so . . . fucking . . . *good.*"

The plus-size hippie announced me and Mara froze with her hands out. Her voice was shaky when she said she's home sick. And on a mission to Africa. And she's sick. And not here.

When Muumuu Chick didn't answer, Mara said, "He's in the room with us, isn't he?"

So I said, "Hello, Mara. Hello, Mara's bloated self-esteem."

As Mara turned in slow motion, I heard the hippie galumphing off in her Birkenstocks. Mara had deadened her eyes on the way around, but the quick raise of an eyebrow acknowledged that I looked worn and shitty from too much booze and Valium and ghosts and dead preachers and too little sleep.

She opened her mouth to say something witty and crisp but then she closed it again and we just looked at each other. Finally, I told her I liked the nose ring and she said, "Oh, goody. I'll keep it then."

I reminded her that my father had died to make her feel like shit for attempting to banter with me. She deflated appropriately and told me how sorry she was.

I explained that the doctors had concluded that after six months of having every word taken out of context and turned inside out by her leftist rag, his heart just collapsed.

Her jaw fell open. I told her I was just kidding.

Mara drew her cheeks in and squinted at me as she stood, the look I always got the half of the time we weren't fucking. She was like, this is how it's gonna be? Then *bring it*.

I opened my mouth to say something else clever and it came out: "God, you're more beautiful than ever," all shaky and breathy. Cary Grant would've done so much better, but her eyes are really *green*.

Mara didn't exactly eviscerate me with words. I think she managed something like, "Okay."

I asked about all the scary foreign places. She said as one bad-ass mestiza she ducked the bullets and wrote the stories. Which naturally linked to my next question: "Why are you here?"

She sat back down, desperate to regain the home-court advantage. But she couldn't help posing and reposing like a nervous schoolgirl and so she decided that, all things considered, she was better off standing.

I decided *I* was in control. And you should know that's an utterly moronic thing for me to decide when it comes to Mara.

I pulled a chair from the wall and sat, so she did the same. Again. And the gravity of it all finally pulled at us. This isn't Wittenberg. We're not Romeo and LaJuliet anymore.

I finally asked what I had to ask: "Did Jenni Sanchez call you?" Without so much as a blink, she asked how I knew, which made it official: Our paths are all tangled up again and they won't come undone easily. Nothing has ever been easy about me and Mara. Not ever.

I explained rather indelicately that Jenni had the phone number in her pocket when we fished her out of the creek behind her house. She'd been beaten to death.

Mara was exactly as surprised as she should've been but no more. I knew that if Mara had spoken to Jenni, she'd have picked up rather quickly that this was the kind of girl who ended up in a creek behind her house. Things just *happen* to girls like Jenni Sanchez and girls like Mara know that.

My voice shook when I told Mara that Jenni's head had been caved in. She was the worst dead I'd seen in a long while.

Mara nodded and volunteered that Jenni had been "fucked up and scared as shit." Jenni told her about the video. She said there were people who were worried she might tell the whole story and that made her think she should.

I asked who those scary people are, but I knew Mara didn't know or she would've told me by now. What she did know was this: Jenni met with a man earlier that night. She liked him okay and even kind of trusted him but she didn't want to get in any deeper. She told the guy she was going to call Mara.

Of course, I asked Mara why Jenni chose *her* to call. She said she didn't know and I believe her. And right there, sitting across from Mara, I started wondering about that phone number in the plastic bag and my assumption that Jenni had written it.

When I looked back up, Mara was standing again, closer, and she had the same expression as Ally Wong. And I flat-out knew she knew about me and Jenni.

I skipped the bullshit and said, "You know why I did it, Mara," trying to sound firm and innocent and defiantly unapologetic. She said that's what she *wants* to believe, that I just meant to stay out of it and keep it clean and let the truth have out.

That's what she *wants* to believe? Well then what the fuck *does* she believe? That I was somehow involved in Jenni's death? Is that what Mara thinks of me?

She read my mind and said at the very least I coached her, right? At the very least, I sent her home and told her to never, ever tell, right?

Mara wanted to say more but didn't. So I said it for her: "And now she's dead."

She nodded and looked out the window and I knew how badly she wanted out of this. I could tell she imagined escaping out that window before things went where we both knew they were heading.

They were heading for me saying this: "Nobody else knows." Mara's jaw dropped and her expression gradually evolved into unfiltered revulsion. I tried to talk fast and explain that if things turned into a circus I'd never find the truth, right?

Right?

But I was too late. She was huffing out scary little laughs and saying, "Oh, shit. Oh, holy shit, you are fucking un*real.* You marched in here to tell me what I can and can't write in my paper? You haven't changed a bit, have you? You're still the most egocentric *dick* I've ever known."

You have to understand that I am not at the wheel once this shit starts with the two of us. So don't hate me for saying, "Well, it's nice to see you're over it and this isn't personal."

She did the eye-slitting thing and said, "Over *what,* Joe?"

To which I said—and you have to admit this is pretty good—"Oh, please. Your paper might as well be called 'Joe Way Broke up with Me.'"

She smiled like a murderer and found a stapler, turned it over in her hands and seemed to consider beating me to death with it before setting it down gingerly. And she said, "Do I gather, then, that you think that when I criticize you and your father's fascist politics—God rest his soul—it's because I'm so googly-fucked in the head over our monumentally forgettable college fling that I'd use my paper to get your attention?"

I tried to pretend I wasn't putting my chair between the two of us when I stood, but she was advancing and her dead-calm voice was setting off all kinds of fight-or-flight that I couldn't ignore. I wondered aloud if we might just forget that I said that part, which made her kick the chair from between us without breaking eye contact.

I raised my hands and said I'm sorry, I'm sorry a million times and can't we *please* just start over? She grabbed her head like it was going to explode and said she couldn't decide what was worse, that I think she's been pulling my pigtails all this time or that I expect her to keep secrets under my order.

I extended my hand to her and she slapped the back of it every bit as hard as Beth had. It's a new thing with women, I guess. Same hand, too, so I whined, "Ow! That hurt!" Like I'm eight or something.

She didn't apologize, so I resumed begging: *Four lousy days,* man. And she said, then what? She gives me four days of silence and I give her *what?*

An exclusive. That's what I'd give her. Her eyes lit up like I'd morphed into Kobe's Apology Ring. She went electric, focused, alive, which I found horribly sad and told her so. She was like, ooh, you're breaking my heart. Stop, please stop.

She clarified that I was offering to tell her the entire story before I spoke to another soul. She could grill me for as long as she liked, pour water on me if I passed out. I asked her why it always had to come back to sex with us but she swatted at the air angrily until I agreed that, yes, that's what I'm offering.

She mulled it over and said, "One more condition: You acknowledge that *I* broke up with *you*. Once and for all. Right here and now."

I'm a grown man. You'd think I'd just have the sense to say it. But instead, I heard myself say, "Well, except that you didn't."

She crossed her arms, smiled, sat down all regal, and said, "And now I'm going to count to ten."

I told her I couldn't believe we'd devolved to this point.

To which she replied, "One . . ."

I reminded her that we're grown-ups. That this is serious shit, right? Remember my father? Remember Jenni Sanchez?

To which she replied, "Two-three-four." Just like that. Really fast. I said some horrible profanity hyphenate that made no sense whatsoever and she said, "Five-six-seven."

So I said, "You broke up with me."

She said, "Hmm?" I glared at her and she said she was counting too loud. Could I please say it again?

So I did: "You . . . broke up . . . with me."

"Yes I did," she said, pleased with herself. "So deal with it."

I reminded her: "Four days." I needed to get out of there before we inadvertently had sex. We're that way. I couldn't do that to Beth. I'm not my father.

Before I could get out the door, she read my mind and said she'd seen me and Beth in the society column a few dozen times. She admitted that Beth was really pretty and blond and some men seem to like that kind of thing.

She asked how we'd met and that was that: I knew she'd been thinking about me, too. It filled me, warm and tingly like the first drink of really good scotch.

I told it by rote, like I had so many other times: When I went in the Ring of Honor at my high school, where Beth's an instructor, my father introduced us.

Mara screwed her face into that so-above-it-all look and said, "The ring of *what?*"

Like a lamb being led to slaughter, I quite earnestly explained that they put the best players' names and numbers on a band around the middle of the stadium and then parade us around while everybody cheers. You know, like that.

She shook her head quickly and said, "Yeah, it's a total mystery why you have issues, isn't it?"

I said, "Goodbye, Mara." And she said, "Goodbye, Joe." And I walked out, just like it was that simple.

(CLICK.)

(CLICK.)

Let's pretend for a second that none of this happened. I didn't stumble upon my father's secret and he never fell face-first onto the manicured country-club turf. Jenni Sanchez could be a fast-food counter at Belden Village Mall for all I know.

So who am I? What is the *truth* of me? Well, let's break it down, shall we?

I am the assistant district attorney of Cleveland, Ohio, which happens to be the global definition of *big fucking whoop*.

I am also the son of Joseph Way, Senior, who was almost assuredly heading for the end of his one and only term as mayor. He would quickly become known as the successful entrepreneur who briefly held public office in a second-tier American city.

These two things along with the fact that I have straight teeth and broad shoulders made me a suitable spokesperson for the Sports Commission as the fairly mundane details of the Browns return to Cleveland were worked out. These factors along with my prudent choice of an equally photogenic mate earned me a temporary place in the Self-Congratulatory Section of local magazines and newspapers in said second-tier American City.

It's not just that nobody outside of Cleveland would wake in midscream if I drove my car off a pier and into Lake Erie. The hard truth is that about nine out of ten people *within* the city limits couldn't care less if I lived, died, or shit my pants on the train.

Here's what I've come to: When skating through life based on Who You Are, lucid self-awareness is something of a no-no. I'm getting the nagging sense that *Being Joe Way* might, in the end, be somewhat less than fulfilling than, say, Being John-John Kennedy or even Being Nicole Ritchie unless I settle into a champagne-for-lunch, Gatsbyesque haze.

These things occur to you when you've just left a very important meeting that ultimately was a roomful of city employees struggling with how to preserve your shallow and utterly meaningless prominence among the handful of people who truly *do* care if you shit your pants on the train. Or become mayor, which now seems to be the more likely *and* ridiculous of the two.

Twenty minutes prior to Chief of Police Evan Collins's press conference, we gathered in the green room together (in this case, Ally Wong's office). Included were Ally, McCale, Bulger, and myself, along with Collins—distinguished, fifty, and black—and our new head coroner, Patrice Holocheck. Patrice is undernourished and overeducated. I'm thinking people have pegged her at forty since she was twenty-five, but she finally *is* forty now. I'd bet a cool yard she carries a Mensa card in her wallet.

Collins said what everybody says about these things: "I think we should give them as little information as possible." He's mayor for the next two weeks, prior to the election, and clearly didn't ask for it. He was sitting on Ally's desk but it seemed more like it was sitting on him.

Ally angrily fired off something like, "And just what would that be?" It jolted everybody until we remembered Ally can't say "good morning" without it sounding like "suck my ass."

Collins said we'd reveal the existence of Jenni Sanchez's video testimony against Ratcovic and announce that no charges will be filed until further investigation. Then we'd say she was found dead in the creek. Drive safely and we'll talk again Thursday morning when the coroner's report is final.

Collins hates the media. He's no politician, which would probably make him a far better mayor than I. He wouldn't go into that cramped room filled with lights down the hall unless he absolutely had to. And he did.

Patrice wanted to know what we would have her say, a question expressed in a passive-aggressive whisper followed by a quick eye flutter that made you want to casually beat her to death. She says everything like that. Everything.

McCale checked in, telling Patrice to stick with the science. He repeated his karate chop indicating the slope of Jenni's back lawn. We still don't know for absolute certain that she hadn't fallen.

And to that, I said, "She was murdered." I never meant to say it out loud. I didn't know I had until everybody was looking at me. My certainty of this earned another knowing look from Ally. But what does *she* know? And how?

McCale shook his head and said, again, that we didn't know that. Bulger waved his hand back and forth at the stubborn idiocy of such a statement, reminding us all that Jenni took nineteen blows, man. *Nineteen.* He correctly said she would've looked like a fucking pinball if she'd fallen.

And here Collins asked the question that set me off on my whole *Being Joe Way* dilemma: "As far as motive, would somebody really kill to be mayor of Cleveland, Ohio?"

He looked at me with a quick laugh and said, "Shit, I don't think I'd *wrestle* you for it."

Before I could ponder that—and I think it bears pondering—I noticed that Ally had dropped her head quickly and cleared her throat. She herself once told me that whole notion of *knowing what you know before you know it.* And here's what I knew right there and then: Ally *would* wrestle me to be mayor. She might shank me or poison me for it, too.

She gave me just the head dip and the throat clear and that's all I needed.

In support of Bulger, Patrice pointed out that the cause of death was massive trauma to the right side of the head, but only because it won the race. She would've died anyway from the internal injuries caused by trauma to her kidneys and lungs.

To which Bulger concluded aloud that Jenni Sanchez was beaten to death. And while I'm not as certain of that as I am of Ally Wong's mayoral aspirations, well, it seems unlikely that Jenni beat herself to death on her way down to that creek.

But you know what? I like McCale. I trust McCale. He isn't *being* anything, right? He's just *doing* and from that doing emerges some sense of what this organism called McCale truly is. But he leaves that for others to worry about and goes about his business. I think that's one hell of a lot of cool.

Well, all that aside, I wanted McCale's buy-in and he could tell from the way I looked at him. So he shrugged and said it would be something of a coincidence if Jenni Sanchez had died accidentally under the circumstances. As if that were too complicated for the rest of us, Ally said, "You mean the fact that she accused a mayoral candidate of molesting her and then got plonked to death that very night?"

And in case we also couldn't identify sarcasm, she then bit her finger to ponder it all.

McCale looked at Ally for a long while, his face as expressionless as ever. As an afterthought, he said, "Fuck you."

"Noted," Ally responded.

Collins got off the desk or took it off himself and walked over to me. He's a big man, the kind you hope will hug you when you're down, not the kind you fear. He asked how I was holding up and I said I was doing okay, all things considered.

But fuck me, man, when he said things might get a little crazy, I laughed through my nose so fast I had to put my hand over it. I mean, *really?* Things might *get* a little crazy? So what do you call this complicated relationship with my dead, aging-in-reverse father?

Off-putting?

And then I had this suffocating sense that I'd just said all of that out loud. Everybody was looking at me like I'd had a convulsion and vomited on my shirt. In a whisper, I asked McCale what I'd said last. Ally threw up her hands and practically yelled, "Oh, Christ. Now Everybody's All-American is flipping out."

I protested that I most certainly was not flipping out, but it appeared that everybody in the room saw it Ally's way. So I stepped up, lowered my voice in the name of credibility, and said, "I need to know, okay? *I need to know.*"

I hadn't considered how much I was revealing until the silence blew in off the lake. The air-handling system seemed to roar. McCale finally asked what everybody was thinking: "Know *what*, Joe?" Ally raised her eyebrows, ending any question of whether she knew Jenni Sanchez had spoken to me first.

So I just said it: "She came to me first."

Collins looked like I'd tasered his scrotum. He stood upright, eyes darting. "What'd he just say?" he asked everybody but me. *"What'd he just fucking say?"*

So I spilled it all: "Jenni Sanchez came to me first. I told her to go home and come back Friday morning and give her testimony to Ally. I just wanted to keep it clean. That's all."

Now the crazy-ass air-handling system sounded like a jet landing. McCale asked if I'd told anyone about Jenni and I quickly said no. Their collective exhale drowned out even the deafening cacophony exploding from the floor vents.

Then I remembered—and said—that Callie knew. How could she not? Collins barked to nobody in particular to get her in here right fucking now. Then he stared right into my eyes and said, with absolutely no malice whatsoever, "You will have less than nothing to do with this investigation."

That's how making it possible for me to continue the important work of *Being Joe Way* became as much an objective of this investigation as finding out who killed Jenni Sanchez.

I'll talk to you later. I just pulled into the parking lot at Redmond's Funeral Home. Time to shop for a casket.

(Click.)

(Click.)

Okay, two things: First, talking into a microcassette recorder while you drive intrigues women. This reasonably hot thirty-something in a custom-color Lexus SUV has spent the last five miles pretending not to watch me.

Second, if you've never been in the casket showroom of a funeral home, you've never really experienced quiet. Everything you once referred to as "quiet"—the library, desolate woods, a bomb shelter—suddenly doesn't qualify anymore. It's the kind of quiet that forces the mind to manufacture whispery white noise before the absence of auditory stimulus drives you slobbering mad.

Redmond's Funeral Home's showroom is small but not cramped, with muted lighting, no windows, and tasteful, library wallpaper over cherry wainscoting.

Oh. And about a dozen caskets rimming the room, mounted on wrought-iron racks. There are *those*.

Nathan, Mom, and I milled and fidgeted in the awesome silence. I pretended to be torn between two worthy casket models, but mostly I thought about my confession.

Callie, of course, had told nobody. Even though she's worked for me less than a year, she's already part of the program. She *gets it*, as we politicos say. "Of course not" was her repeated answer to the question, no matter how many times and ways it was stated.

Both Collins and Patrice kept the press conference calm and factual. Jack Presley, a veteran beat reporter for the Cleveland *Plain Dealer*, asked the pertinent question: "Is there any reason to believe somebody from the Ratcovic camp knew about the girl's statement?"

Collins answered just as I would've: "At this time, we have no specific reason to suspect that Mister Ratcovic or anybody working for him knew about the accusations."

He also said that "Mister Ratcovic," the employees of his law firm, and his campaign staffers have been cooperative and will not leave Cleveland until further notice. Mister Ratcovic and his counsel have agreed to come in for a meeting tomorrow morning with representatives of both the district attorney's office and the Cleveland Police Department. But at this point, no charges of any kind have been filed.

In case you're wondering, "Mister Ratcovic" is code for, "He is totally fucked and you will never hear from this man again. Never-ever."

McCale skipped the press conference. He's a man of precise agenda, and Item One is discerning what Jenni Sanchez did, where she did it, and who she did it with between her meeting with Ally Wong and that violent descent into a muddy creek.

As I stood there, not really looking at caskets, it occurred to me that Jenni Sanchez would be buried soon, too. And that made me wonder who she was before the rasp in her voice and the rings on her toes. Who was she as a little girl? What events conspired to create the version of her I met that day? What was *the truth* of Jenni Sanchez?

Anyway, McCale called my cell a few minutes before I reached Redmond's Funeral Home, which was extremely cool, considering Ally had officially dismissed me from the case. He had a list of three bars Jenni had mentioned to her Mayan friend Elise late that night. The bartender at Quaff's, one of Jenni's regular haunts, had served her a couple of rum and Cokes and watched her flirt with a "preppy ad-guy type." But his pin-striped posse had dragged him off before he went through with anything the wife might find unsavory. So far, nobody from the other two bars remembered seeing her.

So even though Jerald Redmond has this lush, calming voice, I was so deep in thought I almost cleared my bladder when he said, "Hi, folks." Nathan and Mom must've been on their own private islands because we spun in sync on the poor guy. He's sort of lanky and goofy with Carrot Top hair pulled back in a fussy little ball and pop-bottle glasses, but he's the antidote to Ally's Human Rush Hour: Human Xanax. He makes me wanna take a do-do in a sun spot.

I've known Jerald since high school and I could tell from the way he was taking me in that he was concerned by my exhaustion and stubble. I told him I'm fine, just not sleeping well.

Jerald navigates silence masterfully, surfing it, neither forcing pleasantries nor rushing into business. I'm thinking of trying it. He nodded on and on, holding a conversation with our body language and expressions.

When he asked my mom how she was doing, it wasn't rhetorical—he wanted to know. To proceed, his tone implied, I *need* to know. And when she said she was well, he considered it like she'd said much more.

He said "yes" with finality, like a complete sentence, then opened the top half of each casket lid, displaying both the interior and the dignified, black-on-beige strip along the inner rim of wood just above the lining—the price tag. He explained that we'd reached the time when he leaves the family alone to get acquainted at their own pace with the selection and the costs. He made eye contact with each of us and asked if that sounded good. I had to laugh when Nathan sleepily answered, "Yes. Yes it does." He'd clearly been lulled into a Redmond State.

Redmond tilted his head, contemplated Nathan for a moment, then slipped out the door and closed it with excruciating care.

Nathan asked, "Wood or metal?" Mom thought wood. Definitely wood. Our father, in her estimation, was a "woody guy."

Nathan pondered that deeply and asked if I, too, would categorize Dad as "woody." In fact I do and I said as much, but I pointed out that we're the ones who'll actually see the outside while he'll only see the interior.

My mother snorted, equating that with asking other people to pick out your car since they'll be the ones who see it drive by. Finding this conversation not at all absurd, I earnestly pointed out that this wasn't precisely parallel unless you never, ever get out of your car.

Nathan fidgeted, adjusted his tie, and said in his very gayest voice, "I hate to bring this up, but I don't think Dad's gonna see the interior either."

We all agreed. Mom asked if the consensus was that we should get what we like, but Nathan winced, shook his head, and said, "Still, it is *his* casket. Shouldn't it reflect something about his personality?"

So, well, I flipped out. I yelled, "Oh, for the love of *God!*" and pressed my fingers into my temples so hard they met in the middle. And it occurred to me that Mom and Nathan weren't so much looking at me as just past me.

Now while we've established I wasn't transcendent or great or maybe even really good, I *was* a quarterback, right? So I have a feel for defenders creeping up behind me. I knew without looking that Jerald Redmond had reentered the room, was standing behind me, and had heard my outburst. So I dropped my head and held my hands out prayerfully, palms up. "Dear, *dear* beloved God," I preached passionately. "Please help us do right by our father as we choose his final resting place."

I glared at the two of them with one eye.

"Amen," Nathan said.

"Amen," my mom echoed.

I never did turn. I heard the door open and close. Mom snickered first. Then it was a staccato sniff-sniff-sniff-sniff laugh that bent her at the waist. She covered her mouth tightly.

"Jesus, don't bust a blood vessel holding back, Mom," Nathan managed between hiccups of laughter. "You couldn't hear gunplay through these walls."

With permission, Mom let out a big, lusty laugh that knocked Nathan back a step. She was snorting, as she was prone to do on rare occasions of unrestrained laughter. And watching straight-backed Republican Rita Way snort and try to catch each one was funny in any setting, so pretty quick all three of us were doubled over by more hilarity than had ever been shared in the casket gallery at Redmond's Funeral Home. I'm guessing the record was within easy reach for anybody who really cared to go for it.

Eventually, though, there was only so much oxygen in the preternaturally quiet setting, and our flash-flame of laughter flickered, hissed, and went out.

I asked my mom if we should just leave her alone for a bit, let her make the decision. She said, "If that's okay, yeah."

Nathan has no idea I was cut off from the Jenni Sanchez case, so I could still tell him I was headed for the office to tie a few things up. But the truth is, I have a "precise agenda" of my own, don't I? Running more or less parallel to McCale's.

I'm pretty sure a violent intersection is imminent.

(CLICK.)

(CLICK.)

Okay, maybe there's nothing precise about my agenda. Maybe I'm not bravely hacking a path to personal enlightenment through the high grass of my own soul. Maybe I'm being led to an unseemly, unshaven emotional meltdown by the Ghost of Joseph Way and my own self-destructive libido.

That said, it won't surprise you that I got to *The Independent* at about nine-thirty. I was pretty sure I'd heard that Mara lives in a loft on the third floor.

I went to the single red door with the stenciled logo. The blinds were closed at that hour, but I started pumping the buzzer anyway. Over and over and over, more than a dozen times.

Nothing. But I could sense her in there. I could *feel* her. And when I gave the bell a break and walked around in tight, angry circles, it ran up the back of my neck that I hadn't called Beth once all day. Still haven't. In the last year, not one single day has passed without us at least talking on the phone and under the circumstances, it's even more bizarre. What the hell am I doing? And how will I ever *un*do it?

But you know what? I think there *is* a certain order to it all, no matter how twisted or wrong-minded it might turn out. I'm following my own acid-trip-in-a-funhouse version of McCale's Agenda. A shotgun wedding of madness and purpose.

I can't see the horizon, can't see anything above the high pines, but I guess each turn in the nick of time. Here's me, hands on hips on a sidewalk on the Left Side . . . and way down here is me again, standing at a lectern in front of my father's casket on Thursday night.

And only about a million miles of broken glass in between.

Somebody said, "Can I help you?" and it smacked the wind out of me. It sounded something like, *"Harrr?"*

Just a few yards from me stood Y.J. Jiminez, artist and coffee-house magnate. He was walking his tiny white poodle and his raised eyebrow and hand-on-hip stance clashed with his tattooed, forty-eight-inch shoulders. He wore a shitload of eyeliner, like he'd just taken off the wig and pumps a few minutes ago.

You know how I told Beth that Nathan isn't that kind of gay? Well Y.J. *is.*

I pulled it together and tried to put some eat-me in my voice when I said I was here to see Mara Pinkett. Before I could stop myself, I also said I was FBI. The tone just led me there. I even identified myself as Agent Forrester.

He fought a laugh to say, "Yeah, so you're the mayor's son, right?"

After this, I won't be thinking of my exchange with Y.J. Jiminez again. Ever. There's the cute, funny most-embarrassing moment you confess to someone to make them think you're vulnerable and self-aware. And then there's introducing yourself as Agent Forrester of the FBI, only to find out Y.J. knows precisely who you are.

Anyway, he glanced up at the third-floor window and I realized there was a very faint glow coming from it. Seeing me looking that way, Y.J. tied his alleged dog off on the streetlight and advanced a couple of steps, apparently willing to slap or claw me or something if it came to that. The smaller bitch got feisty, too, yipping furiously.

I warned Y.J. to engage the emergency brake right there, you know? I said, "No offense, José, but back off, okay? *Seriously.*"

Yeah, it didn't scare him either.

I picked up a chip of curb, displayed it for him, and chucked it up at the window above us. It rattled the window frame and echoed down the tight street.

Y.J. poked his finger at me and said, "You do that again and you're waking up in the Cleveland Clinic with my foot up your ass."

I chuckled like, Ooh, I'm so scared, and said thanks for the sage advice but you and your lab rat can move along now. I pointed behind him and said, "Oh my *God!* Was that Cher?"

He had to twist his mouth up like an ass to keep from laughing, which made me instantly like him. I could use a friend like Mara has in Y.J. Maybe she deserves him and I don't.

Anyway, I used the distraction to pick up a slightly bigger chunk of driveway, set my feet, and flung it up at Mara's window . . .

To smash right through and into Mara's apartment. Glass shards fell, making all three of us—me, Y.J., and the lab rat—scurry away, hands/paws over our heads. I made a beeline for my car like a vandalous teenager. I could hear Y.J. pounding after me but I didn't look back. Then Mara's voice came from the broken window: "What the hell's going on, Y.J.?"

I turned to see Y.J. pointing at me, the other hand on his hip. I gave up my escape and waved up at her. She said, "Joe? You threw a rock through my window?"

Mara, looking through what used to be her window, and Y.J., in the middle of the street, waited for an explanation.

I said, "Let's all just take a really deep breath, okay?"

Mara crossed her arms to say, "This oughta be good." Y.J. mimicked it to a tee. Even the tiny little poodle put one arm over the other as she lay down to watch.

So I said, "Can I come up?"

She rightfully said that would be a bad idea. When I asked why, she explained that throughout history, we have yet to spend more than five minutes alone without having intercourse. I promised that sex was the last thing on my mind and, besides, I could probably wrap it all up in 270 seconds or less.

She considered seriously, then shook her head. "Nah," she said. "You can't control yourself."

I rolled my eyes and pretended to be stricken, staggering around the sidewalk dizzily. I must've been pretty convincing, because Y.J. got to me quick and steadied me by the shoulders. Like I said, I really could use a friend like him.

So I breathed all heavy and said, "It's too late! Dear God, help me! I'm stricken with jungle fever as we speak! Bar the door, wanton dark-skinned woman! *Bar the damn door!*"

Y.J. shoved me away harshly.

Mara nodded—oh, good one. Then she said, "And yet you're still not getting in."

I told her I needed her help. She said she knew all about the kind of help I wanted. I said I was serious. Finally, she told me to start 'splaining myself. I said, for one thing, I don't speak Spanish.

And then I played my usual trump card: I begged shamelessly. "Please, Mara," I said hypersincerely. *"Please."*

She raised a hand to stop me. "Fine, alright," she said. "Just stop before I yack."

I looked over just in time to see Y.J.'s lab rat drop a log bigger than her entire body. It seemed biologically impossible.

"You're gonna have to scoop that," I reminded him.

"Fuck you very much, Agent Forrester," he said, and flipped me off as he turned and walked away.

That's it. I will never, ever think of the Agent Forrester thing again as long as I live. Too painful.

A half hour later, I grabbed Mara's hand to drag her down the hallway to room 324 in the Savoy Riverfront Inn. I told her this is where it happened and that's when we realized we were still holding hands. I don't wanna make more of it than it was, but we'd never been the hand-holding kind of couple, or a couple at all, for that matter. In fact, this was the first time we'd ever tackled much of anything besides each other.

And we were holding hands. Then we weren't. We both used faux gestures to get out of the clasp and she rallied a reasonable question about where her fluency in a foreign language would figure in.

On cue, a blur of Spanish came from behind us: A middle-aged housekeeper and her young helper dragged a cart from a room two doors down.

Mara said, "Ah." I started to instruct her, but she interrupted, reminding me which of us was the investigative reporter here. Before I could follow her to the already-wary housekeepers, the door of room 324 swung open on its own and a voice inside whispered, "Joe! Hey, Joey!"

I couldn't resist turning to see my father standing near the king-sized bed, waving me in. He looked at least another five years younger now, in his midforties somewhere. He toasted me with a tiny bottle of Jack Daniels and then drained it. I stole a quick glance back at Mara—she was engrossed in conversation with the two women—then stepped gingerly back into Crazyville, aka room 324.

I took in the sweater, the trimmer waistline on the pleated slacks, the man who was so *not* the father I remember. I pasted on as much calm as I could muster and said, "You're getting younger, right? That's the program here?"

He bounced onto the end of the bed with a shrug, tossed the empty booze bottle into the trash, and said that appears to be the case. Then he said, "Pretty cool, huh?"

To which *I* said, "Riiiight. You're wearing a sweater and saying 'cool.' I think I'm just gonna go, okay?"

He jumped up, got a hand on my arm and said he just needed a minute. I said, "To explain?"

He tilted his head innocently and said, "Explain what, Joe?" I jerked away, like, *fuck you,* dead man. I suggested he spend a little less time amusing himself and a little more imparting wisdom. Or whatever it is ghosts do.

He nodded amiably enough and asked what I wanted to know. I didn't pause for a second: I asked if Nathan was right. Was I really a puppet? A science project? That's what I asked first. Not, "Did you have anything to do with Jenni Sanchez's death?"

His answer was, "Define 'puppet.'" But I already knew the answer, right? I buried my face in my hands and he admitted he might have set up a few things along the way. You know, made a contribution here or there to Wittenberg, pulled some strings at the Sports Commission and the DA's office. Those kinds of things.

The ACT score, as it turns out, was all mine. Things that make you go "hmm."

He fidgeted in the silence, something I'd never seen him do. And like a child changing the subject, he said, "You'll find *this* interesting: I can't fly. Isn't that odd?"

Honestly, I don't remember clearing the three steps between

us, but I pistoned both palms toward his chest for a nice, bracing shove. It wasn't like I passed through; I just didn't make contact. My hands were headed for his barrel chest and then I was staggering to fall face-first onto the bed.

I rolled quickly to see my dad blink quickly and say, "Well. That's neat."

He ignored my glare and sat down next to me. "You seem pissed, Joe," he said, patting my shoulder. "We should talk this through."

Once I caught my breath, I said, "It's bad enough I have no idea who *you* are, but you know what? I don't remember deciding I even *wanted* to be a fucking congressman. I've never once envisioned myself *being* a congressman."

He looked away from me and his shoulders fell. He said, "I think it might be hereditary."

I sat up and looked back at him, all his clever, JD-swilling attitude drained and gone. He looked at me like he was seeing me for the first time and a sad smile crossed his eyes but never his mouth.

I heard myself whisper something I hadn't meant to say: "Was *any* of it real? You and Mom, me and Nathan and Kate? Was it all just a movie?"

He couldn't look at me anymore. He dropped his head, turned his wedding ring around and around on his thick finger.

"I can't hand it to you," he said into his hands. "Not this time." And then he looked at me and said, "Find your truth, Joe. That's your thing, right? The truth? Find every little bit of it."

I stood up in a burst, hoping the flurry of action would hide that I was wiping the back of my hand across my eyes. I said something about Jenni Sanchez, something about *you can bet your dead fucking ass I'm gonna find the truth.*

And he said, "Find *your* truth, Joey. All of it."

I sweetly informed him that he wouldn't know the truth if it bit him on the dick and then, with no space in between, Mara said my name. I spun to see her in the doorway, looking as though she'd just watched me arc a piss onto the hotel bed.

I explained that I was practicing my eulogy. She raised her eyebrows and said it needed some work. As she entered, she scouted around, hoping there had been someone else in the room. When it became clear there wasn't, she smiled tightly and said, "Yeah, this has been so nice, but I'm just gonna catch a cab back home, okay?"

I got to her in midturn, held her shoulders, and told her that I needed her. Behind me, my father chuckled and said, "So Cocoa Puff here is your version of Carla Brugano, right?"

The name went into a file as I spun around and fired off, "Why don't you just kiss my ass, old man!" Even as I was yelling, I remembered that Mara couldn't see my father. That's always how these things work, right?

When I reluctantly looked back, her eyes were wide as saucers and she wasn't breathing. "You're having a nervous breakdown," she barely managed. Without hesitation, I said, "Why, yes I am."

Mara bit her lip, came to me, and held me. It was so natural; we just fit, you know? We fill each other's spaces perfectly. The smell of her overwhelms me. It's a lot like fear and I'm nowhere close to understanding it.

As he passed on his way to the door, my dad said, "Four days until I go in the ground, Joey. You know what I need."

My forgiveness, in case you've lost track. That's what he's after, right? *Absolution.*

When I looked up again, he was still there, lingering at the door and watching me. His eyes, for lack of a better word, were haunted. He patted the door frame and walked away. The moment the door closed and latched, a tapping came from the other side. A key worked in the lock and the door opened; the two Mexican housekeepers walked in, clearly befuddled.

Mara and I disengaged quickly and the older woman looked at us, then back to the door. "Ehhhh," she idled out of habit, "How you get in?"

I said it was open. She looked dubious. Then she pointed at me and rattled off a string of Spanish. Mara looked at me, then back to the old housekeeper, and asked, *"Se fue del hotel?"*

The housekeeper nodded. Mara looked at me and I said, *"Huh?"* She waved me off and said *gracias* to the housekeepers, both of whom shot me a disapproving glance as they turned away.

"Huh?" I asked again. But Mara just grabbed my hand and led me from the room, shaking her head. She said, "Let's just get out of here."

Our fingers laced together again, like boyfriend and girl-friend.

Neither of us spoke for the entire twenty-minute drive back

to her apartment. For some reason, I sensed it wasn't something I should be eager to know.

We sat in silence for another minute or so at the curb. When I started to ask, she interrupted and told me to tell her all about me and Beth.

I felt that tumbling and turning again, the rush, the almost-fear. Asking about Beth edged us closer to something, probably a cliff, if history serves. When I started by telling her that Beth teaches social studies and martial arts at the WRA, Mara said, "Why am I so certain this is all gonna end with me getting my ass kicked?"

I started talking about Beth, but in a way I was telling a story to myself: She's Ivy League educated, but she's not a corporate climber. She's got the kind of job that makes it easy to raise kids and stand by your man. She left New York and moved home when her mother had a stroke so she could rehab their old house off the square and take care of her.

It's official, I said. Beth's perfect.

Mara asked, "Perfect for you? Or just perfect?"

I just shook my head, told her that my dad and my best friend Mark set us up a year and a half ago. And until yesterday, it had all been so easy between us. In other words, the opposite of how things work for me and Mara.

She let that settle, swished it around, then said, "The older housekeeper started working there fifteen years ago, and she said your father's been meeting that woman there the second Friday of every month at least since then."

That's right: It was one woman. The same woman for fifteen

years. Moreover, Mara said, she wasn't some young hottie. The housekeeper guessed her about sixty. A little on the plump side. Kinda ethnic.

Without thinking, I said, "She's Italian. Her name's Carla Brugano."

I didn't answer when she asked how I knew. I just stared out the window until I felt the back of her hand brush against my cheek. I caught it, pressed my lips against the palm. It just happened.

She pulled away from me, like my lips were branding her. She opened the door and got out, slamming it behind her and practically running for the door.

I got out meaning to yell something to her, but I didn't. I just stood there, watching her. She seemed to feel me, though, and stopped at the door.

For a long time, we just stood there, staring at each other. A couple of dozen feet of blacktop and my car joined my fianceé and my dead father and a thousand other complications that were always between us.

I finally asked what the housekeeper had said about me. And according to Mara, it was this: I'd come down to the lobby very late, after the bar was closed. I had an argument with the desk clerk.

Mara hesitated here, chewed at her lip. And finally, she added, "And then you left the hotel."

And now, one more thing stands between us. Because on the night Jenni Sanchez was murdered, I drunkenly left my hotel. I didn't have scratches or muddy shoes or any telltale signs of a struggle, but that still doesn't answer the question: *Where did I go?*

There was nothing left to say. I got back in my car and drove away. That was almost two hours ago. And I'm still driving.

(CLICK.)

(CLICK.)

It's dusk on the tee box where I last saw my father as I knew him before. Since then I've known him as a philandering prick and then a ghost aging in reverse, so this place is understandably nostalgic for me.

When I sat here on the bench, under the antique street lamp, I realized that the copy of *The Independent* he'd planted and used as a prop was still there, pages fanned out by the wind. The very first thing I did was turn to page 2, where I knew Mara's glam photo would be. And then I mooned over it before I realized what I was doing and tossed the rag aside in embarrassment.

That feeling, the tumbling in my stomach that's almost fear, I can get it even from a photo of her. From the sound of her voice. From the very *idea* of Mara Pinkett. I've never admitted this to anybody but you, but it's been that way since the very first time I saw her. She was speaking in the quad at Wittenberg, bitching about Shwarzkopf and the Highway to Hell and linking that in some way to the cancellation of a women's-poetry class. It didn't make a speck of sense to me and I wasn't really paying attention anyway, but I had that feeling, the one you get when you're not quite asleep but you dream you're missing a stair step.

That's what she makes me feel. Like I'm out of control, just holding on for the ride.

Nobody's here but I'm still terrified to ask out loud: *Is that love?*

A few days later, I watched her in the library for about an hour before I finally had the balls to approach. I had the cool smile in place and I went so far as to put a thumb in my jean pocket, but my monosyllabic icebreaker—"Hey," after much deliberation—still wedged in my throat enough to allow her that up-and-down, who-the-fuck-are-you look.

It was awkward and fumbling and two days later we slept together for the first time. Romeo and LaJuliet and their spectacular secret. We were the victims of a cosmic practical joke, magnetized by attraction and repelled by virtually everything else about each other.

That's where we put it and that's where it stayed. But now I wonder if maybe, just maybe, all of it was a sitcom conceit, a defense mechanism, a matter of convenience. Did we speak Banterese because it prevented us from speaking the truth?

That said, I like *and* love Beth Pruitt. I really, honestly do.

The thought of not being with her disorients me. She's funny and smart and sexy and she gets me, man. If I fuck things up with her, the line would wind around The Square five times. I just think that's worth acknowledging. It should be said.

But I'm *not* going to fuck things up. When this is over, I'll go to her and get down on my knees if I have to and vow my love to her forever. We'll make babies and watch them cheer and play football under the lights at the WRA. And one day, Shane's name and number will go up next to mine. That's the way it'll be. Because that's the way it's designed to be.

Shit. I have no idea how this will end. No idea at all.

I slept like the dead last night, after I'd finally stopped driving. Through the window when I was pouring coffee this morning, I saw Nathan on the drive, elbows deep in the Mercedes' engine. It was a total disconnect. I wondered if I'd had a stroke and I was mismatching visual elements. Maybe next I'd see a woman wearing a batter's helmet walking a cow down the sidewalk. Something like that.

I poured a cup for him, too, threw on one of Dad's old windbreakers, went out, and said, "You're kidding, right?"

He wiped his hands, took the coffee, gave me the once-over I was getting used to. Apparently I never allowed anybody to see me before I shaved and pressed my hair, because it gets a reaction every time.

Nathan told me not to panic—he still likes *The O.C.* and Banana Republic. He calculated me some more and said, "They're making you stay away from the case." I nodded. Very perceptive.

He asked if I really *am* staying away and I said not exactly. He said I looked deader than Dad and suggested I get something from Dr. Faver to make me sleep. Before I realized it, I said, "I keep expecting Dad to appear again."

Nathan smirked and cut back against the grain, asking, "Who do you think taught Mr. Quarterback how to throw a football?"

My answer: "Well, for starters, not you."

He said, "You think the great man had time for you? He didn't call you 'the little guy' because you were cute, you know. He couldn't even remember your name until you became his last, best hope. Particularly sad, don't you think, considering it's his name, too?"

Nathan went back to work. And after a minute of consideration, I asked if he'd had any Ed Wood moments, like one of the walls fell over so you could see all the lights and camera gear.

He didn't answer, which pissed me off. So I asked, "Is it hard to love him *and* hate him?"

He turned quickly and I spilled a bit of coffee trying not to back off. And he said, "I never hated him. And I don't hate him now."

I laughed. I wasn't buying it. He said something about one of us being a fully evolved personality capable of processing disappointment, and I told him how *extremely* thin that was wearing. He bobbed his head—fair enough. And he admitted that at one time, Dad was his whole world. But even then, he had the nagging sense that he was on borrowed time.

For the first time in my life, the oppressive sadness of that fell upon me. It was so heavy I leaned against the car to bear its weight. Nathan slammed the hood just to scare the shit out of me and laughed when it worked.

He said, "But I got this now, don't I? I hope he's watching when I paint it pink and slap on the BOYTOY plates." He pushed past me on his way to the driver's seat, and I said, "I've been with Mara."

It slowed him for a beat, but he got in the car anyway. He started it before he looked back and asked me to define "been with." I explained that she was sort of helping me. He tried to say, "Define helping you," but I told him to shut up.

I said, "I want the truth."

He said, "That's noble."

I said, "All of it. In about three days."

He said, "If a little unrealistic."

And that's when I decided to more fully explain that Dad needs me to find it, too. Well, technically, he needs my forgiveness before he can move on, which he apparently hopes will be the result of me learning the entire truth. In three days.

When I stopped blathering and looked up, Nathan was shaking his head, his jaw off line. He said, "Yeah, I'd love to hear more about your chronic narcissism, but I have a date with your ex-fiancée, *bitch.*"

I slapped the back of the car to make him stop and explain: He'd talked her into taking the rest of the day off and cruising around in Nathan's new wheels. He waited with eyebrows raised. I finally said, "You know how you said I helped Dad make me into a Xerox of a photo of a painting of a sculpture of a *whatever?*"

He allowed that it was a little harsh. I told him I was planning to go to the old place. To Uncle Roy's.

He bobbed his head, considering. I had him at Uncle Roy, I think. He said that's as good a place to cruise as any and I got in. We were pulling into the ivy-on-brick arched entrance to the WRA before I got the nerve to tell him I'd seen Dad again last night, in room 324 of the Savoy.

He braked right there, right under the arch, and turned a slow, unpleasant smile on me. He said, "Oh do go on."

I more patiently explained *again* that Dad's stuck here. If I understand correctly, I need to forgive him by the time I give the eulogy or he goes to hell. You know, or whatever Not Heaven is. Maybe it's a Super Wal-Mart or the DMV.

Nathan calmly offered to recap. He said, "Not only does your future depend on whatever decision you come to in the next couple of days, so does the fate of our father's eternal soul. It's all hanging entirely on *your* verdict, Mr. Assistant Disctrict Attorney?"

Stupidly, I said, "Pretty wild, huh?"

He said, "Yeah. *Wild.* And while I'd be the last person to suggest your staggering immaturity or guilt over hating your dead father might be at the root of all this, let's at least consider the near certainty that being the spit-shined apple of Super Daddy's eye has made you the most delusional egocentric in the history of, well . . . forever, quite possibly."

When I told him his support was deeply appreciated, *asshole,* and informed him I hadn't asked for this, he put up his hand and made a buzzing sound, like *dzzzt!*

I said if he did that again he'd pull back a fucking stump, *bitch.* So he did it again, over and over and over. And while he did not technically pull back a stump, I did give him the mother of all mouse milkings.

In case you were raised in a convent or as a single child, that's pinching the pinkie into itself. It's horrible. Generally older brothers do it to younger ones, but Kate had taught me because Nathan is a self-important priss and truly needs to have his mouse milked from time to time.

When he finally freed himself, the cool was all gone. He was mincing off his words: "Dad's appearing to *you,* begging for *your* forgiveness. Oh, that's just too precious."

I said, "That's not jealousy I detect, is it, Nathan? Because you're far too *evolved* for that, right?"

He had to admit: direct hit. He said, "Touché." Nathan is nothing if not gracious amid a flame war.

And as he eased the Mercedes forward, around the back of Simmons Hall toward the new gym, I sensed just the slightest movement behind me and the hairs at the back of my neck rose. I turned enough to see my father from the corner of my eye without alerting Nathan. Then I used the rearview mirror to get a better look: Joseph Way had aged himself a few years younger.

My calm lasted about eight seconds before I spun around and screamed, "So why the hell can't *he* see you?"

Nathan huffed and said, "You know what: Fuck you a million, trillion times." And he got out and started marching stiff-legged and angry toward the landscaped entrance to the new gym.

"He doesn't hate me," my father said softly from behind me. "Maybe if he did, maybe if he still felt *something* . . ."

I said, "Maybe he couldn't." And then I looked at my father. He nodded slowly.

I couldn't help look away when I heard Nathan grouse something under his breath as he flung open the gym door.

And when I looked back, my father was gone.

I caught Nathan in the brief corridor between the main doors and the gym itself and we walked in together. I saw Beth, alone at the far end, beating the living shit out of a heavy bag with a frightening blur of spinning kicks and pistoned fists.

I'd never seen her fight. Her teeth were bared; it was only a hair's breadth too scary to be sexy. I made an eek expression and Nathan caught it.

He said, "Yeah, it's probably not a good idea to have a wife who can kick your ass, is it?"

Beth turned to us as we approached. The very first words out of her mouth were, "You didn't say *he* was coming."

She refused to look at me even when I said, "I'm *he* now? One stupid question, and I'm *he?*"

Nathan rubbed his hands together and said, "Oh, goodie. This should be fun!"

Twenty minutes outside Cleveland on a blue highway cut between a series of low-end farms, Beth was still silent in the backseat, arms crossed defensively. I glared straight ahead and pretended not to notice.

Nathan played the disappointed parent. He asked for Mom's sake that we at least pretend to be grown-ups for a couple of weeks. We both said "fine" at the same time, sounding equally adolescent.

Another twenty minutes of stone-cold silence later, the three of us sat on the floor of my first home, the two-bedroom apartment over Uncle Roy's detached garage behind his humble airplane bungalow. Roy was never an ambitious man. I figure he's led as close to a stress-free life as can be had this close to a major U.S. city. He seemed even more fluid in his seventies, like he was born to be this age. He wore a wash-softened flannel shirt over a burgundy Cavaliers T-shirt that was older than me and sipped a beer as he watched us.

I got the feeling that he was neither happy nor sad that we'd come. Those were extreme emotions that might knock his needle off its flat line. He was *just fine* with it.

He finally said, "Honest truth, I never once dreamt that the man who lived with my sister over the garage would eventually become a millionaire, let alone the mayor of Cleveland. That boy was back in the yard with a beer by four in the afternoon, bitching about how hard it was to sell those damn alarm systems."

"It's true," Nathan said. He was laughing at me, so my sense of being unable to shake a lingering acid trip was clearly showing.

Oblivious, Roy went on, telling how my dad was downright *stoked* over pulling together a scheme to handle all the newspaper deliveries for this half of the county. He damn near pulled it off, too, but my grandfather—Roy and my mom's dad—had other plans.

I had to say it to digest it: "My dad was an aspiring paper-boy."

Beth breathed out a "wow" as she stared at a black-and-white photo. Nathan and I skittered over to see it: Nathan and Kate beamed with a two-year-old between them. The littlest was me, of course. I was a beat behind like most toddlers, my face locked in perpetual *"Wha?"*

Nathan took the picture and ran his thumb over Kate's face; she radiated a natural beauty even at eleven.

"I can almost smell her soap," he sighed. "She always smelled like soap."

I agreed: always.

Nathan smiled at me and we made up in the memory of her. Nathan said it was like the sun went down when she died. Then he cleared his throat to keep from crying, stood, and walked directly to the nearest bedroom door. He pushed it open, stepped inside, and I could see him sit down on the edge of the bed.

Beth looked at me and I nodded: our parents' room. She tipped her head to tell me to go with him, but I'd already decided to do just that.

I closed the door behind us. Nathan ran his hand over the quilt and said, "I always loved this bed."

I watched Nathan for a long while, getting lost with him in his memories, and I caught glimpses of another him, flickering in like a ghost broadcast. He was still a child, just as trapped as our father.

That's when I heard water running from the tiny attached bathroom, saw the light in the crack of the door. One step put me in line to see my dad at the sink in a T-shirt. Lean and muscular, he clocked in somewhere in his early forties now, lathering his face to shave.

He began to sing, first mumbling, but then more clearly: "Nathan is leaving tonight on a plane . . . I can see the red tail lights, heading for Spay-ee-ain. . . ."

"He sang 'Daniel' to you, but he put your name in it," I whispered, looking between my father and brother.

Dad turned in midstroke to look at me, but then his eyes fell on Nathan, who was lying on the bed, now, his face pressed into a pillow, breathing it in.

I leaned in, but before I could speak, Nathan said he'd heard me. Suddenly, Dad was there beside me, defying space and time, looking down on Nathan. Frustrated and helpless, he wrang a face towel in his hands.

I just lost it, man. I yelled at my dead father, "Just say something! Say *anything,* you stupid shit!"

It terrified Nathan, pressed him up against the wood headboard. He looked between me and Dad and for the moment, I was sure he saw him.

But then he chuffed off a laugh and said, "Another visit from Daddy?"

I got Nathan by the shirt, pulled him up to a sitting position, got so close our noses grazed. I yelled at him even louder than I had at our father, "You're not so complete! Do you hear me? You're *not!*"

He just stared back at me with slate eyes and a smug smile. He said, "I have no idea what you're talking about."

Bullshit. I said, "He couldn't handle it so he left you and it still hurts. How can you not *see* when it's so clear to me?"

Nothing. He gave back nothing.

When I turned, Joseph Way was back in the bathroom again, shaving and whispering the song: "God, it looks like Nathan . . . must be the clouds in my eyes." He stopped then, looked back at his sons, eyes indeed clouded with decades of regret.

The bell of a passing ice-cream truck shattered the scene, an ambitious vendor taking full advantage of another unseasonably warm day.

Nathan rocketed off the bed. "Ice cream!" he cried happily, and pushed past me on his suddenly giddy way to the door.

Just before he left, he looked back with a flat expression. "See how fine I am, Joe?" he said evenly, then walked out of the room without waiting for a reply.

My father was beside me again and I shoved him hard, making contact this time and knocking him back several steps. I said, "As ghosts go, you are *entirely fucking useless!*"

He threw his towel down hard, waded right back into my anger, and snarled, "You were barely six, for Christ's sake. For you, Kate's death is just an interesting bit of bio, something to put on your resumé: 'My sister died when I was a little boy.' But it's not really part of you, is it?"

I told him to fuck off, but he continued anyway: "The rest of us are carrying the shrapnel, you little shit. We can still feel the impact when we close our eyes."

I couldn't speak. I could barely breathe. By inches, his anger receded. His voice cracked and he started over: "I wanted to fight for your brother. But it turned out I didn't have any fight left in me."

He shrugged and turned away. Walked back to the bathroom and closed the door behind him.

I just need a second or a glass of water or a Valium or something. I'm not sure, really.

(CLICK.)

(CLICK.)

Okay. I'm back. I went with the water.

When I got out front, Uncle Roy watched from the driveway as Nathan and Beth ran to join a huddle of children around the ice-cream truck.

I stood beside Roy and he looked at me but said nothing. I got the sense that he knew something was going on here, something more than mundane rummaging, but he figured that wasn't his business.

After a bit, I asked what my dad was like when he lived here. Roy chuckled and scratched his leg, looked around like he was watching a movie. He said, "Honestly? He and I were a couple of peas in a pod. Joseph liked his beer cold and his overhead low, just like me."

I asked if that meant he was happy and Roy nodded. He said sometimes it seemed to him that Rita and my grandfather dragged Joseph Way kicking and screaming all the way to Benton Heights and the rest of his life. "One day he's calling Reagan a gassy old retard," he offered as evidence, "the next he's winning some businessman award and going on about how the

Gipper and John Wayne are the only significant American men of the last half century. I mean, what's up with *that* shit?"

A few days ago, Uncle Roy telling me my father was "dragged" into his staggeringly successful business venture would've buckled my knees. Instead of asking, I said it outright: "I understand my dad didn't really start up his own company."

Roy said, "Yeah, that story's pretty much bullshit. My dad—your grandpa—he had the connections. He hooked Joseph up with some vendors, but people out in this part of town don't exactly lie awake at night worrying about gettin' robbed, see? So Dad pretty much snatched Joseph Way right outta my back-yard, plunked him down in Benton Heights, and built a little company around him, all nice and tidy."

I just started laughing. Right there, standing next to my uncle a few yards in front of the garage apartment I barely remembered, I couldn't think of one damn other thing to do.

Roy squinted at me, asked if I needed a beer. In Roy's world, virtually everything calls for a beer, even discomfiting laughter. When I shook my head "no," he took that as a clear "yes," slapped my arm, and headed off to fetch the universal tonic. I yelled after him, "Did you know about Carla Brugano?"

It was a wild guess; it seemed to me Roy had ended up closer to his brother-in-law than his sister. My uncle froze, lowered his head. He turned back reluctantly and nodded just a little.

I asked when it started. He said twenty-some years ago, not so long after Kate died. He didn't have the exact date, but I was still just "a pimple of a boy."

I asked who she was and how they met. He said Carla Brugano was his assistant, a girl from "Dagoville," up on North Hill. The wrong girl from the wrong side of town.

I didn't need to build a very big bridge to make the connection. Dagoville, the Left Side. Whatever. Whenever.

Roy nodded, agreeing with something he read off me, and said, "Doesn't exactly fit in the Joseph Way Memorial Museum, now does it?"

To which I asked, "Does anything?" He smiled a little, totally getting it. Just then, Beth and Nathan ran by with their ice-cream bars to disappear into the dark garage. Seconds later, they emerged, pedaling past Joe and Uncle Roy on old Schwinns, racing each other in circles around the lawn.

Roy watched, crossing his arms and smiling sadly, the corners of his mouth weighted by the certainty that the best was over. The rest would be too long by half.

"Nathan and your sister used to do that all summer long," he said. "Rode their bikes right through the lawn sprinkler. Tore my front yard to shit, they did."

I dropped my head and Uncle Roy asked if I was okay. I told him I wish that I could remember Kate better. And I do wish that, so very much. I know I loved her. That I can remember.

It came from him so soft I'm not sure he said it: "Me, too, Joe," is what I thought I heard. He walked away without another word and I went to tear Nathan and Beth from their fun.

It was afternoon by the time we pulled up in front of Beth and her mother's house. Over two summers, with little help,

Beth had nearly restored the Victorian to its original pumpkin with three-color trim. But for the time being, the porch was propped up by an expandable pole.

Beth circled the car and waved to her mom, who was sitting in her wheelchair on the front porch, then leaned in the driver's side and kissed Nathan on the cheek.

She started in without so much as looking at me. Nathan scowled at me and I scrambled out of the car and after her. When I called her name, she stopped for a bit before she turned back. I just blurted it out: "My father was having an affair. For about twenty-three years, I think."

She nodded calmly and pointed out that twenty-three years isn't an affair. It's something else.

I didn't know where to go from there, but Beth put the pieces together for both of us. She said, "And you don't wanna end up like him? Is that it? I'm playing the role of your mother in this twisted Shakespearean drama?"

I stammered some kind of protest, and she took three full strides to get right in front of me. Cutting through my confusion, she said, "Did you know I had two of my black belts by the time I was twelve?"

And, yeah, for a second I thought, Oh my God, she's actually going to kick my ass, right here on her front lawn. I wondered where something like that leaves a guy in the social hierarchy.

When I finally said, "Yes," I meant it to be definitive. But it still came out like a question.

She ignored it and said, "Now, what would motivate a little girl to do that?" Then she moved closer yet. Her eyes went hard and her voice descended to a low whisper. She said, "And what kind of beating would a fourteen-year-old girl have to give her stepfather to get shipped off to boarding school in Boston?"

I heard myself breathe out, "Jesus, Beth."

She said, "And why do you think that little girl didn't move back to Ohio and square up with her mother for *ten years?* Hmm? You ever wonder about that?"

I had. I'd wondered a million things about Beth. About the wineglasses left full, about her leaving and her return, and too many other things to list.

Everybody has a story. Why had I never asked about hers?

She moved closer yet, so close I could feel the heat of her rage radiating. And she said, "Because by then he was dead. And I wouldn't have to kill him."

With that, she pulled the engagement ring off her finger, turned my palm up, and put it there. She said we'd just see where we are when this is all over, and then she turned and walked to the porch and her mother.

Sitting here now with this hole in me, I swear to you, Beth, I don't want to do what my father did, giving only half of himself to my mother and the other half to Carla Brugano. I want the woman I love to know me and I want to know her, every word of every page in her fascinating, surprising story. I want to finish each other's sentences when we're old.

I want to hold entire conversations without speaking.

I'm gonna fix us, Beth. So right now, this second, I'm going to start by going to Mara and doing what my father never could.

I'm going to end it.

(CLICK.)

(CLICK.)

Well, things have taken quite a turn. First of all, my visit with Mara didn't come off as I'd planned.

I made sure to throw only pebbles this time. She'd already had the glass replaced—on the Left Side, Mara can make shit happen. My first throw was off target, but the next one clinked sharply against the new glass.

Mara appeared, raised the window. She said, "Wonderful. It's Romeo again."

When I told her I needed to come up, she said, "Oh, let's just *not*." She wrung her hands and kept shaking her head. I waited her out until she threw up her hands and made a "guh" sound, then disappeared from sight.

By the time she opened the front door, I was having second

thoughts of my own. I told her maybe I should leave after all. She agreed that was probably best.

I got as far as my car door door before she said, "There's something I want to show you."

I couldn't suppress my you-know-you-want-me smirk, and Mara's disdainful eye roll dashed any hope that she'd missed it. She said, "After that, I wouldn't sleep with you if I was dying and your dick was the only cure."

Just the same, we were careful to wedge ourselves into opposite corners of her massive distressed-leather couch. She punched a remote at the bigscreen, pulling up a TiVo menu called "Now Playing"—programs recorded on her digital video recorder.

I looked around at her apartment, which was a little upscale for a soldier of the revolution. She read my mind and snapped, "I'm a journalist, not a communist."

The late news came on the screen, a generic blond anchor with the requisite bob and highlights. Mara shuttled quickly, stopped and backed up . . .

To a press conference. Stepping to the mike, illuminated by photo flashes, was none other than Ally Wong. The long hair had been tastefully trimmed to shoulder length and pulled back demurely. She wore just the right amount of makeup and the perfect navy blue suit over an open-collar blouse that exposed precisely enough milky skin.

What mattered most, though, was that she seemed to have mainlined more Valium than my mother. Instead of spraying a glare across the room, marking future victims, she smiled professionally, even serenely, leaned into the mike, and said, "Thanks for coming," in a warm, honey-dipped voice.

So I said, "Just who the fuck is *that*?"

On-screen, Ally spoke evenly, her gaze turning from left to right and back again, addressing each of the unseen media representatives. Basically, she said that on the night of her death, Jenni Sanchez met with a Caucasian male in his early thirties at approximately midnight for roughly thirty minutes in a bar called Manny's on Ninth Street in Downtown Cleveland. The man wore a suit but no tie. Because the bar was dark, the description of him is vague: He's medium height and has short hair. The conversation grew tense but not loud. Ms. Sanchez left the bar alone. The man left a few minutes later.

It occurred to me that I was officially and completely out of the loop now. Ally continued, saying that she hoped at least one of the estimated ten other patrons who were in that bar would contact the Cleveland Police Department to help us pull together a more accurate picture of the man Jenni Sanchez was with that night . . . and perhaps even what was said.

Mara punched the remote, freezing the "after" image of Ally Wong. She summed up the rest—Ally gave out the phone number a few times and asked the media for help.

"God," I marveled. "It must've taken a bull tranquilizer to bring her down that far."

Mara stared at the frozen image with me and said, "You know what she looks like?"

I did and I said so: a mayoral candidate. That's exactly what she looked like.

I shook it off and told Mara I would need to use the phone in about one minute. She warily asked how we would fill those sixty seconds. I explained that we were going to settle things between us, once and for all. She asked if I remembered the last time we settled things, two years after college.

I did. We had sex for seven hours, yelled a lot, and then she threw a beer bottle at me. I concluded that we all have our peculiar versions of closure.

We both laughed nervously and she chewed at her thumb. I immediately told her to stop because, well, the thumb thing always makes me want to have sex with her. She said, "Right," and put her hand under her thigh. Which made me *look* at her thigh, bare and smooth and caramel-coated just below the faded black CBGB T-shirt she'd picked up in New York in case you weren't sure she's cooler than you'll ever be. Noticing me noticing made her pull the shirt down over both knees.

My breathing accelerated to short bursts. Hers fell into rhythm with it. I reminded her that I was going through some intense shit. She reminded *me* that she saw me cussing out a lamp in a hotel room, so *duh*.

Besides, if there's a worse idea than the two of us, she couldn't imagine what it would be. And with that, we met in the middle of the couch and tied our tongues into a complex knot.

We didn't crawl, scurry, or slide to the middle of the couch. We magnetized. She was there and I was here and then we converged into a single body, mouths devouring and hands finding and grabbing desperately. I didn't just want to do her; I wanted to *consume* her.

Before she could consume me, maybe. Because I know as much as I hunger for Mara, I fear her at least twice that. I still can't explain it.

She toppled me over, onto my back, and straddled me. She breathed, "Damn, you're pretty," just as she put her tongue back in my mouth where it belonged. My hands found her hips and pressed her down onto me and she fell into a circular motion. I thought she was groaning and realized it was me. And then us.

She whispered, "We should stop," warm and wet in my ear, like a threat. My fingers found the slender sides of her panties and I decided to rip them off, throw her on the ground, and pin her hands to the floor over her head. I'd make her admit *I* broke up with *her*.

But then she just wasn't there. I was shaking, gasping, clawing at the air as I broke the atmosphere and reentered the mundane world. She was standing, gripping the arm of a nearby chair, tumbling into it and pulling her knees up under her shirt, turning away from me and looking back.

She said, "I can't." I managed to tell her how desperately I wished she'd come to that conclusion ninety seconds ago.

She shook her head quickly, winced between sexual frustration and anger, and said, "Just get out of my life, you goddamn fucking boomerang."

I deduced that in her sloppy-ass metaphor she'd thrown me out and I kept coming back, because my mind's a steel trap that way. But halfway into reminding her that *I* broke up with *her*, she started wax-and-wiping both hands at me, erasing the notion.

"Will you for once in your life just *shut up*," she seethed.

When I asked what all the hate was about, she said she hated me because she *couldn't* hate me. It was just deranged enough that I totally got it.

I made a little move down the couch, toward her, and she threw a hand up at me and said, "Stay! You get one inch closer to me and I will kick you repeatedly in the head, I swear to God."

I nodded and dropped back reluctantly. I asked what the hell's wrong with us but she didn't have any answers better than mine. I said, "I don't love you," and she said, "Yeah, I don't love you, too, babydoll."

We both struggled not to smile. She waved a hand at me dismissively and said, "Now get me a beer and hit the pavement, okay? I need to masturbate and then wallow in self-loathing."

I reminded her of the call I needed to make. She told me to use my cell. I told her to get her own fucking beer. She said we had a deal, waved at me coquettishly with one finger, and said, "Buh-bye."

That would've been fine, you know? But then she made two little kisses, designed to be the bitchy last word, and that's when we fucked. She didn't even make it out of the chair though somehow I mysteriously ended up beneath her. My head still aches from having my hair pulled back so she could probe her tongue down my throat.

When it was over, she staggered away in a daze, picked up her panties, and saw what we'd done to them. She tossed them at my face, spun on her heels, and headed back to her bedroom. She never even looked back.

This is what we do, me and Mara. This is how it works for us. I don't think there's a name for it. It's so wrong it passes through right on its way back to wrong again.

I headed straight for McCale's place. He lives in a cop apartment: bland, four-story brick building four miles south of downtown in a mostly Yugoslavian neighborhood with a drive-through liquor store, a family market, and a long stretch of closed storefronts.

He opened the door in his gray, monochromatic sweatsuit and gestured me in. The two of us were dead serious because he was truly breaking rank, now. My call had asked for that much and letting me in complied.

McCale's apartment is a kitchenette, a single couch aimed at a ten-year-old TV, and a reasonably new computer that, along with its desk and the files stacked around it, dominates the place.

McCale is a detective now and nothing more. He was married once for a few years and took that one earnest stab at being a human being. It didn't take.

I sat at the bargain-barn oak table marred with newsprint and beer-bottle circles while McCale found two cold ones in the back of the fridge and sat across from me. We clinked bottles and nodded together for a beat, a fast, tight exchange that replaced the bullshit pleasantries one might exchange with a person leading an actual life.

I asked what the hell was up with Ally's press conference and the man didn't even bother to hesitate before asking, "You think she's the one getting something?" That's cop talk: When you're lining up suspects, start by following the money or whatever else is there to be gained.

When I asked if he'd tested the handwriting sample on Mara's number, McCale hitched a second before he nodded. He'd been equally handcuffed by the assumption that Jenni herself had written down the number, which in McCale's world is reason enough to put his head in an oven.

He'd figured the girl had simply scrawled it down after she called information, leafed through a phone book, or found it in the rag itself. He'd *assumed* it and then been shocked when the tests told him the handwriting didn't match.

Dan McCale doesn't like to be shocked. He doesn't golf or bet football or jog or make homemade beer. There's nowhere else to pick up the slack when he fucks up at work.

And for the first time, I said what I'd realized when I watched a tranquilized Ally Wong and her new hairdo on Mara's bigscreen: "I think somebody wanted the world to know what I did, McCale. And that somebody gave Mara's number to Jenni Sanchez."

He asked about "Guy without Tie," but I informed him that Mara said he'd been trying to talk Jenni *out* of making the call. Why would he then give her Mara's number?

In the silence we both took long draws from our beers and the affiliation between me and McCale deepened. It was deepened because by being there, by *digging*, I'd clearly demonstrated something of vital importance: Coming to his home like this, at this hour, proved to Dan McCale that I wanted the truth. Nothing more and nothing less.

In Dan McCale's world—maybe in the world as a whole—there are two kinds of people: those looking for truth and those in their way. There are always too few of the former and too many of the latter, it seems. In the nasty haze of deceit that seems to settle over any dead body, finding just one other person with that exact same objective can be like two children in a cocktail party of adults, drawn together as Best Friends Ever for at least this night.

McCale and I wanted the same thing for different reasons. We wanted to know the Truth of Jenni Sanchez. For me, it was the corner of a larger puzzle. For him, it *was* the puzzle.

I reached into the breast pocket of my jacket, pulled out a folded piece of thick stationery, and smoothed it out on the table in front of McCale: a scrawled note from Ally Wong to me. "Make goddamn fucking sure you mention my name at that rally," it said.

McCale nodded, went to the computer and its related clutter, grabbed a thick expanding file, loosened the string, and rifled through until he found what he wanted.

He returned to the table and laid down a Xerox of Mara's name and phone number. I slid the two pieces of paper together, overlapped them. I finally fitted them so the words *make* and *Mara* butted up against each other.

McCale whispered, "Jesus Filmore Christ," because there was no doubt. None whatsoever. Ally Wong had written down Mara Pinkett's number and given it to Jenni Sanchez. McCale came alive, his eyes flickering, ready to play. He said, "Let's run it through."

I took a swipe. I said Jenni got nervous, admitted to Ally that she'd met with me. Ally saw an opportunity to wipe out both candidates with one sex scandal. Ratcovic's a perv and the Ways are corrupt insiders.

McCale said, "That works."

I went on: So Ally tells Jenni to call Mara, because she figures Mara will eat it up, right? McCale asked the right question: Why would Jenni do it? What's in it for her?

I didn't have to think about that one: money. And it probably didn't take much.

But then I questioned my own scenario: Why would Ally want Jenni dead? McCale smiled, relishing it, and said, "Because Jenni got scared and decided only the truth could set her free."

Bingo. Mara said that the girl had decided the only way out was to tell the truth. The whole truth. Somehow—perhaps from Man without Tie—Ally found out.

McCale turned his beer in a perfect circle and shot down my theory: "If Guy without Tie was working in opposition to Ally, trying to persuade Jenni *not* to call Mara, why would he turn around and tell Ally about it?"

I admitted I have no fucking idea. McCale liked me more for it because when you don't know, you don't know and you say so. That's the way the game is played and most people can't handle it.

That's when McCale went on to confuse the shit out of the whole issue by revealing that he'd dug up a direct line between the D.A.'s office and Lester Ratcovic. He's not a man prone to the dramatic, but he couldn't resist making me ask before he leaned in, eyes blazing, and said, "Your assistant, Callie Burke. She's the connection."

I was about to put my last drink of beer through my nose. I said, "Callie? Callie was a housewife for twenty-five years before she came to work for me."

But McCale played it differently. Suddenly out of nowhere Callie Burke decided she just had to become an assistant in the D.A.'s office at exactly the same time Lester Ratcovic began publicly considering a run for mayor.

He couldn't help drumming "Wipeout" with his fingers as he went on: "Even though she's married to a successful lawyer and could just as easily spend her days getting her toes painted by the pool, she goes to work for you."

I knew where this was going. I guessed that Callie Burke's lawyer husband has some affiliation to Lester Ratcovic. And that he does: They attended Dennison College together right through law school and then partnered in a small firm for ten years.

I took my beer with me to the window and added it all up. The question had changed: It's not who knew about Jenni Sanchez.

It's who *didn't*.

McCale ticked off the names: Me, Callie, Ally, Ratcovic, my father and therefore Jacob Moore all apparently *did* know. He said it like that—"Your father and therefore Jacob Moore."

To my raised eyebrows, he said, "No offense. But the mayor didn't take a shit without Jacob approving the time and place."

I couldn't help but laugh. It was becoming increasingly obvious that my grandfather and then Jacob Moore were the only things that came between my father and his chosen life as a beer-swilling career paperboy who lived over his brother-in-law's garage.

I drained my beer and realized out loud that we were right back where we started: *Just who in the hell is the Guy without Tie?*

McCale stood, too, and shrugged. Then he smiled when he echoed what I'd said just minutes earlier: "No fucking clue."

I need sleep. And I need that tie-less fucker. I need him and everybody and everything else.

I need The Truth. Every last bitter drop of it.

(CLICK.)

ENTRY 17: WEDNESDAY, OCTOBER 13, 9:26 A.M.

(CLICK.)

I'm in my car and it's, what? Nine-something on Wednesday morning. Shit, you know what? This is my last tape.

I just left Elisa Vasquez and the diner where she waits tables and I have that feeling there was something just beneath the words I can't hear yet, something on a different frequency.

Something that matters.

She filled my cup at the breakfast bar with no intention of looking up at me. Elisa is the anti-Jenni. She knows why a thirty-something white guy would ogle her and wants no part of it. It wasn't until I said her name that she realized who I was. She didn't waste any words; just took off her apron and grabbed her jacket on the way out the door.

You can see the six tallest high-rises in Downtown Cleveland from the South Side, rising straight and sure into the cloud-dotted sky. You can also see the sun, but that doesn't mean you can get there from here.

The two of us walked down the decayed sidewalk along the three-block stretch of brightly colored markets, restaurants, and one pool bar. All of it ends abruptly at a barbwired used-car lot with a faded sign that promises, WE SELL TO ANYBODY!

Just beneath it, two teenagers in hooded sweatshirts tied into perfect O's around their pockmarked faces bounced up and down against the saggy fence, taking advantage of the free advertising. That was the end of the line, and they were the sentinels. After that came the twenty-four-hour liquor store surrounded by standing corpses and then a crumbling, graffiti-scarred bridge. People had lost their lives under that bridge.

Elisa wrapped her arms around herself as we walked, each gripping a steaming Styrofoam cup of coffee. She was shaky so I offered my jacket. She smiled a little at my chivalry and said she was more nervous than cold.

Such honesty. I admitted I wouldn't place her and Jenni as friends. She said it was a family thing, really. Elisa had tried to get Jenni to take some classes with her at the community college, but Jenni had her own ideas about how to get from here to downtown.

I said I could see that.

That's when she stopped, got in front of me, and stared right into my eyes. I took the challenge, let her sear right through me. She coaxed a lock of hair behind her ears, tilted her head as she studied me. And then she asked pointblank if Jenni got to me.

I thought for a moment before I decided to admit it. Yeah, I told her. Jenni got to me.

She asked if I fucked her and I said only in my head and just that one time.

Elisa chewed at her lip and nodded slowly. I'd passed the test. I'd answered a hard question with a hard answer.

She's a smart girl, Elisa, so she asked if I'm official. I admitted I'm not. Not anymore. She asked if I'm in trouble and I said up to my eyes. And she kept staring at me, mining for the slightest clue that I was playing her somehow.

I promised I wouldn't let anybody hurt her. I swore to it. And after a few beats, she said, "I believe you."

We walked again and she looked around her life, to the boys leaning against the fence. They stared back at us brazenly now.

She caught my arm, stopped me, and said we shouldn't go any farther. I said, "The world gets pretty small around here."

She laughed coldly and said, "Real fucking small."

And with that, I asked how Jenni had hooked up with Ratcovic. It was a specific question, but Elisa had a bigger story to tell. Before she did, though, she said, "I'm going to tell you everything. Then I'm going to a funeral and you're going to find out the truth of what happened to Jenni."

I said I'd like to be at Jenni's funeral; Elisa said that was a very bad idea. She was right: I was part of the mess Jenni got mixed up in. Part of what killed her.

"I'll go to the funeral and you'll find the truth," she said again. I nodded this time.

But Elisa still wasn't ready to tell her story. She pinched at her lip until it made her eyes water. She said, "I'm trusting you, man."

There was nothing left for me to say. I just waited until Elisa started talking. She said Guy without Tie didn't want Jenni to call the reporter chick. He was anxious and shifty and that scared the shit out of Jenni. He wanted her to stick with the story she told the D.A., no matter what.

But the main thing, the thing Elisa didn't tell the police, was this: There was something very wrong with Jenni that night. She was slurring her words and losing her train of thought. Half of what she said didn't make much sense and the other half made none at all. Every so often, she'd laugh until she cried.

I said it sounded a lot like the kind of drunk you're lucky to forget, that's all. Elisa said, yeah, that's the catch: "Jenni doesn't get drunk, man. I've seen her drink so many guys under the table it doesn't even impress me anymore. It's like she's got some special chemistry or something. She's always in control, especially when a man's involved."

I knew exactly what she meant. Getting pie-eyed drunk and putting herself at the mercy of a man who scared her doesn't add up for the Jenni Sanchez who brushed her hand across my trousers before we even started talking.

And then Elisa Vasquez asked *me* a question: She asked if anybody had seen Jenni drinking really hard. You know, like pounding back tequila shot after tequila shot.

They hadn't. That's the kind of thing McCale would've been looking for, since he still wasn't convinced that Jenni hadn't bounced her own head off every tree in the backyard that night.

I asked why Elisa hadn't told the cops this and she gave exactly the answer I expected: Because hearing that Jenni was fucked up would've given them all they needed to conclude she'd fallen into the creek all by herself. And Elisa has a gut that isn't true. Not exactly.

When I asked why she'd told me, she wiped her eyes with the sleeve of her flannel shirt. After a bit, she said, "Because Jenni said you wanted her to tell the truth and she wished she'd listened to you. And because that's all I want for her now: the truth. Even Jenni deserves that much."

I said we all deserve that much, don't we? I extended my hand to Elisa as a promise, but she pushed right through it and hugged me, pressing the side of her face into my chest. She hung on because she believed in me.

Finally, she pulled back and looked me in the eye once more. Satisfied with what she saw, she ran back to the little diner at the center of her very small world.

For what seemed like an hour but was probably less than a minute, I could just barely breathe, let alone move. An amazing thing happened there on that cracked sidewalk: I saw something reflected in Elisa Vasquez's eyes that paralyzed me.

I saw *me*. Not the one-term mayor's namesake son, not the man at the podium basking in adulation as his name is chanted by a few dozen beer-buzzed construction workers. Not the man who never really brought the Browns back to Cleveland or the Division III quarterback who ended his forgettable career with a stumbling, staggering display of luck. Not even the guy who has spent the last few days with his head three feet up his own ass, babbling incessantly to a microcassette recorder.

Elisa saw none of that when she looked at me because I'm *not* the sum of all that; I'm *not* a Xerox of a shitty self-portrait. What she saw was somebody to trust, somebody who sincerely believes the truth *always* matters.

My father didn't live a lie; he lived *many* lies. He married one woman and loved another. He chased other people's dreams and did work that never called him. He played a role in a movie that wasn't even his own.

When he was alive, Joseph Way, Senior said, "The plan rolls on." But when he was dead, he amended that to, *"Find your truth."* The truth of Jenni Sanchez, the truth of my own father, they matter in their own right but they're also pieces of me.

Find your truth. It's the peculiar wisdom of my dead father, a single piece of sage advice, a method to chart my course so I never, *ever* get as lost as he did.

The time for talking is over. Like McCale, I'll allow the truer, more vivid picture of me to emerge from what I *do*. And I'll see it reflected in the eyes of the people who love me; in the eyes of the people I love.

So, anyway, thanks for listening. And I finally know who all these tapes were for. I know who you are now.

You're me.

(CLICK.)

PART TWO:

Field Work

Mara unzipped her overnight bag with trembling hands and jammed in her toothbrush.

"What're you gonna do, piss yourself again?" she asked. She had to bite her lip and fake a laugh to keep back the tears. She hiked the bag over her shoulder and set her jaw.

This is what I do, Mara thought. When the bullets start flying, I leave. The notion that she was running to Daddy's house to help Joe, to stop confusing him, was starting to feel like a leaflet dropped from the sky . . .

To herself.

She knew the right thing was to go to him, make him realize they weren't in love, never had been. But she knew she would fuck him instead, and that might not be the most persuasive argument.

So, all that considered, she was running away again, to Daddy's sprawling Tudor in a pristine suburb well south of town, a place audaciously called Glad Acres.

There, in Hudson, in a nationally ranked public school, Mara had in the period of a year given up ballet and become a revolutionary, switched from a Whitney Houston bob to dreads and sandals. She pierced her nose. She read Maya Angelou, or at least carried her books. She organized a protest against the Gulf War.

She *became.* People noticed. It was cool.

Somewhere along the line, form evolved into function and the posing took on meaning. She wasn't that self-infatuated sixteen-year-old anymore.

Or was she?

She dropped backwards onto the bed, covered her face in her hands. "Goddammit, stop being so hard on yourself," she cried.

"Oh, I don't know," came the woman's voice from the other room, chilling Mara's blood so fast it gave her brain freeze.

And then Beth Pruitt pivoted into Mara's line of sight, leaned against the bedroom doorway. "I think maybe you're not being hard *enough* on yourself."

With that, the preppy blonde with her shirttails hanging adorably beneath her angora sweater crooked a finger for Mara to *come along,* then disappeared out of sight.

Mara sat frozen on the bed, hands still at her chest, fingers locked, knees raised.

"I have other business," Beth said curtly from the front room. So Mara stood, made a quick stop at her mirror to affect a dead-eye, bad-ass sistah stare, and strode out to the front room.

Beth was sitting in Mara's favorite chair, curled up adorably, shoes off and stocking feet tucked beneath her. Her calm smile was unnerving, but Mara put her hands on her hips anyway. "Are we gonna have a problem here? Because—"

"Do you know who I am?" Beth cut in, ignoring the entire presentation and all the hard work that went into it.

"Yes," Mara whispered. More of a shuddered breath, actually. Beth nodded and said, "Sit."

"Um, *excuse me?*" Mara said, affecting just enough street. "You wanna just pat your leg or whistle while you're at it?"

"Mara," Beth said, dipping her chin a little. "Please come over here and sit down, okay?"

Well, that's better, Mara's jaunty-girlfriend walk said. Moreover, she sat where she wanted—keeping a coffee table between the two of them in the process—not where the smug bitch had pointed. "So how'd you get in here?" she demanded, but Beth only smiled and shook her head lightly—does it matter?

Mara struggled to hold Beth's inspection. She realized that in person, sans the photo-op, Crest Kid smile, Beth had a small scar around the right edge of her lip. Her nose was a skitch crooked, a little more pug than she'd expected.

But Mara couldn't resist glancing at the door. Gauging the distance. Calculating the time.

"Yes," Beth said.

"Yes what?" Mara said, pretending as much to herself that she didn't know.

"Yes, I'd get to you before you could make it to the door."

"Oh, I see," Mara said, crossing her arms. "So you're here to kick my ass, huh? Because you're the big, bad kung-fu girl, right?"

Beth laughed like a girlfriend to Mara, stood, and took in the room around her, purring her approval. "I'm not committed to a plan just yet, so let's just work that out together as we go along," she said congenially.

Beth smugly kept her back to Mara as she studied R.J.'s piece on the wall, tilted her head at the chaos of it. In the silence, Mara determined she should stand, maybe even approach Beth. That would show her. That's what I should do.

"Sit down, Mara," Beth said before she even turned. Mara dropped quickly. Beth's eyes seared as she cleared the space between them with alarming ease to sit on the edge of the coffee table in front of Mara.

I'm not breathing, Mara realized. Three out of four doctors agree that can lead to death. And I don't want to die.

"Try to relax," Beth said, and seemed to mean it. "Okay?"

"Okay."

"So you and Joe . . ." Beth said.

"He told you?"

"No. But now you have."

"*Shit.*"

"I just came here because I couldn't help wondering."

"Wondering what?"

"Just what the hell you think you're doing." Beth's smile wasn't making it all the way to her eyes anymore.

I'm going to lose consciousness, Mara thought. I'm going to pass out and then she'll kick me to death for sure.

"You know how I imagine you two?" Beth asked, her bottom lip trembling just a little. "I imagine that you're just *too much* together, right? Horny little Nick and Nora with the banter and fuck, fuck and banter."

Mara's jaw bounced off the shrinking space between them. "Ooh," Beth cooed, noticing. "Not what you expected? No, I'm not. But nobody ever is, are they, Mara?"

She didn't wait for an answer, turned her attention to the view outside the window and walked to it again. "Cute neighborhood. Very Birkenstock."

"I want you to go," Mara said firmly. When Beth looked back, she added a firm nod to say, *I mean it.*

"And I want you to cease to exist," Beth volleyed back so smoothly that Mara barely noticed she was there, in front of her again. "Like you were never born. Can you do that? Hmm? Because if you can do that, I'll leave."

Mara tried to stand, but Beth caught her wrists, pinned them to the arms of the chair. The blonde's eyes ignited and her jaw flexed as she leaned in.

"You're a fucking psycho," Mara snarled.

"A little," Beth said, her teeth never parting. "But that's just the tiniest corner of me."

"I'll fight back."

"Not for long, sweetie."

"What do you want?" Mara screamed, tears filling her eyes. *"What do you fucking want from me?"*

Beth's shoulders dropped. She shook her head quickly and released Mara's wrists. "I didn't mean to scare you like this," she said. "I'm sorry."

Mara finally found a full breath. She never knew how good it could feel.

Beth examined her manicure and said, "I just want you to leave for a little while, okay?" She flickered her eyes back up to Mara and shrugged. "That's what I need you to do. If Joe and I don't work because we don't work, I can live with that. But if it falls apart because of you, well . . . I can live with that, too. But I'm not so sure about you."

"You're threatening me again," Mara deadpanned.

"Yeah, but now I really mean it."

Mara tried to stand in anger but Beth caught her by the throat, thumb and forefinger knifing under each side of her jaw, cutting off oxygen and transmitting piercing pain signals the short distance to her victim's brain.

Beth mounted Mara, planted a knee firmly into her abdomen, pinning her into the chair. Mara's hands flailed and Beth whispered in her ear, "I don't like the hands, Mara. The hands should stay down."

Mara complied, tucking her hands under her own thighs against the reflex. Her attention skipped wildly from her panicked hunger for oxygen to the searing pain in her throat to the duller but just as profound discomfort of Beth's knee pressing through her stomach to her spine . . . to Beth's sea-blue eyes, just inches away. The last thing she'd ever see.

"If you come back before one week from this very moment,

I will beat you so badly you'll beg me to let you lose consciousness," Beth said. "But I won't."

Mara's eyes locked closed, tears leaking out. The only way she knew Beth had released her was the cool air flooding her lungs at last and the sound of her own starving gasp.

She could make out Beth's shape, opening the door.

"Don't come back," Mara choked.

Beth got in last word as the door swung closed behind her: "Don't make me."

Mara raised her knees and rocked herself, tried to settle her breathing. Just when she'd almost found a rhythm, the phone rang, nearly knocking her out of the chair. She reached toward the new digital phone/answering machine on the end table, then pulled her hand back.

"It's Mara," her own voice said, crystal clear as the salesman had promised. "Keep it real."

Oh, gag me, Mara thought for the first time.

And after the beep, Joe's voice: "I have a couple stops to make, but I'm coming over in an hour or so. If you're not there, I'll wait. It's hard to explain but I've burned through about eight microcassette tapes figuring some stuff out and *God* that sounds overevolved and metrosexual when I say it out loud. Anyway, I'm finished talking to myself and now I need to talk to you, okay?"

By the time the second beep came, Mara had already hiked the overnight bag over her shoulder and found her keys.

Storm clouds gathered on the horizon, and a nearly impercepti-ble mist grazed the golf course just beyond a tree line behind Jacob Moore's house. Jacob licked a finger to gauge the wind, wound up, and chucked the golf ball as far as he could.

"Nice," Rita called, and they walked together toward their lies, just a few yards apart.

She picked up her ball. "That's four, right?" she asked. "I'm lying four?"

"I can get up in three, down in four," Jacob yelled from his lie. "And you're buying dinner."

Rita put her hands on her hips and shook her head. "You know, you really must get some clubs if we're gonna hang out together."

"I'll do just that," Jacob said, hoping she hadn't noticed the catch in his voice.

Jacob loved Rita Way. Always had, in ways maybe only the old can understand. True, it was the love of a man for a woman, but it wasn't exactly romantic, at least not as a younger man knows it.

Jacob simply wanted the privilege of making Rita Way happy. So many times over the years, he'd turned to find her already looking at him. That selfless, truer brand of love forged by age and pain and loss always stole the breath from him. Their eyes spoke so clearly sometimes that they'd both look around to see who else might've heard.

Jacob laughed off the profound effect of her casual words as he threw for the green. "Ow!" he cried, clutching his elbow. "I think you might be onto something with this golf club idea."

Rita took his arm and briskly rubbed his elbow. "What kind of Republican doesn't even own golf clubs?"

She beamed up at him and he pulled her into a bear hug. She stepped into it as readily as he offered it, and they stood like that in the mist, neither one moving to kiss or to stare longingly. Or even to speak.

It wasn't that Jacob Moore made Rita Way *feel like a woman.* She'd given up that bullshit dime-store vanity years ago. With her broad shoulders, sensible haircut, and clear eyes, Rita Way wanted something more fundamental and profound than that.

She wanted to feel like she *mattered.* And Jacob Moore delivered, no extra charge.

He'd earned the right to speak freely of her children without permission over decades of unerring devotion. Back when Nathan was thirteen and too old for such things in Joseph's eyes, his favorite of three rabbits died without warning. The boy was prodded deeper into his private world of leaf collecting and scrawling stories he'd let nobody read while kneeling at his bedside for hours on end.

Joseph stepped in with a solution straight from primetime TV: They held a cute little funeral for Tamale, the whole family. He said a cute little prayer, complete with cautious levity, and put the whole cute little disruption behind them and moved on.

But it was Jacob who actually *talked* to Nathan. He coaxed the boy out, took his grief seriously, let him replay all the wondrous high points of Tamale's brief year on earth.

It never occurred to Jacob that Nathan's Michael Jackson-esque devotion to a rabbit was fueled by a steady diet of cannabis. But it wouldn't have mattered anyway.

Jacob first served as a financial mentor to Joseph, then eventually someone to turn to who most importantly *wasn't* Joseph's father-in-law. More recently, Jacob considered himself the silent partner in the vital business of keeping Cleveland out of the hands of Democrats and perverts.

But not a puppeteer. Not exactly that.

Rita Way never consciously knew that it was Jacob Moore who gave her husband back to her, or at least enough of him, but on some level she understood it. He'd lured Joseph back, inch by inch, so she could enjoy these last five moderately happy, nonlonely years with the love of her life.

So Jacob had a right.

Silent lightning flashed across a Matisse sky, followed by a low, distant rumble. It was so perfect that Rita smiled the broad, careless smile of the younger woman she'd never really been.

Jacob threw once more with a wince, finally making it to the green. "So how in God's name do we *putt?*" he asked.

Rita took his hand. "We don't," she said, dragging him away as more lightning flared in the distance.

Back at the house, Jacob and Rita kicked off their wet shoes on the cut stone back porch on their way into the den. Jacob snatched a pair of towels from a closet.

"I'll make coffee," he offered, drying his dense gray hair with one of them as he handed the other to Rita. She followed Jacob into the kitchen, then slammed face-first into his back with an "umph" when he stopped just inside the doorway.

"You've got one sweet view of the twelfth fairway and the pond there, Jacob," Joe Way pandered as he turned away from the kitchen window. He crossed his arms over his chest, tilted to smile at Rita. "Mother," he said tightly.

Rita made a show of scouting around the room for her purse, found it, and took the shortest possible route to the front door without the complication of a goodbye.

Jacob checked his watch. "I think you should choose which topic you'd like to tackle this afternoon," he growled. "I'm on a schedule."

"So you know why I'm here."

"Sometimes I wish I knew less, Joe." Jacob shrugged, tossed his towel on the counter. "Comes with age."

He started across the room, pausing to smell a vase of fresh flowers on the counter. "Coffee?"

Joe shook his head, pained and nauseated, and asked, "Are those from my mother's garden?"

Jacob nodded and asked, "Is that your choice, me and your mother?"

Joe braced himself on the edge of the counter. "Actually, I plan to suppress that one just as long as I can."

"So it's Jenni Sanchez then." Jacob pulled a mug out of the cabinet and looked over at him. "Was that yes to the coffee?"

Joe didn't answer so Jacob sipped his and waited. Finally, Joe said, "You helped my father frame an innocent husband and father."

Jacob used his right hand on his chest to guide the coffee down. "Innocent? Lester the Molester? Are you fucking serious?"

"I was the one she came to. He never laid a hand on her."

"Ah, yes. You *were* the one she came to, weren't you?"

Joe stepped closer, felt his teeth grinding. "Don't you *even* try to—"

"Blame it on you?" Jacob counterpunched, meeting Joe in the center of the kitchen. "Too late, Joey, because I *do* blame it on you. If you hadn't handed her off to Ally Wong, that fucking mob bitch wouldn't have sent her to Mara Pinkett and we wouldn't be squared off here in the middle of my kitchen, now would we?"

Joe's mouth opened to speak but he hitched once, twice, and then finally asked the more pertinent question: "Did you just say 'mob bitch'?"

"Ally Wong grew up in a Tong family, my friend," Jacob nodded smugly. "She came to the U.S. for college and law school to get out from under the motherfucker of all glass ceilings over there."

Jacob took another step closer to the younger man, crossed his arms, and feigned deep thought. "And just what do you think she banged her head into over here?"

Joe got it. He did the math and it all added up, maybe a little too cleanly: Ally Wong came to Cleveland for an opportunity but was deemed "indelicate and decidedly unelectable." That sort of thing will piss off an Asian mob chick every time.

Jacob asked, "Now what can you tell me, Joe?"

"I don't have to tell you anything, Jacob," Joe said with a quick, tight smile. "I'm not my father."

Jacob bobbed his head, considered, then said, "Then I guess we're done here, aren't we?"

Before he could turn away, Joe asked, "Was my father your puppet? Is that why he broke our confidence?"

Jacob deflated, sunk inward a little. When he finally looked back to Joe, his eyes were moist with tears.

"Joseph told me about you and Jenni Sanchez because he smelled trouble," Jacob explained carefully. "He was worried about you."

Joe's eyes darted between Jacob's. "And what did you do about it?" he asked.

Jacob exhaled long and slow, bearing the weight of his answer. Which was: "I paid your Nubian princess ten grand to forget that phone call ever happened. That's what I did."

Joe started shaking his head halfway through Jacob's sentence. "You're a fucking liar," he said, smiling razor blades as he backed away.

"It's the truth, Joe," Jacob said sadly. "She didn't put up much of a fight, either. Capitalism is apparently the one institution she's at peace with."

"Shut . . . the fuck . . . *up,*" Joe spat, still backing away, thrusting his finger at Jacob just as he had in the hallway of the Savoy Riverfront Inn that night.

"Holy shit," Jacob marveled. "You're in love with that phony bitch, aren't you?"

Joe groped for words but could only snarl as he spun away. Jacob heard the front door open and then slam, leaving him alone with the echo.

He went to the small desk just off the kitchen, found the framed picture of his son at fifteen without having to look. Picked it up and held it in both hands. As ever, he took a long, deep breath before he could face the slender redhead with the embarrassed smile.

"He's turning out to be a tough piece of business, that one," he said to his only child. "Just like you would've been."

"Storm's coming."

Joe's eyes shot open. "What?" he choked, trying to blink himself out of a sleep he didn't know had claimed him.

He'd slipped away there on the bench at the edge of Pier 62 on Lake Erie, waiting for Dan McCale. But the sound of rising winds on the lake and the first real drops of rain on his vinyl Browns cap had lulled him.

He'd dreamed in that brief moment of sleep. He again stepped to the microphone in the First Episcopal Church, opened his mouth . . .

And said nothing. He shuffled through a stack of index cards. But they were as blank as his mind.

I'll start riffing, free-forming, let my instincts lead the way, he decided. He nodded firmly, revving up. Opened his mouth and . . .

Nothing. Nada. Zip. Zero.

Worse, he was naked from the waist down. Worst yet, then, he was naked *entirely.*

No costume. No uniform. No name. Just *him.* It was terrifying, yeah, but mostly it was *exhilarating.*

It was Joseph's voice that woke him. The wind had picked up during his fugue and the temperature was plummeting. Dense, black clouds crept over the roiling lake. A ghost ship couldn't disrupt the mood.

"Storm's coming," Joe echoed dreamily, coughing to clear his throat.

"I'd say you're in the eye of it as we speak."

Joe looked up to see Joseph leaning against the far railing, smiling back at him, arching his eyebrows in approval of his own cleverness. He looked to be past the midpoint of his thirties but shy of forty, wearing a too-small sweatshirt over khakis. Trim and sideburned, this was Joseph Way circa 1970.

He was still the bad boy. And he *could* fill out those khakis. "You need sleep, Joey," he said with genuine concern. "Big day tomorrow."

"I can sleep when I'm dead," Joe said, easing his way back to consciousness. "Like you."

"Yeah, you'd think," Joseph said. "I'm having a bit of a problem, myself. Got any Valium left?"

Joseph waved off his own joke.

"You seem to be wearing it well," Joe allowed.

"Thanks," Joseph said, and spread his arms out. "This is the Joseph Way I see in my mind. Sometimes, when I was still alive,

I'd walk past a mirror and the old man looking back at me would scare the freakin' shit out of me."

"They say your self-image freezes when you're the happiest you'll ever be," Joe agreed.

Joseph walked back to the rail and looked out over the water. "This was me when I still had all three of you," he said. "Man, this was the *real* me. Before Kate died and I lost your brother."

"Do you have any regrets?" Joe asked.

"Are you even listening?"

"Then how come you never talked to me about them?"

"I think that's the biggest regret right there." Joseph's mouth curled at the corners and he wiped his eyes, covered it all with a laugh. "Well, one of the biggest."

Joe measured his next question for a long while: "If you could do it all over, what would you change?"

Joseph stared out onto the lake, shook his head slowly, over and over. "That's a tough one," he said. "Because while you're traveling down the wrong road, you pick up things that you wouldn't give back. Moments . . . people . . . friends . . . you and Nathan and Kate. And your mother, too, as hard as that may be for you to believe."

"It's not so hard."

Joseph nodded his thanks.

"But what would you do?" Joe pressed. "Who would you be if you were really you? If you'd found *your* truth?"

Joseph smiled a little at his son, blinked back tears. He shook his head again, battled it some more. In the end, he settled on, "Just a guy, I think. I would've been just a guy who worked a little, fished a little, kept the beer cold and the over-head low."

Joe nodded. "That's what Uncle Roy said."

They let the silence fall comfortably, never looking away from each other. Joe said, "I'm still not sure."

"About?"

"Anything, really."

"That's because you're not finished."

Joe nodded. Joseph bent down closer to his son so he could look him in the eye. "No matter what, right?" he said, letting the tear stream down his cheek.

Joe nodded, wiped a tear of his own.

"No matter how easy they make it for you to stop," Joseph insisted.

"Yeah." Joe nodded. "I promise."

Joseph stood, stepped back a little without taking his eyes off his son. He almost whispered, "You wandered outside the hotel that night, but then you came back to my room. That's where you went."

Joe looked up and Joseph went on, "You cried. I held you and told you how very sorry I was."

"I let you?"

"Yes. Because that's part of who you are."

"So I've already forgiven you?"

Joseph bobbed his head. "Pretty much," he said.

"But you said—"

"I said what I had to." He held out his hands and smiled sheepishly as he backed away toward the far railing again. Eyes still on Joe, he kicked off his loafers and nimbly mounted the railing. "You just keep going, Joe," he said. "No matter what."

He stood on the railing and spread his hands out like an Olympic diver. "Your mother used to *love* this," he said, smiling wickedly over his shoulder.

Joe scrambled off the bench just as his father leaped. He looked over to see Joseph flail his arms wildly in the air, then pull his knees into a cannonball at the last possible instant.

Joe scanned the whitecaps for Joseph. He wasn't at all surprised that he'd disappeared.

"Joe?"

He spun—McCale was there at five sharp, as promised. "Whatcha looking for? Did you drop something?"

"No," Joe said, leaving it at that. The two men leaned against the railing, side by side, equal in their exhaustion.

"I don't think Ratcovic knew," McCale finally said.

"What about—"

"Callie Burke came to me, believe it or not. Seems she and her husband have been separated for about eighteen months. She'd rather put a gardening spade between his eyes than do him or his perverted old friend a favor. *Her* words."

Joe nodded. "That's why she needed the job."

"Exactly. She even offered to do a lie detector."

"You took her up on it?"

"Two hours ago. She didn't tell a soul, Joe."

Joe took his turn: "Ally's from a Hong Kong mob family," he said casually. "At least that's what Jacob says."

"No shit."

"She was extremely pissed about being passed over."

Joe turned away from McCale's astonishment to look out at the imminent storm. "I don't know, Joe," McCale sighed. "Maybe I just wanna believe she fell. Maybe I wanna believe nobody would do something like that just to be mayor of Cleveland."

He laughed darkly and added, "Even a fucking Hong Kong mob daughter."

Joe turned and faced McCale, seeing a little something he'd never noticed before. "But you're a cop, McCale. You know people are capable of doing almost anything for practically no good reason at all."

"Yeah," McCale said. "I do know that, don't I?"

Joe let a respectful amount of time pass before he got a grip on the detective's arm and said, "I need to know, Dan."

The intensity of it startled McCale but Joe bore on: "I need to know the whole truth by tomorrow night. No assumptions, no settling, no matter how easy they make it. Do you understand what I'm telling you?"

McCale started to speak but Joe cut him off: "I know the consequences, Dan. I do. You can't open this door halfway. When you bring Ally in for questioning she's gonna throw me under the bus. Me and Jacob and my dead father and anybody else she can get her nails into."

McCale unconsciously shook his head in awe as he took in the man next to him. "Okay," was all he said.

Joe slapped McCale's shoulder and started back down the pier and into the mist. McCale watched him. In the end, the one word he could think to say was, "Damn."

Just south of Akron, roughly fifty miles from Downtown Cleveland, rests a 1980s-built suburb of nouveau Tudors on rolling, barren, two-acre lots known quite appropriately as Glad Acres.

Meaning, if you live here, chances are you don't have a hell of a lot to worry about.

A long drive down N.E. 149th Street between farms, sub-divisions-in-waiting, and an arboretum, then a left turn past the cobblestone marker leading to the unlikely upbringing of liberal journalist Mara Pinkett.

With no trees over eight feet to block the view, she could already see the well-lit and immaculately landscaped back porch of her parents' home, the one she'd lived in from age eleven until Wittenberg—a gray number with midnight-green shutters, perched on a low-rising hill.

Mara's purportedly white 1984 Nissan Sentra seemed underdressed cruising between driveways of freshly washed Lexi and seventy-thousand-dollar SUVs rigged for the treacherous terrain between here and the Pottery Barn.

Eight years ago, just after her college graduation, Mara's father had the horrifying audacity to arrange an interview for her at the Toyota regional office, where he'd ascended well past function to vice presidency.

As part of her requisite damning rejection, she'd called him the VP of Oreo Relations, because the only blacks Corporate America could stomach were fluffy and white on the inside.

Their relationship had miraculously recovered from the blow and they'd continued to talk on the phone when he could catch her, here or abroad. Since the onset of caller ID, however, the successful connections had halved, from weekly to twice a month, if not less.

Mara never apologized. He never asked her to. And they pretended her words hadn't hacked their connection to a sliver.

Still, the voice on the other end of the line was always Evers Pinkett, not Norene the mulatta 1966 Miss Teen Ohio and catalog model, even though mother and daughter had never exchanged harsh words.

It struck Mara after she'd smoked hash in a Bosnian hotel room that they hadn't exchanged many words of any flavor since she'd graduated college. She'd cried that day, five years ago, and then never gave it another moment's thought.

Sometimes you run with your legs. Sometimes only with your heart.

Norene Pinkett was a willowy, striking woman with few passions or commitments, eternally peaceful and understanding, always ready with a soothing smile and a pat on the hand before drifting away to pose elegantly on a fainting chair with a "smart" romance novel *(never* a bodice-ripper).

But not once after Mara had fled Glad Acres for good did her mother ever call her. Of course, she'd hollered from the background when Evers called, always hurrying to important business like a midweight coat at the Eddie Bauer in Town Center Square. Possibly a latté and almost certainly a stop at Barnes and Noble. Tell Mara I'll call later in the week.

Now, edging slowly toward her childhood home, Mara acknowledged for the first time that it had been almost a year since she'd heard her mother's voice.

For all its tidy prefab luxury, there was something comforting and familiar to Mara about this house and, in truth, all of Glad Acres. It represented "the good life," where self-actualization was just a mortgage application away. Where trouble with a capital T was grub worms, a run on Velveeta at the Hy-Vee the night before Super Sunday, or sun-freckled Leslie Fryar cranking Nine Inch Nails' "I Wanna Fuck You Like an Animal" a little too high on her Mustang convertible's stereo on her way in from field-hockey practice.

For instance, at no point in her Glad Acres years had anyone knelt on her spine from the front side. Not once, mind you. Not to mention the fact that you could pick up the entire place and drop it twenty miles outside any major U.S. city and it would fit in just fine.

Assured that Evers was thinking the big organizational thoughts in the corner office while Norene was out buying something somewhere, Mara didn't even bother to ring the bell. She just slid her key in the door and imagined the simple, suburban pleasures of marbled rye, turkey salami from the Hy-Vee deli, and caffeine-free Diet Coke.

But before she could turn the key, the door opened inward, pulling her key chain from between her fingers. And there was Evers Pinkett at sixty, a three-dimensional J. J. Jamison, Spider-Man's editor: square jawed and honey skinned, with close-cut graying hair.

He'd wrapped himself in a flannel robe at six-thirty in the evening, which was odd enough. But he was also unshaven and his eyes were red and swollen. He blinked quickly, as if the vision in front of him had appeared several times before only to waft away like steam when he tried to catch it.

His breath skipped in staccato exhales and Mara suddenly wished she'd showered, put on makeup, done *something* to show that she gave a shit what her father thought after all this time apart with only fifty miles between them.

"Mara," his voice croaked. Definitely his first word of the day.

"Daddy?" she said. "Are you sick?"

"Yes," he said. He nodded too quickly. "Nothing serious. Just a cold."

She couldn't expect an embrace; too much had come between them for that. But she yearned to smell his sleepy warmth, to be engulfed by his arms and squeezed so tight she could feel the rumble of his laugh through his chest.

"Some stuff happened," she explained, suddenly afraid that her Glad Acres membership had expired. "I just need to—"

Evers grabbed her hand, still extended where she'd held her key, and pulled her staggering over the doorway and into his flannel-covered chest. She felt his thick arms wrap around her, his face burrow into her neck, breathing her in like a drowning man breaking the surface at the last possible instant.

And instead of the rumble of his laugh, Mara felt the spasm of sobs. "I've missed you, Mara Christine," he cried.

With those words, Evers Pinkett razed Mara's fourteen years of meticulously designed emotional architecture . . .

And held his little girl again.

By Thursday morning, the temperature had bottomed out below freezing. The sun glistened magnificently off frozen trees, cracking them to kindling one branch at a time.

In Rita Way's kitchen, however, it was raining food. Joe turned in the doorway to see Nathan slogging wearily through remnants of syrup-drenched pancakes. When he looked up, his eyes pleaded for help. In the name of all that's holy, *make it stop!*

Rita blurred around the stove, pivoting smoothly away from frying bacon and eggs to pour a cup of coffee for Joe as he sat down across from his brother.

"Nice to see you all smooth and cleaned up," she said, patting his freshly shaved cheek as she set the coffee in front of him. But then she looked closer: "Did you sleep?"

"I was out," Joe said, his eyes darting away. She let it go and went back to her work.

"Mara?" Nathan asked.

"I waited most of the night." Joe shrugged, but couldn't play it off. "I think maybe she's gone."

Nathan read the pain coming off his brother. "I always assumed it was just a horny little game with the two of you."

"So did I," Joe said. He found a section of the paper, picked it up and put it down, a transitional gesture.

"So you're done with my tape recorder?" Nathan asked, one brow arched.

Joe shrugged, nodded. Shrugged.

"It helped?" Nathan asked.

"It may need new batteries," Joe said instead.

Nathan raised his eyebrows—*interesting*. Joe asked, "So did I miss breakfast or are we in the midst?"

Nathan whispered anxiously as he leaned in, "This is inter-mission, man. You have no idea what I've forced down."

To accent his point, four slices of toast popped from the toaster. Rita collected them with one hand, slathered butter on them, and turned the bacon in the skillet in front of her with the other.

"She went cold turkey on the Valium," Nathan explained.

"It shows," Joe said, finally taking in the fallout: the table cluttered with dishes, the counters stacked high with pots and pans, food wrappers, plastic bags, and egg cartons, all resting on a dense blanket of flour and grease.

"Since you asked, I've had a fruit plate, bagels with hand-sliced salmon, pancakes, and sausage," Nathan ticked off with a tight smile. "I really should go off and vomit but God help me I'm afraid to stop her."

"Like waking up a sleepwalker," Joe said.

Nathan nodded rapidly. "And she has kitchen utensils."

"Good call."

At that instant, Rita hopped backwards at a loud pop of bacon grease. She doubled over in pain, covered her mouth in a silent cry.

Nathan and Joe scrambled from the table and rushed to her. "Mom, are you okay?" Joe asked, putting a hand on her back.

She took a deep breath, then straightened and looked at them, eyes suddenly as round and perfect as the plates stacking up around her. With no ramp-up whatsoever, she started laughing through her nose.

Joe backed off gingerly with an "eek" expression.

"You know, Mom," Nathan said, hands reaching for her but not daring to actually make contact, "maybe you should have tapered off a little."

She put up a hand while she gathered herself. "Do you boys remember the only time you saw me cry?" she asked, gasping for breath.

Nathan and Joe exchanged a glance: They did.

"I was right here," she said, "frying bacon, trying to keep it all together. And this spat of bacon grease jumped up and hit me right here." She put a finger to her top lip. "Right on top of my mouth. And I yelled out—"

"Fuck me standing!" Nathan imitated her as the memory surfaced.

"Oh, man," Joe chuckled. "I was, what? Eight?"

"Not even," Nathan said. "It wasn't much more than a year after Kate died."

"You boys gripped the table like an electric fence and your eyes went big as saucers," Rita gasped. "You'd never heard me say such a thing."

"And then Joe started laughing," Nathan said, picking up the story again. "And he said, 'Fuck *me* standing.'"

Rita nodded quickly. "And you said, 'No, fuck *me* standing!'"

"You know what? Fuck us *all* standing!" Nathan concluded, waving his arms out expansively.

Their laughter came to a gradual landing, leaving Rita loose and dreamy, as if she'd put in a good hour of yoga (or had a truly clear notion of what yoga was, exactly, except that Sting and Madonna invented it in their spare time in the late 1980s).

"It finally came clear to me that morning," she said, still smiling, "that things were never, ever going to be the way they were before."

She stared at the brief wall along the entry to the dining room, watching her own private movie projected there. "Somehow, your father and I had to find a way to make that okay."

She paused, then turned to them, tapped her temple. "Politics," she said, still amused. "Very important work, you know."

It was so quiet that Joe could hear Nathan's arteries clogging. Finally, though, he found his voice: "What does that mean, you were trying to keep it together?"

She turned to him, leaned against the counter. Joe's voice fell to a whisper: "We're not just talking about Kate anymore, are we?"

"Maybe we're not," she dared him.

And so he dove in, headfirst: "You knew about Carla Brugano, didn't you?"

"And now, it seems, so do you," she said, slumping in relief. The hint of a smile dared to curl at the corners of her mouth.

"Dad left you," Joe challenged her calm.

Rita looked between her boys, calculating their capacity for this kind of honesty. And at last she said, "But I left him first."

Electricity surged between them, cutting through the haze of cooking smoke that had filled the kitchen in spite of the roaring exhaust vent. Joe and Nathan waited, barely breathing. And she went on: "He wanted so much to put us back together, but I was shattered into a million tiny pieces. He needed me, and I wasn't there anymore."

"It happened just a few days later, after the bacon incident," Nathan mumbled to himself.

"What, dear?" she wondered. "What happened?"

Nathan looked his mother in the eye: "He hit you. And then he hit me."

Rita slumped sadly, holding herself. "Nathan, honey," she almost whispered. "Your father never hit me. He never struck anybody in this family."

"He did," Nathan argued. "And when I tried to stop him—"

"The pills," she realized, and it took the breath from her. "You're talking about the pills."

She rubbed her face with a low groan and said, "God, Nathan, if I knew you thought . . ."

She finally looked him in the eye so he could know what she said was true: "Your father wasn't trying to hurt me. He was trying to *save* me."

"Mom, please," Nathan said, spitting off a nervous laugh. "Not to be indelicate, but that's just horseshit."

Rita ignored him and turned back to her private movie screen, brow furrowed. "They'd given me pills," she narrated. "I don't remember what, just something to numb the pain. But it never quite got the job done. I guess I figured if a couple didn't work, maybe twenty would do the trick.

"Your father grabbed the bottle out of my hand. I was fighting him for it, so he held it up in the air to keep me from reaching it. That's when you came into the room."

Joe glanced over at his brother—Nathan was shaking his head in quick, erratic bursts. How do you erase twenty-five years of false memories? How do you just *unknow* it all?

Rita took a step toward her oldest son: "You surprised him, and when he spun around, he knocked you to the ground on accident."

"She's right," Joe breathed. "Jesus, that's how it happened. I never thought of it before, but I was *there.*"

Rita nodded but never looked away from Nathan. "If Joseph hadn't been there, if he hadn't kept caring no matter how hard I pushed him away, I would've taken every last pill in that bottle."

Nathan shuddered as the fragments of his memory reconfigured and snapped back into place. "Oh, Jesus," he choked out in a sob.

"I sent him away that night, emotionally speaking," Rita went on, nodding steadily. "Part of me knew there was someone else, something he was resisting. So I told him to find love where he could, because there wasn't any left here."

"And he *did?*" Joe marveled too loud. The world came to life around them again, the spell broken. The exhaust fan sputtered. A dog barked in the distance.

Rita struggled for words. Finally: "You just keep waking up, Joe. And then you find the oddest ways to get from day to day, ways you never imagined."

She paused again, nodding into her steepled fingers, settling with it herself, too. "We were friends, and we were partners, your father and I. But we were never in love. Not really. Not ever. Sometimes in this life, you just make do."

Nathan was still reeling, but Joe went to his mother, hugged her. After a bit, he held her back by the arms, looked her in the eye, and said, "I want to talk to Carla Brugano."

"I *like* it," she enthused too abruptly, knocking Joe on his heels and startling Nathan out of his trance. "An *exquisite* culmination to this whole 'getting to know your father as a man so you can avoid the mistakes he made' thing."

Nathan blinked quickly: "Wow."

"Nice summary," Joe added.

"A mother knows." Rita shrugged as she went to the small, antique desk wedged into an alcove and found a tattered, three-ring address book in the second drawer down. She thumbed through it for a second, found what she was looking for, and jotted the information down on a sheet of her thick-stock personal stationery, stacked in a wooden box on the desk.

"I wanted Carla to know it was okay," she explained as she extended the woman's address to Joe. "We exchanged cards for a while. And then, well . . . then we didn't."

At that, a horn honked on the driveway just outside the side door. Rita grabbed her purse and hurried that way. Without another word, she waved at the boys over her shoulder and walked out, the heavy door slamming hard behind her.

Joe and Nathan drifted zombielike to the window in time to see her hop into Jacob Moore's cherry-red Mustang and laugh at something he said.

They pulled out. Nathan finally managed, "Um . . . *okay.*"

A beat later, the space just moments ago filled by the Mustang was occupied by Beth's military-green Range Rover.

"Is it just me, or is everything accelerating around here?" Nathan asked nobody in particular. Joe pushed out the side door and stood there at the bottom step. Beth circled her Rover and finally looked up from the enormous tray of flowers in her hands and slowed to a stop.

Wearing threadbare jeans, an insulated flannel shirt, and a ponytail pulled from the back of an Indians cap, she was good and good for you.

"Hello," she said flatly. "I'm here to plant some things in the sun room, for the wake."

"Right," Joe said. Then quickly: "Thank you."

"They're for Rita, not you, sport. Can I get by?"

"I'm sorry."

"You're sorry you're not letting me by or you're sorry for deciding we're not in love?"

"I'm just sorry all over the fucking place," Joe managed. Beth set the tray on the hood of the Range Rover and then turned back to Joe, arms crossed tightly.

"If this is the end, I insist you do better than that," she said evenly. "I deserve better."

He stared at her for a long time. He took in enough oxygen to begin but the words stuck in his throat. *"Fuck,"* he said, putting his fist to his forehead.

"Aw, that's pretty," she lulled with a quick tilt of her head. But the crack in her voice diluted the impact of her sarcasm.

"I've been through some crazy shit, Beth," Joe tried.

Beth rolled her eyes and mocked his voice: *"I* don't know who *I* am, *I* got lost, *I* had to go on this tweaked-out journey of self-discovery so *I* could cry for *my* father."

Her eyes chilled and she continued: "I suggest you get to the 'me' part real quick 'cause I've got flowers to plant and *Curb Your Enthusiasm* waiting on TiVo, okay?"

"I love you, Beth," Joe said abruptly.

She couldn't stop the tear from escaping. "I know," she allowed. "I know you do, Joe."

"I can't do to you what he did to her," Joe said quickly.

Beth nodded, getting it. "I shouldn't want you to. I don't anymore." She pinched the bridge of her nose, and then: "Well, mostly I don't."

Joe squinted into the blinding elegance of the storm's wake. "Such a week," he whispered.

"Yeah," Beth said, crossing her arms and nodding anxiously. "Crazy-crazy. So, anyway, I sort of beat the shit out of your girl-friend last night."

"You *what?*"

"Oh, you know what? *Fuck off,* okay? I had that much com-ing, I think."

"Jesus, Beth! How bad?"

"Like, this choke thing?" She reached up and gave him a sample. He pulled away in horror and she shrugged sheepishly. "Yeah. And this thing with my knee that hurts like a bitch."

"Is that why she left? You beat her up and told her to get out of town?"

"Her bag was already packed. She was on her way out when I got there." Beth crossed her heart to back it up.

Joe clamped his hands on his head, desperately trying to keep all the pieces where they belonged. "Well, Jesus Christ, Beth, I hope you feel better."

She considered while she retrieved the flowers again. "I do, actually," she decided. "I honestly do."

She nudged him with the massive tray. "Move?"

Dazed, Joe opened the storm door for her. She managed the heavier door herself.

Finally, she looked back. "It was just an overnight bag."

"I don't think it matters," Joe said.

"I'll leave that up to you."

"Jacob says he paid her to leave."

After a long beat, Beth finally settled on, "I'm sorry." Then she let the heavy door slam hard between them: *The End.*

THURSDAY, OCTOBER 14, 11 A.M.

Mara's bedroom was just as disorienting the second time as it had been when she'd first dropped off her bag. Dewy from a thirty-minute shower and coddled in her mother's terry-cloth robe, she looked around and caught her breath all over again.

The room was a time capsule. Same Laura Ashley bedspread. Same sculptured carpet. Same garish Sony boom box. Same framed ballet posters. The ballet tickets and tattered toe shoes still hung from her bulletin board.

She'd been a dancer then, right up until the day she'd stumbled upon an article that chiseled the first chip from her innocence. In her father's *Esquire* magazine, ironically, the writer revealed to her in no uncertain terms that Desert Storm had been a war for oil masquerading as a patriotic circle jerk.

The following Monday, three baby-faced soldiers from somewhere nearby—one Hispanic and two black—were marched around the Brookfield High School gymnasium like trained dogs, the shortest one in the middle straining against a huge American flag while Lee Greenwood's "I'm Proud to Be an American" blared tinny and distorted over the P.A.

But the PTA had underestimated the length of the song, which set the boys on a grueling death march, circling the gym dizzily again and again and again, the small, unfortunate one in the middle shifting the enormous flagpole from one shoulder to the other in visible agony.

At one point, they'd whispered to each other and tried to march out a bank of doors at the south end of the gym, only to be cheerfully herded back to their paces by Principal Breland.

By the time the horror ended, the enthusiastic clapping by the upper-upper-middle-class, mostly white student body had been reduced to an arrhythmic patter. And then the gym fell eerily silent as the spent boys were led from the court for intravenous fluids and oxygen.

"We bombed helpless soldiers in cold blood for oil," Mara realized aloud, but quietly enough that only a few around her could hear. But one of them said, "Right on," so she screamed it before knew what she was doing: *"We bombed helpless soldiers for oil!"* It echoed in the silence.

Her face flushed hot with perverse excitement as a hum gathered momentum, rolling across the bleachers at the assembly.

Then, surprisingly . . . *applause.*

Just a smattering, at first, but then a little more. Not a standing ovation, mind you. But a couple of dozen people cheered

because damn, who *does* that, man? What teenager has enough
sack to wear the wrong shoes in the late 1980s, let alone scream
out in the middle of a decidedly creepy display at another
mind-numbing assembly?

By the end of the week, Mara the pretty, stuck-up ballet
dancer with the face-stretching hair bun had switched to dreadlocks, a nose ring, and a very serious disposition. A week after
that, Randy Kinder, the all-league tailback headed for USC on
a scholarship, finally asked her out.

Of course, she was honor-bound to humiliate him for being
a black man blinded to the injustice all around him, for selling
himself into slavery at the hands of college administrators who
would profit from his toil.

But damn did that boy look fine in a bandanna and biking
shorts, running forties on the practice field.

But the passion grew beneath the fashion. Randy Kinder
and the rest of the world seemed oblivious to The Truth, but
Mara came to worship it as her God.

She devoured political history at Wittenberg like a refugee at
a buffet, shocked to insomnia by the systematic processing and
distortion of reality by the mass media, the manipulative fic-
tionalization of the modern world's palsied, lurching journey
down a trail of blood and tears into a comforting bedtime fable.

Now Mara sat at her vanity, looking into her reflection
under a neatly affixed black-on-white headline: KEEP IT REAL.

She'd faced it every day for the last three months of her high-
school career and the summer after. A challenge to herself.

Now it mocked her. She was home because she was afraid of

knowing the truth, just like them. She was afraid of finding out once and for all what she and Joe Way were all about.

They'd come to an understanding of sorts that had worked perfectly well for all this time, so why fix something that isn't broken? They bantered and fucked, as Evil Sadistic Barbie Bitch from Hell had put it. She figured it would always be there, in its own department, filling a specific purpose in her life.

Now, the death of Joseph Way, Senior had somehow lured "it" out into the light for more diligent inspection. "It" had to grow or die and there was no in between. Not now. Not anymore.

And as navel-gazing goes, wasn't it complicated by her recent awareness that the Mara Pinkett Project had come full circle? Wasn't her righteous passion being devoured, bite by bite, by the very fashion it sprung from? The nose ring he'd mocked, her kingdom, her writing, the paper itself? Hadn't she been going through the motions ever since they peeled off her piss-drenched pants after she saw a mob of African villagers surround and then hack to death three young soldiers? They wrapped her up and shipped her home, shaking and keening, "I wanna go home . . . I wanna go home . . . I wanna go home. . . ."

A tear slid down her face and she palmed it quickly. She opened the center drawer of her vanity, shuffled through the old makeup and college acceptance letters and pictures of friends she couldn't remember to find what she wanted.

Scissors.

She lifted one tightly wound dreadlock, positioned the shears just an inch from her head, and squeezed. With a shaky exhale, she dropped the six-inch dread to the floor, and lifted another. She paused to remove her nose ring and wipe another tear from her cheek.

When it was finished, only a short crop of dense, black hair remained, pressed forward into a Mia Farrow pixie.

It was time to find her father. She needed him now after a decade of pretending not to. She started calling out to him on her way down the stairs.

"Daddy?" She called again as she padded through the spread of kitchen, which smelled so strongly of lemon Lysol it burned her eyes. And then once more, quieter, when she noticed the light on in the finished lower level, peaking through a crack in the door: "Daddy?"

He's down in his office, working at home today, she thought. I'll just tell him good morning, and then maybe I'll call Joe and tell him how sorry I am to miss the funeral, but my father has brain cancer. And gout.

Maybe that's overkill. He had back surgery. Perfect. He had back surgery and my mom's a total self-absorbed, narcissistic bitch who couldn't hide her contempt when she brought him breakfast in bed so I figured I should drive right down here.

And where did *that* come from, exactly?

"Daddy?"

Evers Pinkett spun from the sink at the back of the wet bar in the barely lit den, where he'd just poured his second vodka a full half hour before noon. He was dressed now, in a starched navy button-up and khaki pants.

He'd disinfected himself, just as he had the kitchen, Mara deduced. He'd planned to be sober and clear-eyed and clever and fun. Maybe we should catch a movie this afternoon, hmm?

But it just wouldn't take.

"I thought you were working," Mara said. She looked a good decade younger without the affectations.

"I thought you had *hair*," he volleyed back, and snickered silly in a way that was very much *not* vice president of Oreo Relations Evers Pinkett.

Mara wrapped her mother's robe tighter around herself, ran her hand across the one-inch stand of hair. "I needed a change," she said distantly. "You're drinking vodka at eleven-thirty?"

"You needed a change," he toasted her, "and I needed a drink." He sipped from it, but the sip became a drink and the drink became something else entirely until the glass was empty.

He met her slack-jawed stare dead-on. "What's going on?" she finally asked. "Where's Mom?"

Instead of answering, he filled his glass again and sipped it this time. "Bloody Mary?" he asked. "Is that more suitable, socially speaking?"

"No. Where's Mom?"

"At her sister's."

"Earlier you said Grandma's."

"Did I?"

"So which is it?"

Evers swirled the clear liquor in a small circle. Finally: "I suppose I don't really know *where* she is at the moment."

"How long has she been gone?"

"What's today?"

"Thursday."

"No. *The date.*"

"October fourteenth."

"Quite nearly a year then." He raised the glass to her, sipped again.

Mara eased onto a bar stool across from him. The pine wall behind him was a shrine to Ohio State: a pennant, a commemorative poster of Buckeye Football, his master's degree.

"We're going to a little happy-hour thing at the Hollises at five," he said, nodding, grasping at normalcy. "It'll be nice. They haven't seen you in so long."

"What kind of shape will you be in by then?"

He blinked quickly, like a twitch. "I'm going to the Hollises at five," he said, trying to affect an air of dignity in spite of his thickening tongue. "I hope you'll join me."

Mara heard her breath catch, felt her lip quiver. "What about work, Daddy?" she asked. "Do they know the kind of sick you really are?"

"I'm fairly certain they don't much care, darlin'," he said, attempting an ironic chuckle. "You know, considering they booted my Oreo ass into early retirement last year."

He turned suddenly, hiding from her, and very carefully adjusted the framed Buckeye poster.

"Daddy . . ."

He lowered his head for a beat, then braced himself and faced her. "I'd like it very much if you accompanied me to the Hollises at five," he said, clinging desperately to a shadow of the man he'd been. "I'd love to show you off."

"Okay." Mara nodded quickly, wiping away a tear. "We'll go to the Hollises, Daddy."

She reached up and put her palm to his face. "Let's take you up for a nap first, hmm?" she cooed, nodding to coax him.

He put his hand over hers . . . and finally nodded back.

THURSDAY, OCTOBER 14, JUST AFTER NOON

North Hill is the predominant Little Italy of Northeast Ohio, with some three thousand residents clustered around a single commercial strip going up one side and down the other of the steepest hill in the metro area.

It's all about the food here. It started in the 1930s with DeVito's Italian Grocer at the Hill's summit, luring hungry shoppers from as far as Youngstown to load up on homemade sauces, sausages, pastas, and seasonings.

From this hub, the area thrived on restaurants and produce and meat markets. A walk on the Hill left shoppers' clothes so drenched in garlic they were tempted to eat their own pants.

Rising temperatures had rendered the Hill a motor-vehicle version of Italian roulette—is that a benign wet spot or the last thing a soccer mom sees before parking the SUV in DeVito's produce aisle?

Joe tightened his grip on the wheel and Nathan wrung his hands raw as they engaged the ascent.

"Actually, I already took my tape recorder back," Nathan said. Joe's eyes darted briefly to him.

"And the tapes?"

"I listened to some, right up until it freaked me out. I suggest that you tear out the tape and put it all in the trash compactor until you hear cracking sounds."

"Noted."

"Good."

Then, after watching Joe's knuckles whiten as he drove, Nathan said, "Pretty intense, huh?"

"Don't be a girl," Joe chuffed. "We're fine."

"Not the road, you mook," Nathan fired off, backhanding his brother's biceps negligibly. "The whole thing."

"Oh. Right."

"Who was he and who am I . . . your life and his afterlife. It all depends on which way you turn at the intersection tonight. It's pretty intense."

"You're making fun of me. You think Dad's appearances are just manifestations of some narcissistic delusion, a high-end mental meltdown."

The car swiveled its hips as they neared the apex and DeVito's on the left, making Nathan steady himself with a hand on the dash. "Maybe he did talk to you," he said, eyes darting between the road and his brother. "Maybe that's how you knew about Carla Brugano."

Joe raised an eyebrow, stole a hopeful glance toward his

brother. Nathan refused to reciprocate, cleared his throat instead, and asked, "So how old is he now?"

"Somewhere in his thirties."

"Before—"

"Yeah," Joe nodded. "He seems happy."

Nathan's voice dropped: "We all were."

"You know what?" Joe asked, carefully introducing the Audi to her descent, realizing just how insanely roller-coaster steep the area's steepest hill really was. "I'm starting to feel like I was late for the party, and all I got was coffee and crumb cake and inside jokes I'll never understand."

Nathan smiled at that, and a comfortable silence fell between them. "You were right about me," he said then.

"What about you?"

"About my *completeness.*"

The car began picking up speed.

"Um . . . Joe?" Nathan ventured.

"*What?*" Joe's eyes were massive, now, but he was afraid to tap the brakes.

"Doesn't she work at Altieri's?"

"Yeah. So?"

Nathan pointed at the green-awninged little restaurant as it drifted by on the left. "There it went."

Joe glanced out, instinctively tapped the brakes, and the world smeared wildly out of control, all of the green, white, and red of North Hill swirling around them as the car spun.

"*Fuck!*" Joe croaked as the Audi twirled its madcap way down North Hill. "What do I do?"

"It's either imperative that you tap the brakes or *entirely out of the question!*" Nathan yelled authoritatively, bracing himself with both hands.

Even under the circumstances, Joe couldn't resist turning a slow burn on his brother. With a deep breath, he stood on the brake pedal, lurching the car, now facing *up* the hill, to slam its right tires against the high curb. The left side of the Audi lifted a full foot off the ground and . . .

Landed. A flawless piece of parking. "Nicely done," Nathan managed. Then he pointed farther up the hill. "But there's a space right in front."

Once they'd settled back to normal breathing, the boys gingerly made their way to the door of Altieri's. "I think it's open," Joe said, pointing to the lit neon sign.

Indeed, the door was unlocked. They edged into a dimly lit foyer and paused as their eyes adjusted to the darkness—the lunch rush had been destroyed by the weather. The place was empty.

A pretty, older woman with dyed black hair and too-red lips appeared from a smaller dining room to the left, grabbed a couple of menus from a shelf on the wall by rote, and turned to greet them.

The "welcome" smile on her face froze as her eyes volleyed between them. The realization took her down slow and not at all easy. "Nathan?"

"Yes?" he croaked in surprise.

"You always did have his eyes," she breathed, the menus fluttering in a shaky hand.

Nathan flushed. "Well, nobody's ever said *that* before," he laughed nervously.

Joe took the moment to get a read on the woman who'd wrestled away their father's heart. She logged in midsixties, probably, although the dye job and darkness made it a tough call. The body was pasta-plump, but she'd probably been quite a dish in her day.

A flutter of those here-to-eternity lashes, a flash of the enormous black eyes, and the brokenhearted King of Home Security was hers. That's how it went down, Joe decided quickly. Just like that. The Temptress of North Hill, this one.

"It's not the color of your eyes, hon," Carla explained to Nathan, edging forward just a little. "It's the sadness."

She stopped, tears escaping clamped eyes. Her hand went to her stomach and the empty space inside. "I don't have the right," she whispered shakily.

Nathan glanced at Joe, who shrugged his shoulders uneasily, then back at Carla. "Sure you do," he whispered.

With their permission, she cried.

"I miss him so much," she sputtered, the sobs overtaking her. "I loved him with all my heart."

Joe blinked quickly, like it burned. What was his mother's reaction to Joseph Way, Senior's demise? "He was a good friend?"

A glance at his brother told Nathan the job was his, so he shuffled forward to Carla, let her lean into his embrace. He patted her back, just a little. "Take it easy," he managed.

Joe finally opted for the glass counter with the chocolate mints and stacks of North Hill Chamber of Commerce fliers.

Mixed in with a well-read newspaper, he noticed a large envelope with "Rita" scrawled across it.

"We haven't spoken in years, your mother and I," Carla explained, startling him a little. She'd cleared half the distance to him.

Joe noticed the Sinatra soundtrack only in its absence—the CD had ended and all that was left was the breath-sucking silence of this unforeseen moment.

Only five days ago, if you had told Joe Way his father had maintained an extramarital relationship with a spicy North Hill meatball for more than two decades—or that said meatball had communicated occasionally with his mother—he would've covertly ordered the waiter to start serving you tonic and tonics. Now here he was, suffocating in deafening silence just six feet from the woman herself.

He looked back just as she held up a finger and disappeared into the near-blackness of the restaurant. It was the kind of place, Joe thought in the moment, where too much light provides business rivals a clearer aim.

She emerged from the void just moments later with a massive black purse over her shoulder. She sat on a red vinyl bench near the counter and patted for the boys to join her on either side.

Once they'd complied, she pulled a weathered black leather wallet out of her purse, opened it to a dog-eared photo that she held up to them: a snapshot of Nathan and Joe at ages fifteen and seven. They wore pajamas and each held a pop can in one hand and toasted each other with a champagne glass in the other. A smoky cocktail party was in full swing behind them.

"I was stoned," Nathan said. "Look at my eyes."

Joe smiled, couldn't help leaning closer. By then, the brothers' time together had become rare. The condensed memory of this moment, one of the last few before Nathan disappeared for the West Coast, uncoiled to fill him with a warm rush.

"I remember this," Joe whispered, tracing his finger over the image of his brother.

"They were celebrating adding the security patrol, right?" Nathan asked Carla.

"Yeah," she said, lost in it herself. She tapped a manicured pinky on a face in the crowd—hers. She was smiling silly toward the camera, head leaning back and teeth gleaming.

"There I am," she said. "Your father was taking the picture, and I could never seem to look anywhere else but at him."

Joe gulped quickly at that, looked between Now Carla and Then Carla. She'd been even prettier than he'd imagined, her smile a celebration in itself; you could hear the throaty giggle coming off the weathered photo.

Joe looked up at her as the memory came into focus. She turned to him, met his eyes. "You took me up to bed," he whispered. "My mom didn't tell me stories anymore, so—"

"So I did," Carla finished. "I told you a story that night."

"About a king who loved a peasant girl," Joe whispered.

She smiled, pleased, and laid out several other photos on the black wool matting of her broad lap: Joe in his peewee football uniform, Nathan in his natty new sweater. Slices of the good life.

"You carry pictures of us?" Nathan asked.

She dipped her head, embarrassed. "You're the only babies I

ever had, I guess." Then she fished out a strip of photos, the kind you get in those booths outside the market or in the mall. She held it close to her face, moving it slowly to absorb each frame.

At last, she displayed it for the boys: She was midtwenties, maybe, and at the peak of her contrast, all red lips and creamy skin. Joseph was a decade older, handsome and sure.

They were laughing, kissing, crossing their eyes. A couple of teenagers who'd met too late. And just as Carla had said, she was always, *always* looking at him.

"I don't remember the last time I saw him smile like that," Nathan marveled.

"I saw it every time we were together," she whispered, tracing Joseph's tiny face with her index finger.

Joe bolted up and turned away from them, kneaded at a phantom crick in his neck. Carla was still watching him when he finally faced her again.

"I'm sorry for taking so much of him from you," she said, then closed her eyes and covered her mouth. No tears fell, but her jaw was flexing with the effort.

Joe nodded, put his hands in his pockets, looked around at nothing as he drifted a few steps closer.

"You never married," he deduced.

"No."

"Then it wasn't fair to you, either."

"'Fair,'" Carla repeated, amused at the very notion. "I gave up figuring out the right and wrong of it . . . the fair or unfair of it . . . a long time ago."

Joe nodded. But still: "I need to know how it happened."

Carla bit at her lip and laughed at a small piece of memory. Like a schoolgirl in front of the class, her legs pressed tight together and her fingers interlaced, she began, "I was living at home still, down in Akron in one those pillbox houses in the valley. I'd dreamed of going to college at Miami of Ohio, where my best friend Carol was going. My grades were good enough to get in but not good enough for a scholarship. It just wasn't gonna happen.

"I woke up the Monday after graduation and my dad had circled a bunch of classified ads in bright red ink, left it on the kitchen table for me. One was office manager for J. Way Home Security up near Cleveland, which sounded better than secretary or typist or file clerk. Of course, it turned out to be all three, but I didn't really mind.

"We had our first office on the West Side in a storefront next to a Big Boy, which ended up being our conference room for those first couple of years.

"I wonder what he'd say, but *I* think we fell in love about two months after we met. He scored his first big neighborhood security-patrol contract, and I'd really slaved over that project, making up a presentation so you'd never know we pieced it together over burgers in the last booth on the right.

"So I guess he figured he should celebrate with me instead of Rita, which I was too young and had too big a crush to wonder about back then."

She looked up from her hands, remembering that the boys were there. Joe's eyes fell away from her, and she continued,

"We bought a couple of bottles of champagne and paper cups at the Hy-Vee across the street. Those were the best days of all, I think, before we knew what was happening between us.

"I remember Joseph trying to open the champagne, holding it between his knees. 'I've never done this,' he said, looking up at me, and I could see the boy inside. A boy who never thought he'd be where he was right now, wearing that crisp white shirt and those pleated black slacks, opening champagne to celebrate the beginning of a life I'm still not sure he ever wanted.

"Well, that champagne went shooting everywhere. I started laughing so hard, I thought I'd bust something. Then your father just held the bottle over his head and let the champagne run right down, through his hair and over his face. It was cold and his eyes about popped out and he laughed wide open, like children laugh, you know? We both did.

"But then I wasn't laughing anymore. Not at all. I was just watching him, and I remember like it was yesterday my fingers and toes tingling and my stomach fluttering like I was going to throw up.

"He asked me if I was okay and I said, yeah, sure. He walked over to me all serious . . . and then he poured the rest of the bottle right over *my* head. I screamed and laughed and jumped up and I'll be damned if he didn't catch me before I came down again. He caught me in the air and he held me there in his arms.

"We were jumping up and down together and he was saying, 'We did it, Carla!' That word—*we*—it sounded so beautiful."

Carla gathered her courage and looked between the boys, spoke the words directly to them. "And in that moment, Joseph Way had my heart forever." She nodded once, swearing to its truth, and went on with her story.

"It was there between us. See, love is like a big, pink elephant in the room. You can put a lampshade on it, paint it a different color, pretend it's just physical attraction or some chemical thing, but it's still *there.*"

Nathan looked at Joe. Joe winced, annoyed that his brother felt compelled to underscore the Carla-Mara connection.

Carla continued, "Things got tense between us. I thought maybe I'd have to quit. He was impatient with me over typing and stuff, flustered over the smallest things.

"Then one day at lunch—Big Boy, like always—he called the waitress over and got on her for not keeping up with his coffee. He didn't see her flip him off behind her back, and I decided it was best not to tell.

"But he starts going off on some long speech on service in this country and maybe hippies, I think—God knows he didn't make no sense half the time on that shit—and I just got up on my knees, grabbed his tie with one hand and put the other on the table, leaned over and kissed him.

"I just kissed him, right there in the Big Boy. And his eyes are all wide, and I sit down, just so damn scared he's gonna tell me to get up, get out, and keep on going, you know?

"But instead, he smiles and he says, 'I knew something was bothering me.' Just like that.

"That was it for us. We were in love. The real thing. And

there wasn't nothin' either of us could do to make it different if we'd wanted to.

"Exactly eight days later, your sister died," Carla said. "And that little boy inside your father died with her."

Nathan's breath hitched. He clamped his eyes shut, bit at his thumb nervously. That's exactly right, his small nod said. That's just what happened.

Carla waited a beat and finished her tale: "We had just those eight days to talk about a real life together. After Kate, we never talked about divorce again. Never. We talked about breaking it off a lot, thousands of times over the next twenty-some years. I even tried to date someone else, but it made Joseph so crazy I just couldn't do it to him."

Carla stood, carefully stored away the pictures, zipped up her massive purse. With a heavy exhale, she looked back at the boys.

"Then he died," she said gently. "And you came to see me."

Nathan looked to Joe, raised his eyebrows. Joe nodded to him—good enough.

"Thank you," was all Nathan could say to her.

Joe just tipped his head a little.

But as he passed, Carla caught his hand, made him turn to look at her.

"He was *my truth,* Joe," she said, eyes blazing, voice trembling with conviction. "And I was his."

He met her stare, surrendered his anger. "I know," he said with finality.

She smiled her thanks as Joe and Nathan walked out.

On the sidewalk, Joe's cell phone rang in his pocket, startling him. He dug it out. "Hello?"

"Joe, it's Dan," the detective said. "I'm in Ally's office. We're *all* in Ally's office. I know the funeral's at seven, but—"

"What is it?" Joe asked.

"You'll wanna hear this for yourself," was all McCale would give.

Patrice the prim pathologist and Bulger the rumpled CSI were in the principal's office together; opposites united only by their sweaty-palmed plight, side by side against the wall, heads lowered, eyes darting anxiously.

When Joe entered Ally's office, she, McCale, and Chief Collins paced circles around the doomed. Ally met Joe's eyes without apology. "Well look who decided to fucking show up," she said coldly.

"Good morning, Ally," he fired back. "Love the hair, love the dress."

"No fighting, children," Collins's low voice boomed. "We're in this together whether we like it or not."

"Patrice and Bulger wanna tell us a story," McCale said, his anger glimpsing out behind the fake smile. "I insisted that we wait until you could hear it, too."

Ally strolled in front of the two, her arms crossed. It would surprise nobody if she produced a ruler from her pinstriped slacks and cracked each of their hands.

"You may begin," she said, looking between them disdainfully.

"Well," Patrice said, putting her hands flat on her legs. "It started yesterday morning—"

"Wednesday," Collins informed.

"Yes," Patrice said between her teeth. "*Yesterday.* It became evident during my autopsy on Jenni Sanchez that her wounds hadn't come from a single weapon."

She cleared her throat. "In fact," she said, "it would seem that as many as six different instruments made contact with her body during the course of her struggle. Instruments of different materials and densities."

McCale edged closer to Joe, smiled, and blinked quickly. Patrice cued Bulger with a sharp glance.

"Seemed pretty unlikely that one guy used six different weapons on her," the heavyset man said into his own shoes. "And it seemed just as farfetched that six guys went into her backyard and knocked her around without tearing things up a lot more than they were."

Silence fell over the room as Bulger rubbed his face. "So I went back to the site," he finally said.

"Because, you know, *he's a crime scene investigator,*" McCale said congenially, never dropping his smile. Ally crossed her arms tighter, pretending not to know Joe was glaring at her.

But since nobody else pretended not to know, she uncoiled, exploded all over Joe. "You're the one who started all this, pretty boy," she growled between bared teeth. *"You're the fucking one."*

"Easy, now," Joe deadpanned. "Let's hear the whole story before you put a sword in me."

"Fuck off," she said, including the hand signal in case he didn't get it. A multimedia expletive.

"Oh, yeah, Ally," Collins sighed, crossing his arms. "You're mayor material."

"Could I just finish so you can fire me and I can start drinking?" Bulger pleaded.

"Sounds fair," McCale allowed sweetly.

"So anyway, I went back to the site and really started working over every rock, every tree, every, um . . . well . . . the tetherball pole, too."

"Oh, Christ," Joe said, getting it. McCale cut his hand at the angle of the backyard again. "Huh?" he said, as gleeful as ghouls get. *"Huh?"*

Patrice unrolled a posterboard, taped it to the wall just behind them: It was something right out of a *Family Circus* cartoon: Jenni's madcap, zigzaggy path up and down and back up and finally and forever down again into the creek.

"From the hair and traces of blood, it appears she fell down that hill more than once," Bulger said, wincing. "She fell backwards, rolled and bounced her way down off the rocky ground, briefly got on her feet but then staggered back to hit the tetherball pole and went woozy—"

"She probably *crawled* back up the hill at least once, based on the dirt embedded under her nails," Patrice interrupted as she stood, pointed to the darkest trail of arrows down the drawing of Jenni Sanchez's backyard. "The last time she tried to stand and fell again, she took this fallen tree trunk at the base of her spin, did a full flip, and slammed the top of her head right into a big, rounded rock at the front edge of the creek. That's what caved in her skull."

A long silence fell over the room. "You've *got* to be kidding me," Joe finally said, laughing coldly. "She really fell up and down that hill until she died?"

Bulger and Patrice looked at each other, shrugged, and nodded. "Yeah," Bulger said. "That's what happened."

"There are no hand marks on her body," Patrice added quickly. "I mean, if you're wondering if she might've been pushed or dragged around. There's no evidence of that."

"All six of the, um, the 'weapons' Patrice referred to are between the porch and the creek," Bulger summed up. "And she hit all of them at least once."

Joe stood, found space for himself, staked claim to it. "Okay," he leveled. "Does anybody mind if I just sum all this up?"

"Knock yourself out," Collins agreed. "Jenni Sanchez sure as hell did."

Joe flinched and dove in: "Late Thursday, Jenni came to my office to tell me Ratcovic was harassing her. Worried that my involvement might taint her testimony, I sent her home and directed her to come back and give her testimony to Ally."

"Sounds reasonable," Bulger said.

"Shut up, Bulger," at least three people said, Ally among them.

Joe continued, "So Jenni comes clean about her meeting with me. Ally convinces her to up the charge and—"

"*No,*" Ally exploded. "That part she did on her own. I swear to God she lied first. *Then* she got shook up and told me about her meeting with you."

"And that's when you gave her Mara's number and suggested she pin it all on me?" Joe asked.

Ally shrugged and finally nodded her confession.

"How much?" Joe prodded.

"Couple of grand," she confessed with a wave to indicate the bargain she'd found in Jenni.

"Did I tell you how much I like the hair?" Joe countered. Then, without pause: "That night, Jenni spent time at a bar with a tieless man who tried to convince her *not* to call Mara Pinkett . . . or at least that's what she told Mara Pinkett."

"So where's *she?*" Collins asked.

"Let me finish," Joe insisted. Collins held up his hands in apology. "So," Joe continued, "what you're telling me is this: After that meeting, after all this self-serving machination, all the inept plotting and planning, Jenni Sanchez went in her own backyard and tumbled herself to death?"

Joe looked around the room, daring an answer. "That appears to be the case, Joe," was all McCale could offer.

"That's exactly what happened," Patrice said, trying to be authoritative. When everyone looked at her, though, she quietly took her seat next to Bulger, where she belonged.

"The girl was intoxicated," she added meekly.

Joe shook his head, strolled to the fifth-story window, and looked out. "What about poisoning, Patrice?" he said without looking back.

"Hmm?" she said, clearing her throat. She couldn't see Joe's brow furrow at the stall tactic. When he turned, his expression shifted to neutral.

"I asked, what about poisoning? Anything but alcohol in her system?"

"Just booze," she said. "Lots of it—point-two-o."

"How many drinks is that for someone her size?"

"Probably ten," she said disapprovingly, looking at each of the others. Bad girl, Jenni Sanchez. *Bad girl.*

Joe turned to Chief Collins now, tilted his head. "Chief, what are you suggesting we do with all of this?"

Collins bit at his lip, pointed at Joe—good question—and said, "I think, considering no *real* crime was committed here, we just keep all of the other embarrassing details in house, amongst family."

Joe nodded; it was precisely the answer he expected. In a real world with real problems, it wasn't even all that *wrong,* relatively speaking.

"Are you in, Joe?" Ally asked sweetly. "Or should I call you Mayor Way?"

Joe couldn't help but laugh and shake his head. "And what about Mara Pinkett?" he asked.

"We sort of figured you could handle her," Collins said. "Can you?"

Joe didn't answer. Instead, he looked at his watch, adjusted his tie, and headed for the door. Ally got as far as, "Where the hell do you think—" before the door slammed hard behind him.

Elisa stared across the street at Mrs. Borbon, who leaned against the stenciled window to her styling salon, smoking a cigarette and wondering where it all got away from her.

Mrs. Borbon had a first name once. And a plan.

From the other side of the booth, Joe watched Elisa carefully, gave her time to digest what he'd told her.

"You're saying she just fell down the hill," Elisa said, still watching as Mrs. Borbon stepped on her cigarette and went back to sweep up the mounds of black hair on her floor.

"I'm telling you what they told me, Elisa," he said evenly. "That's all. They claim her blood alcohol was off the chart. She had maybe ten drinks."

Elisa's eyes flickered up, focused. "Ten drinks," she said flatly.

"That's right. Give or take."

"Dude, I've seen Jenni drink a twelve-pack and chase every fucking beer with a shot and keep it totally together."

Elisa shook her head quickly, trying to make the pieces fit back together. "Was she stoned?"

Joe was distracted by something just off the corner of his mind's eye. Something flickering, flitting, finding cover.

"Just the liquor," he said distantly.

"Uh-uh," Elisa said, shaking her head even faster, growing more agitated by the second. "It doesn't add up, man."

Joe could sense it there, in the room, then right there in the booth with them. The thing he couldn't catch, the elusive object just off the edges. The connective device, the glue that brought the scheming and the demise together, made them more than independent, coincidental events.

"Oh, shit," Joe whispered, seeing it at last. "Oh, God."

"What?" she demanded. "Oh-shit-oh-God *what?*"

Joe vised his eyes shut. When he opened them again, he said, "He did it for me."

"*Who?*"

Joe reached across the table between them, took both of Elisa's hands. At first she resisted, but his eyes locked onto hers and she relented.

"I promised you the truth," Joe said. He nodded and she mirrored it.

And then he left.

In his boxers and T-shirt, hair wet pressed back severely from his widow's peak hairline, Mark Stranad smoothed his black Brooks Brothers suit out on his king-sized bed. He laid one, two, and then a third tie across its chest.

And he smiled. Not because there was anything inherently cheerful about Joseph Way's funeral, but because it *was* another significant milemarker on a profound journey for an important family. And once again, Mark was *there,* man. He was part of it.

Joe Way, his best friend, would declare his candidacy tonight. Decades from now, the event would sit atop the timeline, highlighted and marked with a nifty graphic.

And that's what really mattered. He was part of something; he *belonged.* He'd been a team player, he'd made sacrifices, and it was so very worthwhile.

It mattered. *He* mattered. There was a place for him in the world after all. For too long, he'd doubted it.

Most people are adrift by Mark's way of thinking. Disconnected and alone. One day, he would set aside his profound, complicated feelings for Joe and marry, raise his own family. His children would play with their children, Joe's and Beth's, and it would be that way forever. He would always be *there*, with the Ways, where he belonged.

"Nice suit. Gonna wear a tie?"

Mark spun, hands seizing against his chest before he could get control. Now he would have to wait it out, breathe through the attack as the chilled potion flowed to his fingertips and the top of his head.

Joe stepped into the room, perfect as ever in his suede jacket and T-shirt. He got Mark by both shoulders, helped him sit on the bed.

"Take a deep breath, Mark," Joe said, sitting next to him, putting his arm around his shoulder. "I didn't mean to startle you. Just breathe, man."

Mark willed himself to settle—in through the nose, out through the mouth, over and over and over. He couldn't be weak, not here with Joe's arm around him. His best friend, the man he'd die for, was burying his father so on this day, of all the days, Mark needed to step up.

Joe stood and went to Mark's nightstand, found the prescription bottle there. He opened it, palmed one of the large blue-and-white capsules, and returned to hand it to Mark.

"Do you remember when you gave me one of these, back in

high school?" Joe asked, his smile warm with the memory. Mark gulped down the capsule and laughed.

Joe sat next to him. "You played 'Smells Like Teen Spirit' thirty-six times, banging your head and smiling all stupid," Mark said, his voice quivering. "Then you passed out and shit your pants."

"I *pissed* my pants and slept in the front yard," Joe corrected. "The head-banging I'll have to take on faith."

Joe's smile descended gradually, but he kept looking at Mark. "I love you," he said, mouth curling down at the edges in spite of all efforts. "I never told you. I just want you to know that, okay?"

Mark's right hand spasmed on the bed between them. He grabbed it in the other, held it tightly. He looked down, away from Joe, unable to process so much at once.

"I'm not gay," Mark said, forcing a laugh and then hating himself for it. "You don't think I'm gay, do you?"

"No," Joe said. He looked at the prescription bottle in his hand, then back at his friend.

"How many did you give her, Mark?" he finally asked.

Mark stared into the floor for a long while. It started with a nod and it moved down his body until he was rocking himself slowly, arms wrapped across his stomach.

"How many, Mark?"

"Two," came the answer. "I emptied them in her beer while she was in the bathroom. I was worried for a minute she'd slipped out the back, but she finally came back and drank it."

Joe nodded patiently. Then: "Why?"

"Her aunt talked her into lying and then Ally paid her to throw *you* under the bus for all of it. She was going to call Mara Pinkett and tell her that you sent her home."

"Were you hoping she'd get in a wreck? Something like that?"

"Man, she should've passed out right there at the table," Mark said, shaking his head in awe. "I was gonna take Mara's number from her and hope she thought better of it in the morning. I didn't have time to think it through. I sure as hell never counted on her walking out of there like she did."

"You never thought of killing her, Mark? You weren't going to drug her and take her somewhere?"

"No," Mark said. At last he looked up at Joe. "I always thought I'd do anything for you. I'm sorry, Joe."

For Mark, that's what this was about: He'd come up short when he didn't take Jenni Sanchez out into the woods somewhere, dazed and drooling, pop her with a shovel, and bury her so deep they'd never find her.

"Who paid Patrice to fix the report?" Joe asked flatly. "That shit of yours would've shown up."

"That was me," Mark said proudly. He even raised his eyebrows a little.

"Did Jacob pay Mara Pinkett to go away?"

Mark squinted, searched his memory. "I don't know," he finally concluded. Joe's eyes pressed him to *think harder,* but Mark just shrugged. "I really don't know," he promised.

Joe nodded and the sob took him by surprise. "Jesus," he managed. "Jesus Christ, Mark."

Mark looked confused—Jesus Christ, *what?*—and Joe

couldn't stomach it. He had to turn away, walked to the window. "We're going to tell the truth," he said. "We're going to tell all of it."

Behind Joe, Mark considered deeply for a long while, brow furrowed as he did the math. "Do you really think that's the best idea, Joe?"

Joe looked back, his anger dissolving until he settled on just this: "I think it's the only idea."

Mark nodded compliantly and it left a bruise on Joe's heart. "I'm sorry," he managed. "None of it was real. You were following a lie. Do you understand what I'm saying, Mark?"

Mark's eyes hardened. "It's real, Joe," he said, a knowing smile curling his lip. "You'll find your way back."

Outside, a car door slammed. Joe turned to look down at McCale, who stood beside his cruiser, waiting for the sign. Behind him, a marked police cruiser eased into the driveway.

At last, Joe nodded.

It hadn't taken long for Mara to deduce that Evers Pinkett was about as welcome at the Hollis house as Louis Farrakhan at a bar mitzvah. Or that he'd made his way back down to the basement bar earlier than she'd thought.

The Hollises and the three other couples had very nearly broken a sweat doing Bugs Bunny double-takes and mortified eye rolls every time Evers refilled his glass, slurred a word, or stumbled on the step to or from the sunken great room, which he did predictably and repeatedly.

Twenty minutes after they'd arrived, with Mara already over-introduced, he silenced the room to *formally* introduce her, as if they'd just glided into a ballroom instead of a suburban home featuring four disdainful white couples.

He was oblivious to their scorn, but Mara couldn't stomach it. She dragged him across three lawns and straight up to his room, where he fell on the bed and passed out. He'd wedged a lifetime of humiliation into just twenty-two minutes.

"I like the hair," he mumbled groggily as she started out the door. "It shows your neck. Like your mother's."

Downstairs, Mara flicked on the tiny TV on the baker's rack, finally settled in at the kitchen table with the sandwich and soda she'd been craving.

That's where she finally let the tears come. She covered her mouth and heaved steadily under the strain. When it was done, she carefully wiped her eyes with a napkin, took a long drink of soda, and watched the news with only a spasmodic shudder here and there as evidence she'd cried at all.

The local affiliate was showing a special weather bulletin: The temperature would drop back below freezing tonight and there was some chance, some modest chance, that what would start as freezing rain might dump roughly a foot of snow on Northeast Ohio by morning. You know, or maybe not.

Either way, a traveler's advisory was already in effect for the northern half of the state.

"Hope you weren't planning on running back to this guy tonight," Evers's voice boomed through the kitchen.

She turned, her eyes flicking away quickly. Seeing her father as the Drunk of Glad Acres didn't settle easily.

"Headache," he explained, going for the cupboard.

"There's no guy," Mara lied weakly into her hands while Evers swallowed a handful of Tylenol.

He circled the breakfast bar, pulled out a chair, and sat down next to her. "The angry young woman runs home to Daddy and chops off all her hair," he recited. "I'm a self-pitying drunk, not a blind man."

"You're just going through a rough time, that's all," she forgave too readily, realizing she had a promising and fruitful career as a codependent ahead of her.

Evers looked off for a moment. "How 'bout you let me be the parent?" he managed.

"Oh, please do," she admonished tightly.

"Do you love him?"

She froze in midchew. She'd managed to bob and weave her way out of that question for nearly a decade now. "I don't know," she said, sounding like a petulant teenager.

"Did he hurt you?"

"He confused me. We confuse each other. It's what we do."

"Why are you here?"

"He's confused enough, trust me." She laughed a little. "He's something of a mess right now. He doesn't need my help."

"Is this the quarterback?"

She was surprised, but gathered quickly. "Yeah. His name is Joe Way."

"Spaghetti arm, but he had—"

"A great ass."

"I was going to say quick feet, but I was just being nice."

"Then that's what I meant to say."

Evers sighed long and hard. "Love shouldn't hurt, Mara." His lip was quivering. "It shouldn't make you drink . . . or cut off your hair . . . or forget who you are."

Mara blinked at the words, sandwich poised in midair,

because just maybe he'd stumbled onto a point. Evers continued into his hands, "Someone who loves you shouldn't just back out of the driveway and out of your life without a goodbye or an explanation or *something.*"

That's what I did, Mara thought. That's exactly what I did, isn't it? But for now, she said, "Mom couldn't love. Part of me knew it even when I was little. It's not your fault."

He looked angry for a moment, ready to pounce and defend the very woman who'd broken him. Then he tilted his head because he knew as well as she did. He said, "Without my job, without her, without you . . . I don't know who I am anymore."

"There's a lot of that going around lately," she whispered, taking her father's thick, heavy hand in both of hers. She stood and held him, let him cry into the shoulder of his wife's cotton nightshirt.

"I want you to stay here with me. Just for a little while," he said.

She pulled back, surprised. His jaw flexed. He took in a deep breath, and finally looked his daughter in the eye.

"I need you, Mara," he said.

She looked out the window to the driveway, through the floodlight on the basketball court at the first flecks of freezing rain. It's safer to stay here, in so many ways. Better for everyone, probably.

"Okay," she whispered. She turned her head and rested it on his chest.

"Okay," she whispered again.

In the full-length mirror on the back of his door, with a frame cluttered by Cleveland Browns football cards and arena rock-band stickers and careful cutouts of masturbatory female icons of the late 1980s, Joe struggled to add a black tie to his sheeny-white pinpoint shirt.

"Five days," he said to himself. His world had been irrevocably and firmly spun onto its ass in just five days.

He started to laugh at the boggling wonder of it all, but then he realized: I took some blows, but I'm not exactly on my ass, am I?

In fact, Joe realized, he was fully awake, maybe for the first time in his life. Was that what his dead father had been to him? An otherworldly alarm? A wake-up call from beyond?

With the wisdom of death, Joe decided, his father had hung around to make sure his son didn't sleepwalk through life, easily nudged and prodded down someone else's path.

Joe stared at himself in the mirror, in the full light, and wondered how many people ever get around to doing just that. How many people take the moment to really look and see and *decide?*

Find your truth, Joseph Way had said. Heavy shit. *Very* heavy shit.

In the mirror, Joe saw Jacob behind him, lying flat on his childhood bed, staring up at Heather Locklear.

"How long have you been there?" Joe asked as he turned.

"I can't believe you still have this," Jacob said, snickering a little as he sat up and finally stood. He went to Joe, harrumphed over his tie. "What'd you do," the old man asked as he pinched at the dimple, "tie this with your feet?"

When he'd finished, Jacob stepped back, dropped his head, and worried at his own tie aimlessly. At last, he said, "I never gave that muckraking blowhard Mara Pinkett a penny, okay? I'd rather you kept on thinking I did, put everything back together the way it was, and run for mayor, but my motherfucking conscience seems to have ideas of its own."

"Well," Joe croaked, the revelation stuck in his throat. "Thanks for telling me."

Jacob smiled, slapped Joe's shoulder. "Least I could do," he understated.

"Did you tell him to do it?" Joe asked flatly. "Did you tell him to 'fix it' or say *anything* that made Mark believe drugging that girl was the right thing to do?"

Jacob put his meaty hands on either side of Joe's neck, held the younger man's jaw with his thick thumbs so he would have to look back into his eyes. And he said, "No. I did not."

The two men locked eyes. Then Jacob prodded, "Might as well ask the other question, Joe. You know the one."

He did know the question. And standing in front of him was the only living man who could answer it. The time had come.

Joe gulped and waded in: "Did my father know Mark was going to meet with Jenni Sanchez?"

Tears brimmed in Jacob's eyes even as he smiled. "As God is my witness," he said, his voice cracking with emotion, "your father and I had one phone conversation, right after you called him. His only concern was you and whatever trouble you might get into over this. It was the last time I ever spoke to Joseph Way."

Joe nodded in a slow, steady rhythm. He gritted his teeth, but at last he relented . . .

And cried for his father. His fist instinctively went to his stomach to keep it in, to hold it together. Jacob pulled the only son he had left in the world into his meaty arms and held him while he wept. "That's been about five days in coming, huh?" Jacob barely whispered as Joe's sobs subsided.

When Joe was finished, his breath shaky and his eyes red, Jacob cleared his throat and said, "Do you have any idea how much I love you and your family? You, Joseph, Nathan . . ."

"My mother?" Joe asked, wiping at his nose like a teenager.

Jacob shrugged apologetically. "'Fraid so," he said.

"How long?"

"Since the day I laid eyes on her."

"Did you—"

Jacob shook his head firmly, once to each side. "Never. Your father was my best friend."

Joe blew out an exhale, still trying to absorb this in the midst of all the rest of it. "Wow," he managed.

"Yeah." Jacob laughed.

"One more question," Joe said, the mirth falling to something else. "Is she your truth, Jacob?"

No hesitation from the older man: "She is that, Joe Way," he said, his voice trembling. "She most certainly is that."

Joe let that wash over him for a moment, tried it on and found it acceptable. He slapped Jacob's shoulder, startling him, and headed for the door. "At the end of the day, your father was a good man," Jacob said, giving Joe pause. "But he was no Joseph Way, Junior."

Joe looked back and smiled his thanks. "I think that's what he's been trying to tell me all week," he said.

Joe was down the stairs and out the front door of the Way home before Jacob managed, *"What?"*

Dusk had given way to night when Joe found Nathan in the backyard again, under the antique streetlamp. He'd pulled one of the dark-stained Adirondack chairs closer to the tee box and sat there, dressed for the funeral, a thick quilt wrapped around his shoulders. He held a tumbler of something in one hand.

Joe stood nearby, stared out into the woods.

"Jacob's inside," Nathan said as a challenge.

"I know," Joe said.

"They're having chardonnay and popcorn and laughing. It's *sick.*"

"The gall. Should we string him up?"

Nathan considered. "Nah," he concluded. "He's too heavy and I'm too tired."

Nathan's gaze returned to the tee box.

"You're pretty cool, Joe," he said dreamily, turning to look at

Joe. "You should be mayor or honorary fire marshal or something."

"Why, thank you, Nathan." Joe smiled.

Nathan chuckled through the moment. "So our mother has a date for our father's funeral," he threw off.

"Yeah," Joe sighed. "I'm not sure I'm ready to have human beings as parents. Dead or alive."

"It certainly is jarring," Nathan agreed. He pinched at his lip, and without warning came: "So why do you think Dad only talks to you?"

Joe shook his head. "I don't know, Nathan. But I do know he never stopped loving you. I know that for sure."

"I'll have to take your word for it, won't I?" Nathan stood, toasted Joe with the remnants of his drink, and started toward the house. But only a few yards on his journey, he stalled.

"Nathan?" Joe asked.

His brother turned back. "If you get shook up tonight," Nathan said, smiling tenderly, "just look at me, okay?"

Joe had to blink back tears. "Yeah," he said. "Yeah, I'll do that."

Nathan started to turn again.

"Nathan?" Joe said, stopping him once more. "Thanks for teaching me how to throw a football."

Nathan tilted his head and toasted his brother again. "You're quite welcome," he said.

The parking lot behind the First Episcopal Church was overflowing half an hour before the 7:00 P.M. event, at which *not* being seen would stain in ways no excuse could ever cleanse.

Now, guests were parking along the residential street, and the hum and flow gave the solemn event a curiously festive atmosphere. It took excruciating restraint not to wave cheerfully or air kiss.

In the chapel itself, people mingled and consoled, and no small amount of business was done. This was Joseph Way being buried, after all, and any less would be an insult.

Jacob tiptoed the high wire, staying close to Rita's side, but not so close as to sprout vulture's wings.

Joe kept his head down, slipped smoothly through the crowd, always looking at something or someone else, and made it for his first look at his actual father since he'd told him to eat shit and die in that hallway at the Savoy Riverfront Inn.

Up two burgundy-carpeted stairs to Joseph's position of dubious honor, surrounded in flowers and candles.

Reluctance suddenly thickened the air, but Joe cut through it and cleared the last few feet to the casket in spite of himself. And no matter how slow you walk, eventually you will get somewhere.

Under even marginally normal circumstances, this would be Joe's last moment alone with his father. Time for a solemn goodbye. But after getting to know the ghost, Joe felt little connection to the lifeless husk arranged in the box.

Dead Joseph's hair was fluffier and whiter than Joe had ever seen it. A smidge Beethoven, even. His face was puffed out to smooth wrinkles, his cheeks a cheery red. He was something of a blow-dried poodle of a man, Joe thought, unable to suppress a small smile.

"You should see this, Dad," he whispered.

"No shit," Joseph's voice came from beside him. "I'm so . . ."

"Fluffy?"

"Exactly."

Joe finally turned his head to look: Joseph wore a black suit, appropriately, but businessmen also wore black suits back in the mid-1960s, when Joseph was thirtyish. The clothes hung on him the way designers intended, and he held himself like a man accustomed to being watched.

His was the pansexual appeal of youth—deer-eyed and long-lashed, slicked-back hair falling foppishly over one brow—instead of the weathered masculinity of an older man's allure.

He was sleeker, thinner in the shoulders, but he looked very much like the son standing before him.

"No matter how old and wrinkled I got, when I fantasized about singing like Tony Bennett, this is what I looked like," Joseph said, arms spread. "I am smokin', huh?"

"Yeah, but breaking news? You *suck* at singing."

"That's why they call it a fantasy, dickless."

"You never struck me as someone insecure about aging. Or somebody who would use the word *dickless*."

"I was never secure enough to *acknowledge* my insecurities. I'm seeing a guy now, though, talking some of that stuff out."

"You're dead. Isn't it a little late for therapy?"

"I may be dead, young man, but I'm still *learning*. That's what matters."

"You certainly *sound* like a guy in therapy," Joe said snidely. They shared a smile. Father and son, leaning against a casket and bantering like friends. Not altogether horrible, Joe decided.

"What's he doing?" Beth whispered to Nathan as she walked in and joined the group collecting around Rita. The two scrutinized Joe from fifteen feet away.

"Son of a bitch is talking to Dad again," Nathan spewed petulantly, drifting away from her confused expression.

Not realizing that the guests had started to flow in, Joe unconsciously mirrored Joseph's jaunty posture—the young version, not the dead one—leaning an elbow on the casket.

Crane Parker slowed to a stop, saw Joe gesturing toward the deceased's head, chatting amicably. "*There's* something you don't see every day," he commented to his wife.

Joe and Joseph fell into a brief silence, letting the mood shift to a more serious discussion.

"So it turns out you had nothing to do with this mess," Joe said. "Sorry about, you know . . . thinking you were a murderer and all that."

"Apology accepted."

"Jacob's dating Mom. That's gotta piss you off, huh?"

"He's been pretty patient, if you ask me."

Joe's face screwed up and he shook his head quickly, still unable to digest the notion, which made Joseph laugh. Together, they looked out at Jacob shielding Rita from the sea of well-wishers, answering their questions as she grew weary of it.

Already, he was her man. Even for the months of propriety that would follow, there was no getting past it.

Joseph turned to his son, watched him until he looked back. "I was doing the same thing to you I let them do to me," Joseph said. "I never made a single meaningful choice all by myself."

"Yeah, I figured it out. The whole 'find your truth' thing. Nice cover with the forgiveness crap." Joe caught Nathan simmering, watching him, and waved to his brother. Nathan flipped him off.

"He needs to talk to you, Dad," Joe said, moving his lips as little as possible. "And I think you need it, too."

"That's up to him, Joe."

Joe turned too late, looked through the air his father had occupied and right at the husk in the box.

Ten minutes later, after the elderly Reverend Charles Means had charmingly stumbled through a mercifully short presentation, Joe moved into position.

One last time.

He stood straight, looked out on the family, friends, and fans of both him and his father.

Faces filled with heartbreak. Faces filled with confusion.

This is about more than one man's death. It's about the death of a dream. The death of an illusion. It's about jury-rigged icons and fool's gold in a fool's paradise.

But more than all that, it's about getting up and starting over.

These are good people, Joe thought. A little misguided, sometimes. Maybe a little naïve. But, as Jacob had put it, *essentially good.*

He looked out at the people who'd watched him grow up in his father's image and now projected him as the one who would fill the void.

He looked at Rita, who smiled proudly. Then Jacob, sitting beside her, who put a hand over hers protectively, steadily meeting Joe's eyes all the while.

Then Nathan, who subtly nodded encouragement. Mark Stranad mouthed "get 'em, Joe," just as he had in high school so many times, raising a thumbs-up that lifted the hand cuffed to his own, which belonged to Dan McCale.

And finally, Beth, who didn't look away but didn't smile, either. Maybe she would be his best friend, but probably not. The notion of losing her entirely nearly made Joe cry, but he put it aside for the moment.

"Um," Joe began unsteadily, gesturing at the cameramen and reporters poised as inconspicuously as possible along the sides of the room. "I, uh . . . the thing is . . . I'm not going to run for mayor, so you can all leave now. I'm Joseph Way, Junior, and I'm the assistant district attorney of Cleveland, Ohio. That's what I do. That's the work that calls me. My only plan is to do it better. That's all."

The room hummed with disappointment. Nathan stood and hurried over to whisper to the media throng. But nothing really happened until Jacob Moore stood with a heavy groan and turned his steely eyes on them. In a flash, the cameramen and reporters made a beeline down the aisles to the thick doors at the end. Within moments, it was like they'd never been there at all.

Joe nodded his thanks to Jacob. Closed his eyes, steadied himself on the dais, and brought in a deep breath. The room fell silent again.

"I finally got a chance to get to know my father over the last few days," he began again. A hum of mild confusion rippled through the congregation. Joe opened his eyes.

"What I learned is that he wasn't at all what I thought he was. He wasn't what any of us thought he was."

Another wave of murmurs shuddered across the room, then the mourners held their breath in unison. Just like in Joe's visualization five days earlier, they were waiting for a punch line they could really get behind.

"He was *more,*" Joe continued, his voice gaining strength. "He was a person, a human being with all the glorious inconsistencies and imperfections that come with the condition. He was spectacular, and ordinary. Righteous, and selfish. Strong, and fragile.

"He had regrets. There are things he'd like to do over. Decisions he wished he'd considered more deeply . . . or even made at all. He wishes he could've been more awake in his life. More *there*. That's what he told me."

Joe smiled at the squints and furrowed brows and whispers about his sanity.

Then he continued, "When my sister Kate died, Joseph Way was shattered. I never saw it before, but he was. And when he put the pieces back together the best he could, they didn't exactly fit. He wasn't precisely *him* anymore. He was a projected image, a glorious statue, everything a man should be but never really is."

He looked at Beth; she gave him the suggestion of a smile he craved. "But in the end," he went on, "he learned that the consequences outweighed the rewards. He learned that the thing you become expands until it eclipses the person you are. It eclipses *your truth*. It keeps you from doing the work that calls you. It keeps you from being with the one you love."

Joe glanced at the back of the chapel. There would be no last-second dramatic entrance from Mara. The doors were still.

And so he looked to Beth again. She nodded a little to encourage him. Joe exhaled and shook his head, marveling in her. Maybe she *would* be his best friend.

And he wondered, *Can you truly love someone who isn't?*

"I'll miss my father," he finally managed. "Wouldn't it be easier if he'd kept on carrying us—me and Nathan and Kate—trudging his way through the sprinkler? Wouldn't the world be clearer if we kept seeing it through his eyes? Wouldn't we be safer, forever nestled in his bed, smelling the warm, woody strength of him enveloping us, covering us, protecting us?"

He let the silence complete itself. Nodded with his own conviction.

"And here's my father's answer, to me, to all of us: Don't build beautiful walls around your heart. Carve out doors and throw open windows. Let the sun and the wind and the rain and the truth come in. You can't be protected from life's peril without being deprived of its bliss. Eat the world. Gobble it up. Have a ball. Don't stand in shadows and don't cast them on others. Fall to the ground in shame, wither in humiliation, then stand again and stare at the sun in defiance.

"To honor my father," Joe went on, his voice rising again and a small smile breaking through, "love your men and women with such force it leaves you deliriously weary at the end of every day. Kiss your babies a million times. Hold them closer, smell their sweet breath, take them inside of you. And when the time comes, nudge them onward and let them fall and skin their knees and come up laughing. Help them carve their own doors and throw open the windows on their own hearts. *Help them find their truth.*"

Something caught Joe's eye, and he did a double-take—a woman standing alone at back of the church. He squinted at . . .

Carla Brugano. The love of his father's life. His truth that never quite was.

Rita Way shifted sideways and glanced over her shoulder, following his eyes. As she and Carla made eye contact, they exchanged a brief smile.

Carla Brugano is here, he thought. And Mara Pinkett isn't.

Joe collected himself, smiled down at the gathered, and brought his eulogy for Joseph Way to a close.

"Oh, yeah. My dad wanted me to tell you one more thing: It's seventy-two where he is, there's no humidity, the beer is impossibly cold, and he's up three strokes on Kate after the front nine."

Laughter erupted, and the crowd began to stand three at a time, then five, until all three hundred mourners were on their feet and applauding: the first standing ovation in the history of the First Episcopal Church.

Joe turned away from the thunderous applause, toward the casket, to a picture of Joseph Way that was standing on an easel beside it.

He stared at the image for a long moment, then Joseph Way, Junior smiled at his father. And he was sure his father smiled back at him.

Outside, the sleet had turned to snow, as tentatively predicted. Inside the Way family great room, a roaring fire warmed the guests at the wake.

Nathan and Joe locked eyes from opposite ends up the cavernous room. Nathan shook his head to his brother, telegraphing his wonder over the upbeat mood among the mourners. An amazing achievement, indeed.

"Joe?" He turned in time to see his mother beside him. Jacob lowered his head and fell back graciously.

Rita smiled to her son, grabbed his face in her hands, and pinched his mouth into an O.

"*You,*" she said. "You are something, aren't you?"

"Yeah," he said, gingerly removing her hands and holding

them. "And thanks to Dad, I finally took the time to figure out what that is."

"You are *Joe Way,*" she said, her voice low and sincere and filled with admiration. "All day long."

Joe considered, nodded, and said, "I should give him something in return, I suppose."

Rita's smile was stiff as her eyes fluttered down to Joe's empty wineglass. "You haven't been into my Valium again, have you?"

Joe kissed her cheek, spun away, and bore through a tight throng of guests to the kitchen. He picked among a cluster of open wine bottles until he found his merlot, nearly empty. He looked some more and found a full one, scanned the room for the corkscrew. He finally spotted it lying on the counter beside the sink, nestled among empty food platters.

It was then that he caught sight of his father in back, past the pool at the tee box again: He'd settled on midthirties and dressed for eighteen holes right up to the cap with the fluffy ball on top. He seemed oblivious to the icy rain, as if it were forever seventies and mostly sunny on his plane.

Probably is, Joe decided.

"He's out there?" Nathan's voice quivered from beside him.

Joe looked at his brother and in that very instant knew what his father wanted back from him.

"He gave me my life," Joe whispered as much to himself as to Nathan. "I'm supposed to give him *you.*"

"Oh, *please.*" Nathan tried to laugh. But Joe grabbed him roughly by the shoulders, made him look out the back window.

"Stop hiding, Nathan, and start looking for him," Joe demanded between gritted teeth. "Keep looking until you see him, goddamm it!"

Nathan breathed hard through his nose, glaring angrily back at his brother. "Do it," Joe demanded. "Do it or I will kick your ass all over this kitchen."

The door to the dining room swung open. A sixtyish woman in a Scotch plaid sweater raised her eyebrows at the two brothers. *"Out,"* Joe demanded. She dropped her wineglass to crash on the floor, turned tail, and ran back where she came from.

Joe clutched Nathan's jaw in his hand, turned his face to look out the window. "Let it hurt. Let him back in."

Nathan squinted hard into the darkness, toward the streetlight and the tee box. *"Try,* Natie," Joe coached, letting loose of his brother's jaw, now.

"He's out there, waiting for you."

Nathan gripped the edge of the counter with the effort, tears filling his eyes, jaw muscles flexing and unflexing.

And then his breath hitched. His arms quaked with the flood of emotion. "Oh, God," he whispered. "I see him."

"You do?" Joe marveled.

"And what a horrible, *horrible* hat that is."

"Go to him, Nathan," Joe managed. "Go talk to Dad."

And he did. In the backyard, past the pool, Nathan Way stopped a mere ten feet from his father. His lips moved to speak, but nothing came out.

"Hello, son," Joseph said, leaning rakishly on his Big Bertha driver. "I've missed you."

Nathan nodded distantly, blinked away tears. "I'm still gay, by the way."

Joseph took a step toward his son. Nathan edged back just that much.

"And I'm still the father with the hollow space in my heart where I used to keep my skinny, cowlick-haired little Natie," Joseph said.

Nathan looked down. Around. Stuffed his hands hard into his jacket pockets like a ten-year-old might.

"I let go of you," Joseph continued. "And I just stood and watched as you got smaller and smaller in the distance. I always figured one day I'd have the courage to strike out and find you again and tell you how nothing else—nobody else—could ever fill that space."

Nathan was perfectly still. The fidgeting and shaking were gone now. He looked up at his father, his face filled more with frustration than anger.

"Jesus, I don't think I can do this," he said.

Joseph put his arms out, palms up. "This is *me*, Nathan. When I was happy and my life was filled with love. And I never, ever loved anyone quite like I loved that eight-year-old boy who snuck into my bed every Saturday morning and pressed his cheek against my back."

Nathan kept his arms crossed, but he made no attempt to hide the tears streaming down his cheeks.

"And you know what I had to die to figure out?" Joseph continued, taking another tentative step closer. "When you were getting smaller and smaller, it wasn't you slipping away.

It was *me*. It was me being led away from my own life.

"I never stopped loving you, Nathan. I just got very lost."

Nathan nodded, then strode stiff-legged into his father's arms for the first time in twenty-five years. Joseph held on to him, soothing his sobs as though he'd never let go. He kissed the top of his son's head as only a father would.

"You're a braver man than I ever was," he whispered, then pulled out of the hug and held Nathan by the shoulders, taking a long last look. "I'm so very, *very* proud of you, Natie."

"Okay, you win," Joe said from behind them. Startled, they both looked around to find him standing there with a grin on his face. "I forgive you. For real."

Joseph chuckled. "That's great, Joe. Thanks a bundle. But it was never about that, remember?"

"Yeah, well, I thought you'd like to know," Joe said.

"Thanks for him," Joseph said, nodding toward Nathan.

"Thanks for *me*," Joe volleyed back.

Joseph turned his eyes back to Nathan. What else was there to say?

"See ya, Dad," Nathan said. "Say hello to Kate?"

"I'll do that."

Nathan walked to Joe. Joe toasted his father and the two brothers turned away.

But Joe sensed something and stalled. He turned back to see his father still standing there.

"*What?*" Joe demanded.

"Finish it, Joe," his father admonished, poking the driver in his direction. "You *finish it*."

Nathan looked at Joe, who shrugged back. Their father's eyes widened and he checked his watch. "Oh, shit. Me and Kate tee off in twenty minutes."

Nathan blinked quickly and shook his head. "What, is heaven some kind of country club or something?"

"It is for me," Joseph said, then saluted. "Now go skin your knees, the both of you."

Joseph turned and started walking toward the woods, vanishing on his way in.

After a few moments, Nathan put an arm around Joe and aimed them both toward the house. "And as they walked back toward the house," he said carefully, "reality finally began to take shape again."

Beth emerged from the darkness in front of them. "But then the ex-fiancée appeared, leaving the older brother to seek his reality alone," she said.

Nathan nodded gallantly. "Which, as one brave homosexual, he did without hesitation," he said as dissolved into the darkness.

Beth tucked her hair behind her ear, crossed her arms.

"We're done with the narration thing," she checked. "Agreed?"

"Absolutely." Joe stood completely still, holding his breath.

"So, um, nice work on the eulogy," she went on, edging a couple of feet closer. "I meant to tell you earlier, but I was pretty busy."

"Busy with what?"

"Trying to throw back open the window to my heart, actually," she said. "I'd closed it off and painted it over a few days ago."

Joe heard himself say, "You know me."

Beth snorted a quick laugh. "Yeah, well, you're not that complicated."

A long silence fell between them, but neither moved to leave. Beth blanched like she'd been poked and finally said, "Eventually we'll be friends."

Joe meant to nod but his head wouldn't comply. Strange. Instead, he said, "Right."

But his voice cracked. Even stranger.

Beth kissed his cheek quickly, then wetted her thumb and blotted out the lipstick mark.

"Have some balls, Joe," she said. "If you love her, go get her."

And she turned and walked away, leaving him there in the freezing rain.

"And stop checking out my 'inspirational ass,'" she yelled without looking back.

"Right after you get over yourself," he yelled back.

She flipped him off without breaking stride. And he never did stop looking, even after she was gone.

Mara sat on the edge of her father's bed, watching him sleep. It was seven o'clock, and she'd been up for almost two hours.

She'd put on coffee, picked up the phone to call Joe, then decided against it. Showered, picked up the phone to call Joe, decided against it. Dug out a jeans shirt and pajama bottoms her mother had left behind in the rush to abandon her sinking husband, picked up the phone to call Joe . . .

Decided against it. Nothing was ever easy between them. *Nothing.*

Now, she had something more productive in mind.

"I think it's an indoor day today," she whispered, gently nudging Evers. He blinked and looked out the window; the warming air had caused fog to descend like a blanket of white, making time of day irrelevant.

He turned over, away from her.

"I have a special father-daughter project in mind for us," she said a little louder, nudging him so he swayed back and forth on the bed.

He blinked, focused.

"Here," she said, handing him the ice water, three Advil, and a multiple vitamin from the bedside table. "You're gonna need your strength."

"You're an angel," he choked dryly, then gulped the pills down with half the glass. "From hell," he added.

He squinted at her, struggling for focus. "Did you say something about a project?"

They started behind the bar, one bottle at a time: Gray Goose vodka, Tanqueray gin, Glenfiddich single-malt scotch, Jack Daniel's Kentucky sipping bourbon—the best avoidance tools money can buy poured right down the drain.

Eleven bottles of vintage merlots and cabernets, all hearty and aggressive, the way Evers liked them even before they'd become more habit than hobby. He uncorked, Mara emptied.

One bottle of beer at a time from the refrigerator. Pop and pour, pop and pour.

When it was all done, they'd filled two bright-yellow garbage bags with cumbrous, clinking glass. Evers stepped into his weathered fishing boots and dragged the bags down the walk, disappearing into the thick fog.

Mara stepped onto the porch in her Chuck Taylors, a sudden sense that he wasn't coming back. He'd disappeared into the fog and his own heartbreak, never to return.

Just a beat later, he faded in, a smudge of blue and brown at the center of a gray canvas, sky and ground indistinguishable from each other.

He slowed to a stop ten feet in front of her, hands on hips. She crossed her arms and nodded.

"Okay," she said.

"Okay," he said.

"What were you doing out there?" she wondered.

He smiled a secret and pushed on by and up the stairs to a shower.

An hour later, Evers and his daughter sat on the kitchen floor against the cabinets, sipping hot coffee. When she was younger, she'd liked it there, with the heater vent blowing up the back of her shirt, and he'd sometimes joined her on the floor, genuinely enthralled by her meandering tales of Adventures in Junior High.

"How did it happen?" Mara asked now, inspecting her cup with her fingertips. "How did it all come apart?"

He looked into his coffee for fresher answers, found none, and shook his head. "After the job was gone, I started to drink to fill in the spaces," he said. "The central premise was that I was finally getting a chance to let go." He smiled, even laughed weakly at the notion. "Did I ever."

"But on the phone—"

"You didn't know because I didn't want you to know."

"And Mom?"

"She actually did say she was going to visit her mother, like I told you. A couple of weeks later, she called to say she was going to keep traveling, see some people she'd lost touch with so I could have some time to pull it together. Somewhere along the line, *I* became the one she lost touch with."

"She never came back?"

He shook his head. "She called every couple of weeks to say she wasn't ready to come home. I think it was the third or fourth call, she very politely asked if I'd be home to let some people in to pack up clothes and jewelry for her."

"She never explained why?"

"That never came up. But I was no picnic, Mara. There was something my father said once, and I just never got past it: 'You can stop being perfect when you can stop being black.'"

The words hit Mara right between the eyes, and she was crying before she knew what was coming. She covered her mouth, doubling over with the pain.

Instinctively, she crawled the short distance to her father, curled up against him, and again felt his thick arms envelop her. Bracing against her sobs.

"There now," he lulled. "It's all gonna be fine, Mara."

At last, she settled against him, hiccuping aftershock sobs that grew farther and farther apart.

And then she heard the car horn from outside. Her father pulled away from her, stood, stopped at the kitchen table to pick up the coat and overnight bag she'd somehow overlooked, and strode to the front door.

"Daddy?" she called after him, cutting through the dining room to catch up. *"Daddy?"*

He opened the door and she could see through the fog to the canary-yellow taxi idling in the driveway.

"That's for you?" she whispered, confused. He showed her the cell phone in his coat pocket.

"That's what I was doing in the fog," he explained, finding her hand and holding it. "I'm taking a thirty-day vacation at the St. Joe's Substance Abuse Center."

"But I thought—"

"I'll do what I need to do . . . and you do what you need to do. We'll meet back on the kitchen floor, say . . . November thirteenth?"

A tear slid down her cheek, but she managed a smile for him.

"You don't owe me anything but your love, Mara," he said. "That's all I expect from you. And I *do* expect it."

A hint of the old Evers Pinkett. There was nothing left for her to do but nod.

The cabbie honked again, oblivious to whatever drama was surely taking place inside, considering the destination.

Evers took a deep, frightened breath. "I'm off."

Mara took his face in her hands and looked him in the eye. "Be strong, Mr. Pinkett," she said.

With a kiss on her forehead, Evers broke away and faded into the fog. The cab backed up, disappearing from view entirely before it even reached the street.

Good plan: You do what you have to do, Daddy. And I'll do what I have to do.

Which for now is go back to the kitchen floor and huddle against the counter with hot air blowing up the back of my nightshirt, wondering what the hell to do next.

Only a minute and change later, a bracing crash came from from upstairs. A window breaking in. Mara scrambled and slid across the kitchen floor, made it to her stocking feet and through the dining room again.

She started for the stairs, then suddenly froze. Instead, she veered to the front door and opened it.

There, in her father's front yard, was Joe Way. Well, presumably, because for now, he was just a red stocking cap and what appeared to be bright blue pajamas under a beige corduroy coat. But he was famous for throwing things through windows.

"Joe?" Mara called, edging down the walk and into the white.

"Oops, I did it again," he said, stepping forward with a shrug.

"Snowball?" she asked.

"Snowball," he confirmed.

"Nice outfit."

"Nice hair."

Nice banter. Again.

The two of them stood there, just a few feet apart. She fidgeted at her thumb like a younger girl. "I'm sorry about the funeral," she mumbled. "I had some stuff here that—"

"So I'm deeply into this whole 'truth' thing now," he interrupted.

"Is that right," she deadpanned.

"From now on, no matter how easy it is to go the other direction, I'm following the truth all the way through."

Joe looked around with a wince. "Even when it leads here," he said, not bothering to hide his disdain for Glad Acres.

"That's really profound, Joe. I hope you won't think less of me if I ask what's in it for me."

"Not at all. Out of everything I've done in the past twenty-four hours, coming to see you, standing here . . . this scares me most of all."

"Facing up to the fact that you love me?"

Joe took a step closer, his eyes darting between hers. His lips opened and shut but words never found their way out.

"I think that's your cue, Romeo," Mara finally stage-whispered in irritation.

"I don't," Joe choked out, amazed.

"You don't *what*?"

"I don't love you."

Her shoulders fell. She squinted, tilted her head in confusion. "Mara?"

Her quick laugh surprised her and she covered her mouth. "Sorry," she said, shaking her head. "It's just . . . I'm not crying, am I?"

"Not on the outside, no."

"If I loved you . . . and you came all the way here to tell me you *don't* love me . . . wouldn't I be crying?"

"Maybe it's too big," Joe surmised, nodding and squinting like someone who actually knows something. "Maybe you're in shock."

Mara looked precariously close to vomiting. "Yes, that's it, Joe," she said flatly. "I'm in shock from the heartbreak you've inflicted upon me."

"Well, that's my guess."

"Actually, I'm shocked and awed by the staggering breadth of your narcissism, even under the most emotional of circumstances."

And with that, she punched him in the chest as hard as she could, knocking the air from him. "Oh, God," he managed between desperate gasps for dry, frozen air.

"I *never* loved you," Mara snarled.

"I . . . I . . ." Joe battled for the words.

"You what?"

Finally: "I said it first."

Mara's eyes widened. Joe waited for the next blow to land.

And then she started laughing. Relieved, Joe joined her because, in the end, the notion of them being *in love* seemed epically absurd all of a sudden.

When Joe finally settled, he said, "He said 'finish it.' This had to happen. I had to come here."

Mara nodded, getting it. And then they nodded for too long, solid proof that they were truly, finally *finished*.

"See ya," she said, flipping him off as she backed away.

"Not if I see you first," he returned, flipping *her* off. Mara disappeared into the fog, but returned just a moment later.

"Way to fuck up a perfectly cool ending," he scolded.

But the banter was over for her. She said, "Someday I want someone to love me like that preppy, psycho-bitch ninja assassin loves you."

And with that, Mara Pinkett turned and walked into the mist and out of Joe's life.

Forever.

Beth erased the blotchy piss-yellow wall, blanketing it in a thick coat of rich taupe with a roller. The harsh past surrendered one smooth, wide line at a time.

As metaphors go, she hardly had to pull a muscle getting from here to there. The past was a part of her, as surely as that piss-yellow paint would always be there, no matter how many coats of taupe she slathered over it.

But it wouldn't define her. She'd vowed that much a half a life ago, at just fourteen years old, when her mother had sent her away.

Three years ago, after four years of boarding school, six years at Brown University, and two years teaching lilting French to East St. Louis gangbangers, she'd come home for a comically imperfect reunion.

First of all, this wasn't exactly "home"—she'd lacked a real sense of the word ever since her father died when she was nine. The four-walled structure she'd endured with her mother and stepbastard had been her little corner of hell on earth but never, *ever* her home.

For that matter, her mother wasn't exactly her mother anymore. The stroke had cleansed her sins, leaving her quaint and needy.

The truth was this: Beth had returned to Northeast Ohio because she'd finally been offered a job at Western Reserve Academy, which was an integral part of the overall remodeling effort that Joe Way was to complete.

Or not.

She hadn't *really* returned to care for her cuddly kitten of a helpless mother. That became part of her bio only later. It never occurred to anybody that the whole thing was a massive coincidence, a masterstroke of mischief by a dry-witted God.

But it was exactly that.

Their initial reunion, more negotiation than emotional flashpoint, was the stuff of cutting-room floors. In the rehab ward of the Cleveland Clinic, witnessed by nobody, occurred this scintillating exchange:

Beth: So you had, what? A stroke?

Mom (slurred): Well, that would seem to be the case.

Beth: There's this old house just off The Square in Benton Heights.

Mom: Oh, I get it. I have to help you buy it, right?

Beth: Well, we could put you in a nursing home and hope they don't whip you with electrical cords or anything.

And, after a stare down . . .

Mom: Oh, fine.

And so they bought the ramshackle Victorian casting a shadow of blight two blocks east of The Square and Beth set herself to the task of putting it all right.

Painting and plastering was easy. Not bashing in her mother's brains with a serving tray had been a struggle on more than one occasion. But time, like thick coats of taupe paint, can cover a lot of piss-yellow misery.

Nine months ago, they had an exchange that led to a brief spurt of mutual laughter. Beth made a crack about the sprawling size of Maddy's underwear and, instead of taking offense, Maddy actually laughed. The droop of her mouth and the guttural "huh-huh-huh" in turn made Beth laugh.

She found an excuse to go upstairs and broke down in a bone-rattling sob on her childhood bed, fingernails cutting tiny lines in the palms of her hands. She'd managed to keep her mother at arm's distance for more than a year. Scraping their scarred hearts together for that fleeting instant of mutual laughter opened old wounds.

Edging closer to her mother focused attention on the space between them: The Betrayal. The space had quietly seeped inside her, nearly devouring her into a void of bitterness and self-loathing.

So all those years ago, she virtually sat herself down at a drafting table and designed Beth Pruitt, Version 2.0. Ivy League Beth. Prep School Instructor Beth. Married to the Mayor Beth.

She ingratiated herself into the tapestry of Benton Heights so deftly that most people assumed she'd always been there. In the end, she found herself a prisoner of her own design, irrevocably woven into a world Joe Way felt compelled to turn away from. Who could've possibly seen *that* coming?

Nine months ago at the dinner table, after the underpants laughter and the crying and between the wet, clacky chews that made Beth threaten to Cuisinart *everything,* Maddy spoke to her broccoli instead of to Beth.

"I heard you crying upstairs," she said.

"I stepped on a carpet tack," Beth tossed off.

"I'm sorry," Maddy whispered into the vegetable. "I should've known."

"It happens," Beth said, knowing full well that her mother was talking about her perverted stepfather, not a carpet tack. Still, she added, "Little fuckers are everywhere."

"I'm sorry," Maddy said again. And so Beth had to leave the table and run back upstairs to cry on her childhood bed again.

Here and now, as Beth painted, "It's too dark," came the slurred voice from behind her.

"Try really-really hard not to express every thought you have," Beth fired back without turning. She resoaked the roller and went back to the wall.

"It's depressing," Maddy slurred.

"Good, because you're *way* too cheerful. It annoys me."

Beth finally turned, and she and her wheelchair-bound mother shared a smile. It still stirred and tumbled inside her, but Beth no longer felt the need to run upstairs and cry.

"I'm going to the porch," Maddy said, struggling to get there. Beth rested the paint roller in the tray to help her.

Outside, Beth chose to slump into the wicker rocker for a rest and enjoy the rising temperature under the cloudless autumn sky.

When she looked over, her mother was staring back, the way she often did. Someday, she'd find the rest of the words. Beth reached over, took her mother's limp left hand from her lap, and held it. For now, it was enough.

Then Joe Way cleared his throat respectfully. Beth looked up to see him there on the walk in a bulky ski sweater and jeans, wet hair combed back and left to fall.

His right hand came from behind him to present a large bouquet of mixed flowers.

Her laugh was quick and wounding. "Yeah, *right,*" she said.

"You wanna push me on inside so you two can have some privacy, hon?" Beth's mother spoke up.

"Not at all," Beth said coolly, standing and crossing her arms to let Joe retrace the perilous turns of his own journey.

So Joe went for, "Hey."

"'Hey,'" she repeated to her mother. "I hope this gets better, don't you?"

"Mrs. Pruitt." Joe nodded nervously. She smiled on one side of her mouth, nodded back.

"Did I ever tell you how 'deeply in like' Joe is with me?" Beth asked her mother. At that, Maddy struggled desperately to get turned and head for the door, saying, "I really think I should—"

Beth got a firm grip on the chair. "It's okay, Mom," she said sweetly.

Joe stepped to the bottom of the stairs, extended the flowers. "You want 'em?" Beth asked her mother, who nodded eagerly. "Just toss 'em on up," Beth said to Joe.

He did and she caught them, gave them over to her mother without a second look.

"They're lovely!" her mother cooed.

Beth leveled an icy stare on her ex-fiancé. "Is that it?" she said, but it was getting harder and harder to *not* smile because, well, here he was, all showered and shaved and apologetic.

Joe looked Beth in the eye and shook his head ever so slightly. To be looked at like that, with *awe,* it almost blew her cover.

She rallied in the nick of time with, "What're you doing here, Joe?" These things aren't meant to be easy.

"I ended it with Mara," he said. "I ended it for good."

"And now?" Beth prodded.

"And now I'm here to fight for you."

"Oh, I see. Well, it's gonna take one hell of a performance so I suggest you get on with it."

Joe nodded. Twisted his neck, loosening up. "Okay," he said. But then he crumbled under the weight of her expectations.

"So this is what 'fighting for you' looks like?" Beth said to her mother between derisive chuckles. "I'm profoundly under-whelmed."

"I really wanna go inside," Maddy pleaded, but Beth locked a fist on the arm of her wheelchair before she could.

Joe bounded two steps for the save and said, "I truly *am* so deeply in like with you, Beth."

Inspired by her curiosity, he took one more step and rushed on, "We can't be friends because that's what we've been since the day we met. *Best* friends."

Beth straightened and crossed her arms. "This is the 'friends' speech?"

Joe's eyes filled with tears. "This is the *everything* speech. Because that's what you are to me: my best friend . . . the only woman I'll ever love . . . the person I want to grow old with. You're something Mara Pinkett could never be. Something nobody else could be."

"Oh?" Beth said, her cheeks sucking in and her voice cracking. "What's that?"

Joe took the last step; Beth didn't retreat. Only when he was right in front of her did he say, "You're my truth. The one thing I'll always know for sure."

Out of the silence came Maddy's slurred voice: "That's pretty good."

Beth bobbed her head in agreement: Yeah, I guess.

"This was all part of his plan," Joe said, smiling and shrugging and crying all at the same time. "I had to go all the way to Glad Acres to get to here, on your porch, telling you that I'll love you forever."

Beth never bothered to ask *whose* plan or what the hell is Glad Acres if not a psychiatric hospital. Instead, she cleared the last twenty-four inches between them and lifted her chin and opened her mouth so he could kiss her.

Which he did.

This was the kiss their children and grandchildren would tire of hearing about. This was the kiss they'd describe to disinterested dinner partners on Alaskan cruises.

The kiss that would get them through petty arguments and wandering eyes and the slick-sloped valleys that so assuredly follow the peaks in a lifetime of love.

This was that kiss. This was their truth.

Like what you just read?

Then don't miss these other great books from Downtown Press!